Killer Protocols

David E. Manuel

Zarina,
Meet Richard
Paladin!

Copyright © 2011 by David E. Manuel

All rights reserved

This is a work of fiction. All the characters and events portrayed in this book are either products of the author's imagination or are used fictitiously.

Cover design by David E. Manuel

Cover photographs by David E. Manuel and Susan C. Sanderson

All statements of fact, opinion, or analysis expressed are those of the author and do not reflect the official positions or views of the CIA or any other U.S. Government agency. Nothing in the contents should be construed as asserting or implying U.S. Government authentication of information or Agency endorsement of the author's views. This material has been reviewed by the CIA to prevent disclosure of classified information.

ISBN-13: 978-1468186376
ISBN-10: 146818637X

Killer Protocols

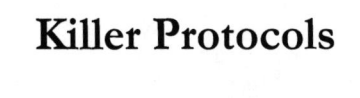

Chapter I
A Perfect Place for a Homicide

I DON'T GO to New York unless I have to. I sure wouldn't go there for pleasure. Maybe some people believe all that crap about it being an exciting place filled with great stuff to do. Me, I'm not interested in opera, Broadway shows or art galleries. I get sick every time I hear some East Coast twit say it's "convenient" that there's a subway system overrun with pick-pockets and punks or that the streets are teeming with cabbies who rip you off for a two-block fare. Best I can tell New Yorkers are a bunch of loud-mouthed, shit-for-brains assholes who think getting mugged is a cultural experience.

New York is pretty compelling proof that this country is on a downward slide. The place was overcrowded and polluted long before raghead terrorists leveled the Twin Towers and coated the city with toxic dust. I suspect people who live there have a higher percentage of lead and asbestos in their systems than a World War II Liberty ship. But New Yorkers are a tough lot. After 9/11, the bankers who own most of the city and damned near all the rest of the country dusted off their silk suits and went right back to robbing the country blind. And the rest of the inhabitants picked themselves up and went back to work serving those bankers their fancy coffees and scones; or resumed mugging the bankers and their servants to make a buck. I'll admit, I admire New Yorkers a lot for their grit and determination. But I avoid the place as much as possible. Since I got out of the army, I make it a habit to stay out of war zones.

I'm not alone in my assessment of New York. Hell, New Yorkers obviously feel the same way: just spend a day in the city and see how pissed off everyone who's stuck there is. The first few times I visited the place, I used to keep count of the number of times I heard someone say "fuck off" or "fuck you, buddy." I gave that up. It's not that I can't count that high—although math's not exactly one of my skills—but it does get boring.

An old army buddy once told me some guy named Oswald something-or-other wrote an entire book about the sorry state of New York and most of the rest of the country, some rant called *The Decline of the West*. Joe Sprague and I got drunk one night in North Carolina, right after we'd gotten kicked out of the army, and he started rambling about this Oswald guy and the West and how everything we believe in is being undermined. At the time I thought he was just drunk and a little nuts, but I've since learned better. I keep meaning to read the book, by the way.

So I don't go to New York often. But when I go I take the train. I live in Fairfax, Virginia, several miles across the Potomac from Washington, D.C.—a place trying real hard to catch New York in the decline race—and it's pretty easy just to take the subway to Union Station and hop on the Metroliner. My office is close to Union Station anyway—not that I have a 9 to 5 job or anything—so I can check in on the way out and on the way back just to see if any new assignments have come in.

Believe me, the Metroliner really beats taking the air shuttle. Sure, transit time is three hours as opposed to

75 minutes by air. But I can walk into Union Station at 6:55 a.m., buy a ticket from the Amtrak ticketing machine, walk right onto the train which pulls out at 7:10, and I'm in New York, downtown at Penn Station, by 10:15. Take the plane, add the hour you have to wait in the lounge before boarding, and the hour-plus cab ride from LaGuardia or Kennedy into the city, and I figure you really only lose twenty minutes max on the train. And what you get in return is a bigger seat, room to walk around, fewer hassles from stewards and stewardesses trying to make you believe they care about your comfort, and the peace and quiet of half-empty railroad cars. Because most people going to New York from Washington just hate to lose that twenty minutes, so they fly. And that's fine with me, because I like the empty, hassle-free train ride.

I also like the fact that I can get all the way into downtown New York without having to pass through a metal detector. Makes it a lot easier when you're packing a gun, which I usually am when I'm heading to New York. Because, like I said, when I go there it's on business. And my business is killing people.

Get one thing straight. I'm no murderer. Killing someone without a good reason is a crime. There are sick bastards out there who get a thrill killing innocent people. I'm not one of them. I've got a real good reason to kill people. This country's at war, has been for a long time. September 11 was just one of the more obvious attacks by our numerous enemies. Just ask the president; there's a whole axis of evil people out there, and 'axis,' in case you didn't know, means 'shitload.' Or something like that. Ridding the world of the scum who are enemies of decent people is a full-time profession. Lucky for me.

Hey, I have bad days. Sometimes the blackness comes over me, the sick sensation everyone gets from time to time that their life sucks. Sometimes I wonder if maybe I shouldn't have bailed out of my rotten marriage, shoulda stuck around to help raise some kids, shoulda found a decent job selling hardware or cars or something.

Then I remind myself. I didn't do that crap because I got lucky. I'm a lucky guy.

Which is why I was sitting on the Metroliner bound for New York City on a hot Tuesday morning in June. Tuesday's the best day for taking the train if you're trying to avoid crowds. Tourists, people visiting relatives, college kids heading home from school or on their way back to campus, they don't take the Tuesday train. You run into them on Friday or Sunday. Attorneys, bankers, stock-brokers, and sales representatives on their way to meetings to discuss important amounts of money typically travel on Monday, Wednesday, or Thursday—don't ask me why. Tuesday sort of falls in between all the various flurry-of-activity days.

Of course, there are always a few businessmen on the Tuesday train, and I often wonder if some of them are in the same line of work as me. Anybody who watches the ten o'clock news or occasionally reads the crime page of any major newspaper knows that a lot of people die unexpectedly and violently every day, and I know I'm not the only professional adding to the toll. But it's not exactly the kind of thing you inquire of the guy sitting across the aisle, now is it? So I just sit there, looking businesslike in the same kind of comfortable but professional coat and tie all the other New York bound, briefcase-laden travelers are wearing.

I don't particularly like carrying a briefcase, by the way. A good army rucksack or shoulder-bag is vastly superior for hauling a days worth of items and miscellany, and they afford plenty of space for useful things like a change of clothes. And there's very little risk of some New York vagrant or street punk trying a grab-and-go of a rucksack slung over your shoulder. A briefcase might as well have "steal me" stickers all over it. But businessmen don't carry rucksacks, so I compromise on New York runs and just keep a firm grip on the handle when walking around the city.

Of course, there's not much of value that I carry. I never stay overnight in New York, so I just pack a sandwich, maybe a newspaper to scan on the train, that sort of stuff. And, today, a medium-blue nylon windbreaker wrapped around a compact .38 revolver sporting a 3-inch-long silencer. These last items wouldn't be making the return trip.

The assignment for this particular Tuesday was a relatively simple one. As always, I'd been given a name and a few relevant details. I don't work on deadline or anything, but usually it's assumed I'll finish the job within a week or so. This assignment was a guy with the United Nations, a mid-level bureaucrat with an office in the UN Secretariat building. I'd come up a week earlier and staked out the entrance at about 3:00 p.m., figuring he'd probably be the type who leaves work early. It's a safe assumption in New York that he'd take the subway to and from the office, but in my line of work it's a good idea not to make too many assumptions, as I had discovered during last week's reconnaissance. This guy had walked out of the UN at 3:45, hiked up 44th street to Broadway, and hailed a cab. I could deal with that.

So on this hot Tuesday afternoon at 3:30 I staked myself out at the end of a dark ally opening up to 44th street, just a little ways from 2nd avenue. I was positioned so I could see people approaching from the direction of the UN and intercept my quarry with just a couple of steps. Just like clockwork, I spotted him heading toward me right at 3:45.

Today's client was from some African shithole—Mali, I think—and had worked at the UN for years. I had no idea what he did there. Most of the time, I'm left pretty much in the dark about specifics. I had his job title; Third Undersecretary to the Secretary of the General Undersecretariat or some such horseshit. That told me exactly nothing. But I usually try to figure out what it is that makes each one of my clients so special. In this case, I figured Mr. Mohammed Hassan Abdulkar Mohammed was probably some kind of spy or terrorist or something. I mean, he looked more African than Middle-eastern, but with a name like that, I suspected contacts with al-Qa'ida or Palestinian terrorists.

Looking him over for the second time was enough to piss me off, too. He was wearing a three-piece suit that I'll bet was silk or fine wool. Hey, I'm no fashion expert. But Mr. Mohammed Mohammed sure dressed like he was one. And he was wearing a watch that I'm certain was mostly gold. Add to that at least three rings on each hand and a very nice leather briefcase and you get the picture of somebody with lots of excess money burning a hole in their pocket. And man, did that piss me off. Here's some lousy foreigner living great in New York City where thousands of good Americans are struggling just to pay the rent. This was a guy who deserved what I had in mind for him.

So this is how I played it. He was about thirty paces away when I stumbled out in the street in front of him, doing my best imitation of someone who's had a few too many. I staggered up to him and threw my left arm around him. Oh, he tried to sidestep me, ignore me, keep walking, but I've had plenty of experience at this. Maybe other people on the street think I'm just a friendly drunk falling into him, but I've actually got a real good grip on Mr. Mohammed Mohammed.

"Hey, buddy. Come have a drink with me. Waddya say?" Playing a drunk is ideal for getting away with murder in New York. Everyone else on the street was just happy I'd picked someone else to annoy. People made absolutely sure they looked the other way.

"Let go of me, you fool. What do you think you are doing?"

Mohammed's English was impeccable. I was surprised, but not enough to lose my grip. I pulled him into the alley.

"I got something to show you, buddy. Come on." Mohammed was struggling, but I'm smart enough to know that staying fit is part of my job. I run about fifty miles a week and work on my upper body strength constantly at a northern Virginia gym. No way he was going to break free. I dragged him around behind this big dumpster that dominated the alley—the thing looked like it hadn't been emptied for days. Mohammed kept trying to yell, but I had pretty quickly moved my left hand up to his mouth to keep him quiet. And the whole bit—grabbing him and dragging him into the alley—took less than a minute. He never really had a chance to figure out what was happening.

Draped over my right hand was that nylon windbreaker. Under that was the silenced .38. I squeezed off one round into Mohammed's midsection to stop him from struggling and, well, sort of to get his attention. Then I shoved him down behind the dumpster.

The look on Mohammed's face was a classic of disbelief. One of the things I've learned in this job: no one expects to die. Not in a back alley in New York. Not in the garden of their lovely Savannah, Georgia home. Not even in bed. People always greet death with disbelief.

I didn't relish Mohammed's shocked expression for long. Efficiency is critical in the execution of a premeditated killing. I aimed the .38 at his skull and shot him two more times. One bullet is not a sure thing. Lots of people get lucky and survive that in this age of modern medicine. Major metropolitan areas are littered with hospitals sporting expert trauma teams—and what does that tell you about the state of our civilization? But plugging your mortally wounded victim five or six times is, well, unprofessional.

Don't get me wrong. I appreciate as much as the next guy taking pleasure in your work. And, believe me, you haven't lived until you've emptied the magazine of a high-power handgun into some unsuspecting son of a bitch. It's an awesome feeling you get seeing that look of total surprise followed by a glimmering awareness that this is the moment of death. And if you're really lucky, and I mean grab-your-wallet-and-head-to-Vegas lucky, those fading eyes will focus on you and your smoking gat right at the last moment in an acknowledgment that the bastard understands just who blew his ass to Hell.

I acted fast, now, quickly feeling inside his coat pocket for a wallet, which I found in the right breast pocket. I grabbed that and his nice leather briefcase and headed toward the other end of the alley—I'd made sure to select one with two exits. I walked up two blocks away from the river, ducked into another alley, opened his briefcase and threw it on the ground, scattering lots of papers Mohammed had been carrying. I opened the wallet and pulled out Mohammed's cash—there was a lot of that—and tossed the wallet down, too. Then I resumed walking at a brisk pace to the nearest subway station, still carrying my briefcase, the windbreaker, and the revolver.

This is the diciest part of shooting someone. Carrying the recently-fired revolver meant I'd be up shit creek if a cop stopped me. I could have ditched it in the alley, too, but it's best to dispose of the murder weapon well-away from the crime scene. The key to getting away with a New York killing is to make it look like one of the hundreds of senseless murder/robberies that occur there every year—that's why you go ahead and rob the victim. If the cops find a silenced handgun in a nearby dumpster, though, they get suspicious. So I headed for the nearest subway stop and hopped the first train. Once aboard, I shoved the windbreaker-wrapped .38 into my briefcase and resumed the look of a typical office-worker headed home.

The best place to dispose of a gun is someplace where no one will be surprised to find one. There are lots of potential spots that fit this description in New York, but on this occasion I selected Harlem. Once I'd gotten out of the vicinity of the UN, I simply made the appropriate transfers to get me there. Needless to say, I was increasing my odds of getting mugged. But I don't worry much about that. At 6'2" I'm a pretty imposing target for street toughs. And I can look very mean when I want to. I exited the subway in a rough-looking neighborhood, located another of New York's thousands of overflowing trash dumpsters, and deposited the .38 without incident.

You can bet that gun eventually made its way into some teenager's possession. But I'll wager it never gets used again. A .38 revolver is a great little weapon, in my book. It's compact, makes little noise—almost none with a silencer—never jams, and holds enough rounds to make sure of your victim with a few to spare. But kids today want a sexier piece, an UZI or AK-47. They wouldn't even contemplate an armed-robbery or revenge-killing without at least a flashy 9mm automatic with a 20 round magazine. Yeah, my used .38 would make a great set of training wheels for some young punk just getting started, but that's about it.

I made my way back to Grand Central Station without incident and hopped the Metroliner for the return to Washington. I haven't done a lot of jobs in New York, but past experience had taught me that the return trip would be relaxing. Once I'd settled into my seat and the train pulled out, the rocking of the car, soft clacking of the wheels on track, and the tension of the job fading put me in a state of comfort I doubt many other people ever achieve. Most passengers bring a book to read or bury their heads in business papers to occupy the time, but I just stare out the window and appreciate the scenery of the good old USA America truly is a wonderful place, fading to be sure, but still great; especially once you get out of New York.

That day I reflected a lot on how lucky I am. In fact, I don't think it's just luck. There are forces at work in the universe larger than any of us. When you're a front-line warrior in the battle of good versus evil, you begin to realize that something's guiding you, directing your every action. I'm not a religious person. As a kid, I was dragged to church like most people, but I got pretty sick of the self-righteous bullshit of the Christ the Redeemer Baptist Church in Fallbrook, North Carolina. In my experience, people who go to church all the time are either feeling guilty about themselves—usually because they're screwing somebody else's wife or husband, stealing money from the company till, or committing some other petty corruption or crime—or are seeking escape from being hopeless losers. Lecturing impressionable kids about the evils of sex and alcohol probably makes these people feel a little less miserable and powerless for a brief period of time. By the time I was eighteen, I'd discovered the joys of beer and back-seat sex and was ready to say good-fucking-bye to Fallbrook, churches, losers and hypocrites. I joined the army.

But I didn't become an atheist. There's a God, and he's got a plan for me. That's about the only way I can explain finding that ad in *Hustler* looking for someone "physically fit, preferably with military experience, interested in making a difference." Something guided me past the centerfold that day, encouraged me to jot down the phone number before putting the magazine back on the rack of that 7-11, made me call the number and arrange an interview. Some higher power had selected me to go to that run-down motel in Alexandria, Virginia and ace the interview in that moldy room. When the mousy little man I met there stuck out his hand and said, "Congratulations, you're hired," I knew my destiny had finally been fulfilled.

I'd figured I'd be working for some super-secret spook organization like the NSA or CIA. I think every kid in America thinks those are the front-line fighters of America's secret wars. Now I know better, of course. I've been in the government long enough to know that those agencies would never touch someone like me. They hire lawyers and accountants who are already predisposed to become mindless bureaucrats pushing papers from one meaningless office to another. They can't really do anything about enemies in the United States, either. They're focused on places like London or Paris where they can get good meals and stay in five-star hotels.

I wasn't hired by the Department of Homeland Security, either. Turns out DHS doesn't really do anything to make America safe, either. Mostly they just make people miserable trying to get through airports onto planes. No, the real work of securing the USA from our countless enemies falls to people like me working in compartmented programs so secret no one ever hears about them. At least, I assume there are others like me. "Super compartmented" means you don't get to meet anybody else in the same line of work. My boss explained that to me the first day.

So I kill people on behalf of the U.S. Government, but they don't make movies or television series glorifying my work. Nobody leaks details of my life for screenwriters to use in fantasies about CIA spies or Secret Service agents. I work in obscurity.

I'm a staff employee of the Environmental Protection Agency.

Chapter II
Life as a Killer Bureaucrat

MY TRAIN PULLED INTO UNION STATION a little after 9:00 in the evening, so I decided to head over to my office and write up my report. I prefer getting everything wrapped up the same day whenever possible. It's not really that I want events fresh in my mind: I have no problem remembering the details of my work days and even weeks afterwards. I like closure, however. Keeps life simple.

And, yes, there's paperwork, even in my business. Nothing gets done in this world without forms being filed and memos being written and forwarded to bosses. Where the U.S. Government is involved, paperwork has to be on record—usually in quintuplicate—before money can be released. Certainly nobody gets expenses reimbursed without filling out an itemized list of every Lincoln penny disbursed. Sitting in an uncomfortable chair laboring over a keyboard in a poorly lit office or cubicle is part of every government job—at least if you want to get paid. And I like getting paid.

Of course, what I write is complete bullshit. I can't exactly type up a memo to the president saying "went to New York and gunned down a U.N. employee named Mohammed." I have to give my boss "plausible deniability." That's the phrase he uses. But my reports aren't that much different than what goes on throughout the government. Calling a spade a spade is just not the way bureaucrats do business. Face it, would anyone in their right mind pay 70,000 dollars for a commode? But call it an "air-deployable toxic waste disposal unit" for a B-52 and Congress will get downright patriotic as it hands over the money. Similarly, I don't list as expenses ".38 revolver, parts for home-made silencer, nylon windbreaker for concealment, three .38 cartridges." For this job I expensed the gun and silencer as a Blackberry, the windbreaker as a coffee table book, and the bullets as ball-point pens. I put them down as "courtesy gifts" that I gave to a foreign official.

The official term for language that satisfies the accountants without revealing what's really going on, according to my boss, is "euphemism." Yeah, government wonks love those big words.

So I strolled over to my office, powered up my computer, and started typing. Getting all the t's crossed and i's dotted usually takes me about an hour, and with our office nicely located in a converted townhouse about halfway between Union Station and the Capitol Building, I figured I could be done and back on the subway for home by 11:00. As always, I wrote up an expense report and a Memorandum for the Record. It read:

SUBJECT: New York Consultation with Subject of File 38^/55-45-65@4A21

Officer traveled to New York per instructions Memorandum A3Q9931204. Explained U.S. policy set out in EPA-100031G to subject of File 38^/55-45-65@4A21 per guidance EPA-X-9631. Presented subject with courtesy gifts itemized per attachment A.

And that constituted Mr. Muhammed Muhammed's official U.S. government obit. Rest in fucking peace.

I don't just make up the document and file numbers,

of course. There really is a File 38^/55-45-65@4A21. It's one of a very long series running from 38^/55-45-65@1A01 to 38^/55-45-65@9Z99. My clients all come from these files, although I don't get them in any particular order. But it does seem that the government has a lifetime of work for me.

Memorandum A3Q9931204 was the cover memo my boss sent me attached to 38^/55-45-65@4A21. And I use EPA-100031G because my boss told me always to reference this when writing up my assignments. It's some kind of policy document relating to U.S. objections to the Kyoto Protocol.

EPA-X-9631 is a personal favorite. It's an internal EPA instruction advising all officers to "seek out and work with local officials whenever and wherever possible to insure proper disposal of human waste from urban and rural areas."

I should point out that "paperwork" is a misnomer for my job. I don't actually print any of this stuff out and put it in inter-office mail. I don't even e-mail my reports. I have a computer, but it's not connected to any networks and certainly not to the Internet. My boss calls it a "stand-alone," a computer for work so secret that it can't be trusted to hackers or nosy system administrators. I save my reports to 3 1/2 inch floppy disks and place them in the safe next to my desk. My boss and I are the only ones with the combination. I assume he opens the safe every now and then to check my work. I know he opens the safe occasionally, because I get my assignments on 3 1/2 inch floppies that he deposits in the safe.

This night I was getting ready to save my work and lock up my disk when I heard someone moving outside my office. I quickly blanked the screen.

"Why, Mr. Paladin, you are certainly working late tonight." It was Sharon, the administrative assistant. "But you always work strange hours, don't you?"

Mr. Paladin's me, by the way. Richard Paladin. Sort of. I'll get to that.

"Didn't expect to see you here, Sharon." It was 10:30. I had no idea what the hell she was doing in the office. Usually she was out the door at 4:30 on the dot.

"Oh, I was having drinks with some friends of mine over by Capitol Hill. Decided to leave my car parked here. Came upstairs 'cause I had to pee." She smiled. I don't think she was drunk, but she'd definitely had enough to knock back a few inhibitions. "You know, Mr. Paladin, you really should demand a new computer. That old PC they got you using is just sad. They must have dragged it out of some equipment archive just for you. I'd be insulted. It can't even connect to the e-mail system."

"Oh, I make do. I don't need anything fancy in my line of work."

"Right. Your line of work." Sharon, of course, didn't know what my line of work was. No one in the office did except my boss, the director of this EPA outpost far-removed from the central office. I didn't really know what any of the rest of them did, either.

This mutual ignorance could have been alerting, except I had a cover story. Before I moved into the office, my boss made sure to tell the previous secretary that I was being transferred over because I was a notorious malingerer and non-performer. Since it is almost impossible to fire anyone in the government, senior EPA managers had decided—so went the cover legend—to send me someplace where I'd be given a desk in a converted broom closet and cut off from all contact with the rest of the Agency in hopes that I would get the message and resign. He explained that he was sharing this information with her because, as the office administrator, she needed to know about it, but he emphasized to her that she should definitely keep the information to herself. Of course, telling a civil service secretary to keep juicy gossip to herself is like asking a mountain lion to stop eating meat; as expected, she informed the rest of the staff before I ever showed up, so they stayed well clear of me.

"Seems like you just come and go as you please, Mr. Paladin." Well, everybody except Sharon stayed clear of me. She'd been assigned to the office about six months earlier; every day she seemed to get more curious.

"I put in my hours. Long as I do that, I get paid. That's all that counts."

"You are so right, Mr. Paladin. I'm one contented kitten, long as I'm getting laid."

Usually I act pretty cool and distant around Sharon, but sometimes she could catch me by surprise. I must have raised an eyebrow.

"Oh, what did I say? Why, Mr. Paladin, you must think I'm very fresh." She was still smiling, a big, toothy smile. Sharon was actually quite pretty. "Of course I meant to say 'paid.' I guess maybe I've had a little too much to drink."

"Sure you're okay to drive?"

"Oh, I'm fine. Just a little tongue-tied is all." She smiled. "I don't have that far to drive. You know, my apartment's only about ten blocks from here."

"Surprised you don't walk to work. Aren't we supposed to be saving the environment?"

"And let that parking space they gave me go to

waste? Besides, you wouldn't want me out on the streets this late all alone, would you? " She batted her eyes at me one last time before turning and walking away. I'd noticed before that she had a very nice ass, but I took notice again that night.

This wasn't the first time Sharon had flirted with me. She clearly suspected that there was more to me than my cover story. After all, most losers aren't 6-foot athletic-looking guys. And if I really was some kind of malcontent, that probably just interested her even more. I'd learned back in the army, when I was on my way to getting kicked out, that being the platoon troublemaker or discipline problem is a real turn-on for some women, especially officers' wives.

And I was sorely tempted, too. I enjoy bedding a good-looking babe as much as the next guy, and Sharon had all the looks and personality that said she'd be very good in the sack. I'm not so shallow I can't appreciate being in a good relationship, either. We could have had some great times in the sack and out. But I also knew that a big part of Sharon's motivation getting involved with me would be to find out what my story really was. And that meant screwing her would be decidedly stupid. I kept reminding myself of that.

Not that I've been particularly smart in my life where women are concerned. Did I mention those officers' wives?

With Sharon gone, I turned my monitor back on and resumed saving my report to disk, then locked the disk in the safe. Turning out the lights in the office, I started thinking how lucky Sharon was to have a parking space. This time of night, the drive to my apartment in Fairfax would be less than half an hour.

Riding the subway, I probably wouldn't get home until after midnight. But there were only two parking spaces in our building. The boss got one, Sharon the other. Good administrative assistants are hard to come by in the government. In fact, even bad ones are hard to come by. Few people are willing to do filing, answer phones, type, keep office supplies stocked, handle payroll forms and timesheets, for the $37,000 a year Sharon was getting. In fact, in the six months or so I'd gotten to know Sharon, I'd noticed that she was smart and efficient in addition to being very sexy, which left me wondering why she was content to stay in such a low-paying job. Anyway, when managers find someone like her, they load on all the perks—like a parking spot—they possibly can. Guys like me have to take public transportation.

Of course, I also was making about twice as much as Sharon and qualified for the "Metro Check" program as well, which covered most of my daily commute. Or not so daily, in my case. Like Sharon had said, I tend to make my own hours. And if it looks like I might be a bit short some months, I can always fudge my expense reports. That's one of the perks of guys in my business.

I hiked over to Union Station and hopped the Red Line train to Metro Center, where I transferred to the Orange Line train for Fairfax. All the trains are color coded in the Washington, D.C. area. There are Red, Orange, Blue, Green, and Yellow lines. I've read they're considering building new White and Purple Lines. I have no idea who came up with the idea to use colors; probably some government psychologist with previous experience as an adviser for Sesame Street. Either that or someone who took way too much LSD back in the 1960s.

My apartment's about two miles from the last stop on the Orange Line, and I like to walk it, even late at night. It's a good way to unwind, and I figure you can't get too much exercise in my line of work. I get a perverse pleasure out of strolling through Fairfax, too. What used to be a pretty traditional southern town with diners and run-down gas stations has been transformed into brick front shopping centers filled with Barnes and Nobles, Body Shops, hyper-modern self-service filling stations, and chain restaurants all trying to look European or San Franciscan. When I first moved to the area, I'd stop by a new restaurant for a cold beer a couple of times a week on my way home. It was always a disappointment. Every one offered new micro-brews with effete-sounding labels like Harlem Hopfest or Manhattan Malt. Waiters and waitresses alike all turned out to be twenty-somethings who wanted you to know they were working their way through business school so they could get jobs ordering nobodies like you around. The last straw came at a place called Buckingham Brewery and Seafood Establishment. I'd strolled in and taken a seat at the bar, "manned" by some snooty chick.

"Are you waiting for a table, sir?" She said sir like she really wanted me to know she didn't mean it.

"I'm waiting to order a beer."

"Oh. You're just here to drink, then."

"Yeah, if that's okay."

"Why not? What may I serve you?" There's a particular mannerism of youth today where they act very polite without ever bothering to look at you that makes me regret occasionally that so few of my clients are youngsters.

"Well, how about a beer."

"Draft or bottle?"

"A draft beer would be great."

"What kind?"

"How about a Miller Genuine Draft?"

She grimaced. "We have five beers on draft. Annandale Ale brewed locally by the Annandale Brewery. Mahatma Pale Ale—that's an IPA. Auslandexport Weiss—a German wheat beer. Stornoflovitz Pils—a Slovakian lager. And Lebdernachtgut Red—that's a red ale from Oregon. One of those do?"

"How about the lager." At that point I figured a commie beer was better than nothing, and since the fall of the Berlin Wall, Slovakia was probably less pinko than Oregon.

Now she looked at me. It's hard to believe eyes so young can already display so much contempt. "Figures."

I swallowed the beer fast, dropped ten bucks on the counter, and left swearing to remember to keep a six pack in the fridge and head straight home from then on. And I would have, too. Except the next night, I stumbled across Dan's Bar.

There aren't too many run-down looking places left in Fairfax, but just a bit off the main, halogen-lit boulevard, a couple of blocks behind one of the myriad Starbucks, there's an ancient strip mall with one of the last, small corner groceries left in America. I'd walked past it dozens of times without taking a second look. But something that evening drew my eye. I noticed that the corner of the shopping center housed a separate establishment. The area wasn't all that well lit, so I had to take a few steps into the parking lot to make out the name above the door. And there it was, in rather faded black, block letters on a dirty white sign:

Dan's Bar. I decided to go in.

It was with some significant trepidation that I entered. I wasn't worried that the place might be too rough for me or anything. Some of my hang-outs back in North Carolina were known more for knife-fights and shootings than fine food and drink. Maybe I was worried that the external appearance was a ruse, that inside I'd find the same craft-brewed sushi-culture crap that had taken over the rest of the region. I opened the door and walked in, ready to bolt if it looked like everyone was drinking lattes or blended beverages. But it was dark and smelled like cigarettes. I went on in and sat at the bar.

"What'll ya have?" The man behind the bar looked to be in his mid-50s, wiry and weathered. He was wearing baggy shorts, a flannel shirt, and a baseball cap sporting an Atlanta Braves "B" on the front.

"What do you have on draft?" I was cringing inside, waiting for him to list a dozen beers I'd never heard of flavored with raspberry or peach.

"Budweiser."

"Budweiser?"

"That's what I said."

I was having trouble believing my luck. "The one from Czechoslovakia?"

"Budweiser. Brewed by union employees in the USA." He gave me a look like I'd dropped in from Mars. "You want something else, there's a TGIF up the street."

"Bud sounds perfect." I'd finally found a home.

Dan's was a real neighborhood bar, and Dan actually was the guy behind the bar. Dan Stigler bought the place in the late 1970s when Fairfax was still a southern town, not a Washington suburb. Somehow he'd resisted all the development and maintained a safehaven for his regulars, a mishmash of redneck construction workers, handymen, hardware retail clerks and other normal Joes who were grateful for a place where they could have a few beers, smoke too many cigarettes and age badly. I felt a bit self-conscious when I first started stopping by; I mean, I stay pretty fit, so I don't have a large butt-crack to display over my barstool. But Dan didn't seem to mind.

It was after midnight when I finally made it to Dan's the evening after the New York trip, and the place was empty except for Dan and me. I wasn't worried I was keeping him from closing, though. A sign behind the bar reads *Closing Time 2:00 a.m. and Not a Minute Earlier!*

"Well, if it isn't Richard Paladin. You been burnin' the midnight oil again?" Dan drew a draft Bud and placed it on the bar in front of me.

"Saving the world, Dan. You know that."

"Shit. More likely sittin' in your office looking at Internet porn. What the hell could be so important at the damned EPA?"

"Secret stuff, Dan. You know I can't talk about it."

"Secret, my ass. The only secret you got is just how much of my tax money you manage to piss away."

"Really, Dan, you know better. Why, the Environmental Protection Agency is at the forefront of the greatest war this nation has ever fought."

"The war on terrorism? What the fuck does the EPA have to do with that?"

"Why, no, Dan. The war on the environment."

"How much longer before you win that one?"

"Don't know. Environment's putting up a tough fight in places. But we'll beat it."

"Sometimes I'm not so sure you're kidding." He

looked concerned for a moment, then grinned. "You civil service types are so full of shit."

We'd had this same conversation now dozens of times. It was our inside joke. Usually we hammed it up some if there was a new customer present. Nights like this, we just did it out of boredom. Dan always enjoyed running down civil servants.

Of course, Dan had been a civil servant himself, before he was proprietor of Dan's Bar. I didn't find this out until I'd been coming in for several months. It's not something he's proud of. But one night, when it was just the two of us, he suddenly drew himself a draft, got a faraway look in his eye, and told me how he'd come to Washington years ago as an idealistic college graduate.

"Things were different back then. Us college kids were gonna change things, make things right. Not like kids today, getting business degrees or computer degrees and thinking how they're gonna get rich. Naw, I did an undergraduate degree in Political Science and got a Masters in Public Administration. Guess I figured I was gonna be that guy from the government who's there to help."

I suspect that Dan was also avoiding the draft with a student deferment. But I kept that speculation to myself.

"Arrived here in 1971, fresh-faced and eager to start work at the Department of the Interior. Had a lot more hair back then, too."

Dan had taken a position with the Bureau of Indian Affairs. He'd grown up in South Dakota and watched way too many Hollywood Westerns where noble Native Americans get screwed by duplicitous whites. He showed me a picture of himself on a field trip to a reservation, wearing a coat and tie and looking like a typical young do-gooder dreaming of building schools and community centers for grateful Comanches and Navajos. He'd become disillusioned after five frustrating years.

"All the bastards wanted to build were casinos. I didn't sign on to help create some fucking Indian mafia."

I had no idea how long Dan and his bar could hold out against the tide of development in northern Virginia. I liked to believe I was doing my part holding back the flood of McMansions, dropping by a couple of times a week for three or four beers. But I'm not much for kidding myself. Spending thirty or forty bucks at Dan's couldn't stop the inevitable any more than plugging one Mohammed Mohammed could make much difference when thousands more are being bred every day.

But a man's got to try.

I drank for an hour or so while Dan cleaned the place up before closing. Then I dropped a twenty on the bar and headed for the door.

"See ya next time, Dan-o."

"Right."

My apartment's just a few blocks from Dan's. It was close to 2:00 a.m., so the streets were deserted. I enjoy the dead quiet after all the stores and bars and restaurants have closed. Everything feels cleaner.

I let myself in when I got home, headed for the fridge, and popped the top on a Miller Genuine Draft. Early hours of the morning are when I do my best thinking, especially while enjoying a cold beer. I've got an old TV I bought cheap, too, hooked into the cable provided by a previous tenant who surreptitiously split it off from a neighbors' service. Fox News popped up when I switched it on. It's mostly self-righteous blowhards who like to talk tough about the war against ragheads but who look like they'd be much too worried about mussing their expensive hair-dos to actually do anything in their lives like sweat out a combat situation in a foxhole. Maybe someone with a sense of humor named the network 'Fox.' But it beats the other news channels. Most of the people on Fox are white and don't try to impress you that they're better-educated than everyone else.

This morning's rant was by some guy with puffy red cheeks assailing liberals who believe non-Americans have rights. I had to admit, what he said made a lot of sense. But I can never get past thinking TV news commentators all look like they'd wilt like delicate flowers if they had to face the kind of shit I deal with routinely. It's too true that this country's getting soft, but Mr. Fat-Face Foxman just looked like part of the problem to me.

"Buddy," I tend to talk back to news on the tube. Probably comes from being a loner. "You might want to stop worrying so much about foreigners in Trashcanistan and pay some attention to the rotten apples right here at home."

That reminded me; there'd been a new disk from the boss when I'd opened the safe, and I've found looking over a fresh assignment is a great way to unwind. I switched off the TV and sat down at the dinette table I'd bought at a garage sale months before, powering up the aging laptop I'd liberated from the office—it had been stored behind a filing cabinet for months, maybe years. I hadn't bothered to inform anybody at work that I'd taken it—given the amount of dust I'd had to blow off it, I suspect it had disappeared from government inventories just after the Berlin Wall was torn down. Yeah, it's not great security, bringing work home, but I didn't figure I needed to tell my boss. Fucking management doesn't have to know everything.

The disk contained the usual information: a name, age, addresses for work and home. This one even had a photograph that looked like it had been pulled off a passport application. I studied the picture of Mrs. Gladys Thurington, resident of Joplin, Missouri, for some time. She wasn't bad looking, actually. Gladys was in her early 40s and worked at someplace called Borderline Books. I was a little surprised, actually, by the remarkable transition from Mr. Mohammed Mohammed the raghead African to Mrs. white-bread middle-America Gladys Thurington.

America's all about diversity these days. I guess it makes sense that the country's enemies are a diverse lot, too.

Chapter III
A Boss, a Bud, a Nosy Broad

THE NEXT MORNING I WOKE UP with a slight headache. Late nights and Miller will do that. I opened another one for breakfast to kill the pain and drank it with my usual boiled egg and toast. I guess that makes me sound like some kind of alcoholic, waking up and grabbing some "hair of the dog." Hell, maybe I am. It was 8:30 in the morning.

I threw on shorts, a t-shirt and running shoes and headed out for a 5 mile run up to the university and back. I've been starting every day with a run since my time in the army, and not some lame middle-age executive jog with an Ipod and earphones. I like to warm up for the first mile, then mix in one-minute sprints with one-minute cool-downs for the next couple, and end it with a progressive build over the last two miles until I'm going a steady 8 or 9 mile-an-hour clip. Most of my assignments aren't very physically demanding, but I figure it's still a good idea to be able to hot-foot it outta someplace without pulling up gasping for air.

Back at the apartment, I showered and threw on some khakis, a long-sleeved blue shirt, brown suede shoes and brown belt, a tie, and navy-blue blazer. I hate suits. Don't own one. Khakis, tie, and blazer are a compromise, and I'm sure some of the pinstripe bozos out there look down on me, but it makes me look businesslike enough that I don't stand out. Besides, some senior EPA bigshot came by the office once to look us over, and she was wearing flip-flops, for Christ's sake. I wasn't going into the office today, anyway.

I got in my car and headed toward highway 50. I don't drive anything fancy, just a cheap Ford Escort I bought when I moved to Fairfax. In North Carolina I'd always had a Ford F-150 pick-up, of course. I'm not really sure why Ford makes anything else. You can throw a variety of crap in the back, and there's plenty of room for two or three in the cab on those rare occasions when you're not alone. But white-collar northern Virginians don't drive F-150s. That's what the rednecks who fix the plumbing, rotting windows, and damp basements in their overpriced homes drive. The white-collar residents drive huge SUVs, Mercedes, Audis, or BMWs if they can afford it, else they drive Japanese imitations. I'm trying not to look like a redneck, but I can't stomach giving a ton of money to the Krauts, and I sure as shit wouldn't be caught dead driving a Jap car. The Escort's a Ford, at least.

Where I was headed was about a 45 minute drive if you take I-66 to the 495 Beltway, connect to 395 and the Duke street exit into Alexandria. I never go that way. I like to head down highway 50 into Annandale, cut through a few back streets to Falls Church, meander through Arlington down to Glebe road and then head south to Alexandria. That takes 1 1/2 to 2 hours, but it's more pleasant than taking your life in your hands on Washington's freeways. It's also better if you want to make sure you're not being followed.

I took Glebe to Mt. Vernon Drive, ducked back into the neighborhood and found a place to park. Then I walked the three blocks or so to a beat-up restaurant with outdoor seating and an awning sporting the name

"Wafle Shop." How someone can own a restaurant and not know how to spell "waffle" beats me. The clock on the post office across the street read 11:30. I grabbed one of the empty tables under the awning and started perusing the menu, like I hadn't been there dozens of times before and didn't know what I might find.

"There you are, Paladin." My boss sat down across the table from me. He's a little guy; dweeby-looking, really. Soaking wet, I bet he wouldn't weigh more than 130 pounds. Always wears a dark suit that seems a size too big. Today he was sporting a pink tie with the white button-down shirt he'd picked out that morning from what was certainly a row of white button-down shirts in his closet. His ties were the only colorful thing about him: I'm betting his wife bought them for him. Add wire-rimmed glasses, short but always-disheveled hair, and a little pencil mustache and you've got a guy who looks like he'd be at home in some book-keeping firm in Ames Iowa. Hell, for all I knew, my boss, Addington Riffelbach, might actually have had a degree in accounting. He had the name for it. But he was no accountant these days. A few times I'd actually caught myself wondering how he wound up with the EPA. Only a few times, though; I didn't really care.

I looked across the street at the clock on the post office. 11:35. He was always punctual.

"Hope you didn't have any trouble finding the place, boss." We always greeted each other the same way. I could probably sound more professional if I said it was a signal and counter-signal, but it wasn't. It was just ritual. Habit. Routine filling the void of not knowing what else to say.

It had been Riffelbach's idea to meet outside the office on the day after I filed the paperwork for an assignment. We'd eventually settled on the Wafle Shop and agreed to 11:35—I made it a habit to arrive 5 minutes early. Once we'd agreed to the arrangements, we never discussed it again, meaning no one at the office would ever overhear the time or place. And the Wafle Shop was far enough away and obscure enough to make it unlikely we'd run into anyone we knew.

The point of these meetings originally had been to give us a venue to discuss the assignments more openly in case there were problems or last minute developments—damage control—we needed to deal with. But there never were. I'm good at my work. And I'd learned early on that my boss really didn't want to hear any details or even discuss the jobs at all. His arrival was acknowledgment that he'd opened the safe and read my reports. We met, the job was behind us, we'd have lunch and discuss baseball or traffic or the weather, then we'd move on.

Except this day. We ordered—buckwheat pancakes, two fried eggs, bacon, and coffee for me; a spinach salad and mineral water for him—and settled in to wait for the food. Then he surprised me.

"Sharon said you were working late at the office last night."

"Huh? Well, yeah, I was writing up . . . you know. I do that all the time, come in after a job to write it up."

"She was pretty curious. Wondered if I had you working on some special project. Said it's funny how you're supposed to be some kind of malingerer yet you work such late hours."

"She's the nosy type. I didn't expect to run into her that late, though."

"What was she doing there?"

"She said she'd been out drinking with some friends

and stopped in to pee. What'd you tell her?"

"That you were probably in late to use office equipment illegally in pursuit of some personal project or business you didn't want any of the rest of us to know about."

"Gee, was that smart? That'll just make her nosier."

"Yes, I am aware of that." He scowled. "I guess I couldn't think of anything better to say. Might be a good idea if you don't come in evenings for awhile."

"When am I supposed to do my paperwork?"

"Just come in during the day. No one's going to look over your shoulder. Besides, your next, er, assignment will take some time to complete, I think. And you'll have to be away a bit. Maybe she'll find something more interesting to be curious about."

"Not likely. Sharon's been nosing around me for awhile. I don't think she buys that malingerer story any more." I'd been concerned about Sharon for some time but hadn't known how to bring it up. Now that he had started the discussion: "Seems to me we're going to have to do something about Sharon."

"Do something? What are you suggesting? You want to take care of her, like one of your, uh, clients?"

He said it so matter-of-factly, like he'd been considering it. I was stunned.

"No. That's not what I meant at all. I work with her. If something happened to her, there'd be police checking into all of us. I meant maybe we should bring her on board, brief her into the program. She's smart. I could use her help. Hell, she could type up my reports."

"No." He looked up at me, staring with emotionless eyes. My boss is one cold fish. "As I have told you many times, your work is known only to you and me.

We don't 'bring other people on board,' as you put it."

"Right."

"You haven't, have you?"

"Haven't what?"

"Brought someone else on board."

"Of course not. I know how sensitive this project is."

"Good." He was still staring at me. The look was an odd mixture of faraway and intense. "We want to keep this as compartmented as possible."

"Yeah, I know. I remember what you told me from the start. Just you, me, and the people you report to."

There was silence. The waitress brought our food. He looked down at his spinach salad, picked up his fork and started munching delicately.

"Yes, of course, the people I report to."

The rest of the lunch was uneventful. He made a few comments about having attended a Washington Nationals game at RFK. He thought it was good that the city finally had a baseball team again. I've been a Braves fan since Dale Murphy played and can't forget that the Nationals used to be the Montreal Expos. I have a hard time respecting anyone or anything that's spent that much time in Canada. We exchanged several meaningless platitudes about baseball teaching valuable lessons about life and overcoming adversity. The check came. He paid it. I figure he claimed these meetings as business lunches.

"Guess I'd better be getting back, Paladin." He liked that name, liked using it. I'd gotten fond of it too. Had a nice ring to it. It had been his idea from the start, my assuming a new identity when I moved to the area and went to work for him. He even provided everything I needed; driver's license, social security card, a birth certificate. I moved to Fairfax and became Richard Paladin.

It seemed pretty obvious my boss had connections with some spook department that could come up with well-documented identities. For trips like the one I'd be making soon, in fact, he kept the safe in my office well-stocked with envelopes, each containing a throw-away identity kit. Every piece of identification had my photo, too, obviously taken from a passport photo I'd attached to my original job application. But each ID photo had been subtly doctored—hair color slightly altered, eyebrows thinner or bushier, face made fatter or thinner—so it resembled me enough to be usable but would prove difficult to match to my actual face if it turned up out of the blue. Whatever spook department Riffelbach used was good.

I waited about five minutes after he had gone before heading back to my car, then drove a roundabout route back to Arlington, just to make sure no one had followed him to the meeting and then started following me. Once I'd established that I was clean, I headed to the main branch of the Arlington library. It was time to start pulling together information about Joplin, Missouri.

Library's have always been great places for research, I guess. That is, if you want to know who won the Battle of Hastings or have suddenly lost your senses and decided to read a Shakespeare novel or something. Before this job, I almost never set foot in one. But modern public libraries have something invaluable. They have publicly accessible Internet terminals that you can use in complete anonymity. I'm certain they're monitored, of course, so if you start pulling up porn images or instructions on how to make a nuclear bomb, you're going to get a tap on the shoulder. And if you decide you have to check-your e-mail, you might as well just sign the monitor in indelible ink. But checking out hotels, businesses, and tourist information for Joplin, Missouri wasn't going to get me noticed.

The library wasn't too busy, not surprising for early Wednesday afternoon. The main Arlington branch is large, two stories and lots of books, CDs, and DVDs to browse. There were maybe a dozen customers meandering about, mostly women. Years ago I suspect libraries were filled with women on weekdays, husbands at work, children at school. The numbers have dwindled because so many wives have to work to provide additional income so their families don't go broke.

To the right of the main desk are the Internet terminals. Half of the ten terminals were occupied—one elderly gentleman dressed in a natty brown suit and four obvious homeless people enjoying the air conditioning. I installed myself at one of the empty machines and began surfing.

It's important, when conducting Internet research—even in the anonymity of the public library—to conduct a lot of very broad searches that get to the information you're looking for without giving away what it is you're specifically seeking. For example, say you want to know a cheap place to stay in Joplin, Missouri that's within a couple of miles of a particular Borderline Books store. The easiest way, of course, would be to plot the location of the bookstore on one of the many mapping sites, then search one of the travel sites for a map of hotels, overlay the two and start comparing prices. Simple, indeed, except that now one of the major Internet search engine companies has a permanent record that a user in Arlington made that specific search. When someone working at that store then turns up dead, a search of that search-engine company's databases can produce a list of everyone who made such a specific search. I'm betting that would be a pretty short list.

That might sound paranoid, thinking Joplin cops are that sophisticated and have access to search *Ask Fred's* records. I'm sure lots of people would scoff at that notion. I don't. My old buddy, Joe Sprague, is serving hard time in a Tennessee prison for being cavalier about Internet searches. When the Knoxville police did, in fact, query a national Internet service provider for any record of someone searching for information about and directions to a specific abortion clinic that had been blown up, lo and behold they came up with one user. And since Joe wasn't even careful about using a public library—he did all the research at his sister's house in Barnwell, North Carolina because she conveniently had broadband service—he not only made himself easy to find, but complicated things further by making it a federal crime.

I began with a Google search for "Missouri Compromise" and read the Wikipedia entry that popped up. There I found a link to a Missouri history website, checked out some facts about Missouri's colorful past, browsed a few Missouri newspapers online, and eventually made my way to *The Joplin Globe*. After reading some very boring articles about city politics, I clicked on a link to www.joplinmo.org. What I learned there is that Joplin is a pretty small town with one shopping mall, two museums, and 130 churches. It looked more than anything like a great place for a visitor to stick out like a sore thumb.

I didn't bother looking up any hotels or motels. Joplin didn't look like a place that attracts many tourists. I doubted I'd need a reservation.

A plan was beginning to formulate in my head. First was the logistics of getting to Joplin. Clearly, I wouldn't fly there. Airline arrival and departure information is practically a permanent record that cops can go back and peruse years later. I wouldn't want a record of my arriving in Joplin and then departing. Best would be to fly someplace about a day's drive away—looking at a map, I picked Dallas—and then rent a car. Of course, I'd use one of my phony identification packets for all this.

Some people might wonder why all the caution if I was going to do the job in alias. Those are the kind of people cops want committing crimes. Your average detective is no genius, but you'd be making a big mistake assuming they're stupid. The more layers you can put between yourself and the victim, the better your chances of getting away.

Of course, there's also the question of why I would worry about this at all, since I would be doing this job on behalf of the U.S government. Surely I'd have some kind of get-out-of-jail free card. Actually, I assume I do. But that misses the point that secret, compartmented programs have to be protected, and that includes keeping them from the Joplin police or the FBI. Hell, that's one reason why I take pains to make sure I don't have a tail, even in Washington. Maybe Joe Citizen in Indianapolis believes the Federal Government is one big monolith: he's wrong; Federal agencies are rivals, all competing for money and trying to make each other look bad. That includes blowing the lid on some other Agency's programs that could prove embarrassing if made public. Pulling a job like this one off correctly would mean my secret program would remain secret and I'd be able to continue doing my job. The more distance I could put between my persona in Joplin and Mr. Richard Paladin, Washington-based EPA employee, the better. I decided to burn two aliases, one for the trip to Dallas, and another to use during the operation in Joplin.

The final security layer on this job would be choosing a method of execution that would give the cops a convenient way to close the case once they realized there wasn't an obvious perpetrator. This means making it look like suicide or an accident. For that, though, I'd have to go to Joplin and do some surveillance on Mrs. Thurington. A well-disguised killing has to be tailored to fit the victim.

I also didn't want to risk two trips to Joplin the way I'd made separate trips to New York to survey Mohammed and then kill him. No, I'd set myself up in Joplin, look over the target, devise a plan, execute it, then head home. I considered flying back from a different city—maybe St. Louis—under yet a third persona, but rejected the notion. Whoever made the trip to Dallas would return from there a week or so later. One-way flights just look too suspicious.

After finding out what I'd set out to learn for the preliminaries of my plan, I headed back to my apartment. I've got some good sets of road atlases and maps there. Figuring out where Borderline Books is wouldn't require the Internet—I'd been provided the address, after all. I'd go ahead and find the best way to drive from Dallas to Joplin as well. All the final preparations, like finding a travel agent I'd never used before and buying airline tickets to Dallas, would have to wait until the next day, when I could stop by the office and pick up a couple of my alias packets.

The drive back to my apartment was terrible. I'd screwed around in the library long enough that I hit the rush hour. Washington has far and away too many people, and they are all on the roads between 5:00 and 7:00 p.m. I'd decided to return via Hwy. 50, pretty much a straight shot to Fairfax. Once I entered off Glebe Road, of course, traffic came to a virtual standstill. Fortunately, I'm the patient type. I had plenty of gas and a decent air conditioning unit in the car, so I cranked up the AC and turned on the radio, content to listen to the two morons on the afternoon drive-time program screaming at each other about Washington's plans to build a new baseball stadium for the Nationals. One guy seemed particularly upset about discussion to locate the ballpark in Anacostia, a traditionally black neighborhood. He didn't put it in exactly those terms, of course. He kept talking about the "logistical difficulties" of people going to a "distressed neighborhood" at night. Clearly he was afraid of getting gunned down by some angry black teenager. I knew better, of course. I was living in Charlotte when they built the new football stadium there. All the poor people who had been living in the neighborhood their whole lives were forced out by the real estate developers, business owners and various other well-heeled citizens who benefit from taxpayer-funded sports facilities. That angry black teenager would no doubt be even angrier after his family got screwed and forced to move to the middle of nowhere, but he wouldn't be in the area any longer to threaten Mike and Morris, the two gun-shy radio personalities.

Traffic had been inching along for half an hour

when I came upon the cause of the trouble. Two vehicles were pulled off to the side, a Saab 9-3 with all its windows, headlights and tail-lights smashed in, and a large black SUV just ahead of it with a scrape mark on the front passenger-side panel. Five police cars were ringing the accident site—the police cars were actually blocking the highway and causing all the traffic congestion. A woman leaning against the front hood of the Saab was sobbing. Several cops milled around, occasionally waving at cars like they were trying to direct traffic.

One came up to my car and tapped on my window. I rolled it down.

"We're closing the road for about thirty minutes. You might want to shut your engine off."

"Sure, officer." Some people would have started yelling at the guy. I know better. I'm always nice to cops. "What's going on?"

"Lotta glass on the road. We're getting a fire crew in to sweep it up and make sure there's no gasoline spillage."

"Wow. Must have been some wreck. Where's the other vehicle, the one that hit the Saab? Already tow it away?

"Nah, not yet. Just two vehicles, the Saab and that SUV."

"Man, that must be one sturdy SUV." I was impressed. This might be a vehicle I'd need someday in my line of work. "I mean, the Saab looks totaled and that SUV just has a little scratch."

"Oh, the collision apparently wasn't that serious." The cop was grinning, obviously with an amusing story he just couldn't wait to tell someone. "The lady driving the Saab was trying to enter the highway. Guy in the

SUV sped up to cut her off—happens all the time—and clipped her right side-mirror. She pulled over and he did too. She thought he was gonna apologize and give her the name of his insurance company."

"That's not why he pulled over?"

"Aw, fuck no. He was pissed she'd scratched his car. He gets out with a baseball bat and bashes in all her windows, then goes to work on the rest of the car. Road rage, man. It's something to see."

"Wow. That's unbelievable."

"Yeah, we got him handcuffed in the back of one of the cruisers. Some government big shot. He was waving his business card around, telling us he works for the Vice-President. Man, this town is full of assholes."

"Guess he's in some serious trouble."

"Shit. We'll take him in and book him, but he'll get off with a slap on the wrist. Veep's gotta lot of clout, you know. The woman works for some government agency, too. I doubt she'll press charges when she realizes the guy can make trouble for her. Anyway, shut off your engine and be patient and we'll have you on your way as soon as possible."

"No problem."

I shut off the engine and watched the sobbing woman for awhile. The cop was right, of course. If your boss is powerful enough, there's no crime you can't get away with. I could testify to that personally.

When I left the library, I had every intention of spending the evening in my apartment studying maps and atlases, boiling down the outlines of a plan in my head into specific routes and locations. After sitting in traffic for three hours—it hadn't improved much even after I made it past the Saab-SUV accident site—I was pretty well exhausted. Instead, I parked at my apartment complex and hiked over to Dan's.

"Well, must be my lucky week, you coming in two nights in a row." Dan looked the same as the night before; he might have been wearing the same worn flannel shirt and baggy shorts. There were a couple of regulars at the bar. Other than Dan and them, the place was empty. I sat at my usual stool. Dan placed a draft Bud in front of me.

"Got any chow tonight, Dan? Didn't get a chance to eat dinner." Dan doesn't have a kitchen, but he usually had something going in a crock-pot behind the bar and keeps some frozen pizzas in a small freezer by a microwave.

"You're in luck tonight. Got some of my homemade chili bubbling away. How about it?"

"Sounds great."

Dan grabbed a bowl from under the counter, flipped the top off the pot, and spooned up a healthy serving of a dark, reddish brown mess of meat and beans in a thick sauce. As soon as he set it in front of me I ladled a large spoonful into my mouth. It was real good, hot and pretty spicy. It had obviously been cooking away for hours, meat completely tenderized, beans almost dissolving. I hadn't had a good bowl of chili in ages.

"Want some saltines with that?"

"You bet."

He handed me a bunch of those packets of saltine crackers you find in salad bars. I tore open a handful and crumbled them into the chili, stirring them in to add some crunch to the texture of the meat and beans.

"Just like your mom used to make, I'll bet." I couldn't tell if he was being sarcastic.

"Yup. Just like homemade." Actually, my mom had been a lousy cook. She'd try to make traditional southern dishes like collard greens and produce something that tasted like mowed lawn grass boiled in piss. But I didn't figure Dan needed to know that.

"So you been slaving away today, government man? I figured you'd take the day off after sitting here so late last night."

"Had an important meeting. And started doing research for a new project."

"Anything interesting or the usual government make-work?"

Often I wondered what Dan would say if I told him the truth. How would he react if I said, 'Oh, nothing major, just a middle-aged woman in Joplin Missouri I've got to assassinate.' I've thought often of telling him something just like that, deadpan, to see if he'd believe me. Then I could always pass it off as a joke. It gets so boring, keeping your super cool job a secret all the time.

"Ah, usual government bullshit, Dan. Forms to fill out, papers to file. Endless meetings listening to crap. You know the drill."

"Yeah, I remember. Guess it pays the bills."

"That's right."

"So didn't you tell me you're in the toxic waste division?"

I spooned more chili into my mouth, trying to remember what I might have told Dan about my work. My boss had given me a cover story to tell people who asked questions like what division I was with, and it was indeed the toxic waste section. He'd even given me a couple of articles to read about Love Canal, pollution in Lake Erie, superfund clean-up sites and so on. I'd read enough to realize the world is pretty much saturated with chemical shit that's going to kill us all and there's nothing much anyone in the government can do about it.

"Yeah, that's right."

"Must have been a lot of buzz in your office today."

I froze. I didn't have a clue what he was talking about. I didn't panic. "Yeah, big buzz. Hey, how'd you hear about it? I mean, it's been the buzz in the office for weeks, but I thought it was still under wraps."

"Christ, it's all over the news."

"Oh, no. Like I said, I've been in some technical meetings all day. How much is in the press? Lot of details?" I was praying he'd provide some details so I could talk around whatever the hell I was in the dark about.

"Details? Plenty of them. Some people are gonna have a lot of explaining to do."

Okay, strike two. I figured I had one more stab to figure out what he was talking about. After that, he'd start wondering how I could be in the dark about something involving my office, how I could not know something all over the news that was so relevant to my job. This could lead inevitably and quickly to curiosity about what I really do and why I would lie about where I work. I decided to try a riskier strategy, throw out something and hope it hit the mark.

"You're right about that. Tell me, did the news have anything about the woman?"

"Huh?"

"The woman." I was banking that any government scandal would involve sex in some form. It's usually a safe bet. I crossed my fingers. "You know, the woman he was having sex with."

"Oh, man! They mentioned something about there

being more to it than monetary payoffs. I guess I should have figured. A big company like Ameri-Chem, yeah, sure they'd set the inspector up with a hooker, too. Pretty sad, when you think about it. All those poor kids in New Jersey playing in a schoolyard next to a PCB dump, and this clown covers it up for a few bucks and a good screw. It's a fucked-up world."

It is, indeed, a fucked-up world. But he'd just saved my ass. "Yeah, Dan, some things are beyond belief. But his ass is in the can now. I'm just glad New Jersey is not my area of responsibility." I made a mental note to start actually reading the *Washington Post* news more often. I look through the paper every day, of course; mostly the obituaries.

"Yeah, I'll bet you're glad." Dan moved to right across the bar from me and leaned close. "So maybe some other big company is providing you with pussy to ignore a little pollution?"

"I'm not an inspector, Dan."

"Then why do you travel all the time?"

"I do special projects." Why was Dan suddenly so interested? "And, by the way, I don't have to take hand-outs from some corporation to get laid. I can manage that all on my own."

"I guess you probably can." Dan looked me over, like he was seeing me for the first time. "You're sure not the typical fat slob civil servant I'm used to, are you. So what exactly do you do for the EPA?"

"I've told you many times, I can't discuss my work. It's classified."

"Right. You've told me that before. Well, then, enjoy your chili, Mr. Paladin." He winked and went back to wiping down the bar.

I finished eating, quaffed my beer, dropped a twenty

on the counter, and left feeling uncomfortable. Two people in less than 24 hours getting curious about what I really do was unnerving. I decided consecutive evenings at Dan's was a mistake I wouldn't repeat soon.

The next morning I got up early, had coffee with my toast and boiled egg, did my ten-mile run and went into the office. I needed to pick up two of my alias packets. I also wanted to make sure Sharon hadn't turned me in for inappropriate use of government equipment after her conversation with my boss.

"Good morning, Mr. Paladin." She had that sly smile as always.

"Morning, Sharon. How are you today?"

"Missed you yesterday. Guess you were off on one of those projects that seem to keep you out of the office."

"Nah, I was just screwing off. You should try it. Good for the soul."

"Well, I might, if I had something better to do than come to work."

"Oh, come on. I'm sure you could find something better to do than work if you put your mind to it."

"Why, I like my job, Mr. Paladin."

"Nothing wrong with that, I guess."

"But I'm always open to suggestions."

"Suggestions?"

"For something better to do during the day." My God she was a tease. Suddenly I couldn't think of anything else other than what she and I could be doing right now instead of work.

"Yeah, well I better get to my office. Got some paperwork to catch up on."

"Okay, Mr. Paladin. Go get yourself caught up,

then."

I why I'd suggested bringing Sharon into the project the day before. I could tell she was interested in me, but I could also see that she was just amused by me because I clearly didn't fit in with the other EPA wonks in our office. No doubt she felt a little sorry for me because, from her perspective, I was being mistreated. That translated to a big dose of pity, in my book, and although I was getting increasingly interested in seeing just how far Sharon might take this little game, I am not the kind of guy who's interested in a pity-fuck. Deep down, what I really wanted was to get Sharon alone somewhere and scare the shit out of her by telling her just exactly what I do, describing in detail what a dangerous and important guy I really am, then bang her brains out while she moaned "Oh I just knew you were a real man Mr. Paladin!"

It's always that inner cave man that gets guys in trouble. I headed to my office to open the safe and retrieve my alias packages. On the way, I grabbed the office copy of the *Washington Post* in order to catch up on the news and figure out the full story of what Dan had been talking about the night before. I also made a mental note to find a hooker somewhere soon and get myself laid in order to quiet the urge to have sex with Sharon and fuck up everything royally.

I found the article I was looking for on page A9. It really wasn't much of a story. Some mid-level EPA manager—Dan had been wrong about him being a line inspector—had buried a report citing Ameri-Chem as responsible for disposing of thousands of gallons of PCBs in a landfill near some small New Jersey town. The stuff had been sitting around an Ameri-Chem warehouse for decades and the corporate managers feared some EPA inspector would find out about it and force them to take care of it safely, which would have cost a fortune. So they bought a landfill through a subsidiary and buried the toxins, figuring it was all stored in barrels so no one would ever know. Of course, some locals in the town saw barrels being trucked in and got suspicious. They called a local newspaper, who called a local EPA official for a comment, who then assigned an inspector to take a look, and so on. Sure enough, a few tests revealed that the barrels were obviously leaking. The inspector dutifully wrote up his findings and noted the proximity to a local playground, etc. I mean, these stories are a dime a dozen. The report would have been buried anyway. As I can attest, the EPA is focused on a lot of other things these days besides kids breathing in a few PCBs. Talk about old news.

But then some genius at Ameri-Chem decided to phone someone he knew at the regional office and call in a few favors—favors to the tune of thousands of dollars worth of free vacations, golf trips, expensive dinners, and promises of post-retirement employment made to the EPA's Upper East Coast Regional Office director. The director obtained the report, sent it back to the original inspector with about three dozen unanswerable questions, and then called the inspector personally to mention that he was considering a suitability review to get the guy fired. Sure enough, the inspector called the *New York Times* and the rest is history—or actually just journalism, I guess. People being incredibly stupid is always news.

What made no sense to me was why Dan Stigler would focus on this very ordinary story and use it as an excuse to pry into my line of work. That was something I'd have to do some digging into. But it could wait. Mrs. Thurington came first.

At lunchtime I pocketed a fresh alias envelope and headed out for a travel agent I'd never used before. Travel agents are getting harder and harder to find in this day of Internet booking for everything from hotels to plane tickets to rental cars. Fortunately there are still a few people left who prefer dealing with a real person over a counter to the anonymity of the Web. Thumbing through a Yellow Pages I'd liberated from someone else's desk months before, I found a travel agent in Silver Spring. Admittedly, I could have done everything—bought airline tickets, rented a car—on the Internet at the library in alias since each envelope always had a couple of credit cards. But I sure don't use my street address when I'm using a phony ID, and setting up P.O. boxes or front addresses where I could receive mail is pretty impractical since I use one or two different identities with every major job.

I stopped by Sharon's desk on my way out. She was busy typing away at something.

"I've got a bunch of meetings out of the office this afternoon, Sharon. I won't be back today."

"Sure thing." She didn't even look up. I hadn't often seen her so engrossed in anything.

"Must be something pretty interesting you're working on."

"What?" She'd barely heard me at first. "Oh, Mr. Paladin. Sorry. Just typing up the quarterly report on the Kyoto Protocol Public Relations Initiative. It's due next week and our wait-til-the-last-minute boss of course handed it to me 15 minutes ago."

"That's too bad. Guess you'll be busy the rest of this week. Kyoto Protocol Public Relations Initiative, huh?

Boy, that sounds scintillating, Sharon. My condolences." I headed for the stairs.

"Do you want to look it over before I send it out, Mr. Paladin?"

I laughed. Sharon did have a sense of humor. "And what on earth would give you the idea that I'd give a rat's ass about some idiotic public relations initiative on the Kyoto Protocol, Sharon?"

"Oh, nothing." She smiled. I resumed my path to the stairs. "It's just that you're listed as the program manager."

I froze. My mind raced, searching for an explanation. Maybe it was some kind of joke Sharon was playing on me. But the boss did have me putting a Kyoto Protocol memo on all my reporting. Was he really listing me on a Kyoto project as part of my cover? But then why hadn't he bothered to tell me? Or had he told me and it had just slipped my mind? How could I let something like that slip my mind? I decided I'd just have to bluff my way through yet again.

"Geeze, you know how I hate memos, Sharon." I turned toward her and gave her my sincerest look. "I mean, I already spent hours last week discussing this report with Riffelbach, and I'm sure he knows what to write better than me. But you're right, I better read it. Tell you what, I'm not sure I'm going to have time to look it over before the deadline, so why don't you just give it back to Riffelbach for review and send it when he's satisfied. But, if you wouldn't mind, could you make me a copy so I can at least read it when I get a chance? Just to make sure we're all on the same page."

"Why, no problem, Mr. Paladin. I'll just leave a copy of the final report on your desk."

"Thanks, Sharon." Yes, I definitely wanted to know

what the hell was in this report with my name on it. But I had an assignment, and that came first. Dan Stigler and the Kyoto Protocol would have to wait until after my date in Joplin.

Chapter IV
The Traveling Salesman

TEXANS think everything about their state is bigger than life, and this includes thunderstorms and tornados. They brag about the life-destroying forces of nature that ravage their cities, towns, farms and ranches the way fathers brag about sons who have turned out to be successful lawyers or baseball players. In this regard, Texans are no different than any of the other peoples inhabiting the Midwest. Kansans, Arkansans, Iowans, Ohioans, Nebraskans and Dakotans from North and South all seem to think that being beset by hailstorms, floods, blizzards, drought, and whatever other apocalypses nature can toss their way is a reason to be exceedingly proud. When I landed in Dallas—my flight had dodged around, between, and under huge thunderheads during the last 45 minute approach to DFW—the guy at the car rental counter literally puffed out his chest as if to announce having just won the Nobel Prize and told me, "Gonna be some big storms blowin' through here this afternoon!" I signed the rental contract—as Jock Desplanes—grabbed the keys and headed to the parking lot before he could wax eloquent about hailstones the size of meteors or something.

Just north of the Oklahoma border, though, I had to admit he had been on the mark. I was sitting in a roadside park waiting for what seemed to be a category 9 hurricane to pass. Not being able to see beyond the front of your car is a sign it's time to pull over in my book, especially since the drivers all around me seemed to respond to the weather by speeding up and using their horns more. I was lucky to see the roadside park sign at all. I pulled in, shut off the motor, moved the seat-rest back, and closed my eyes, figuring the rain slacking up would eventually wake me. I don't figure I'm ever in a big enough rush to risk getting killed on the highway. Besides, carrying two sets of IDs in different names was not something I'd want to explain to a cop after coming around in a hospital.

The trip had been uneventful prior to the thunderstorm. I'd bought a round-trip ticket for Dallas on the Saturday morning flight—returning in two weeks—from the Silver Spring travel agent that Thursday afternoon. She'd been curious, of course, what was taking me to Dallas on such short notice, commiserating that I wouldn't get a good fare. She was a fairly young, mousy-looking thing with little green-plastic-rim glasses that she probably thought made her look smart. Once the charge was approved to Cedric Dibald's black extra-platinum VISA card, she became downright friendly.

"I've never been to Dallas myself. I'll bet it's a nice town." She was waiting for the tickets to print. I always ask for tickets instead of E-tickets if I can get them. "So is this a business trip?"

I could tell I was being evaluated. Amber—that was the name on her deskplate—was hoping to figure out if I was a successful businessman she might want to get to know better. Athletic-looking guys with decent lines of credit and no signs of a wedding band—like the little white line on the ring finger where there usually is one—are not all that common in the Washington area. Hell, I doubt if they're common anywhere in the world.

But Cedric Dibald definitely wasn't available, and although Richard Paladin wouldn't have minded an evening or two with sweet little Amber, making that introduction would be a bit complicated. I nipped the conversation in the bud.

"Got a call yesterday from a buddy of mine in Fort Worth. He scored a couple of passes to a hunting ranch out by Abilene. Gonna spend a couple of weeks hunting deer." She had the look of a tree-hugger.

"Oh. Well, I've never been hunting. But that sounds interesting, hiking in the forest, tracking animals and all that." Give her credit for open-mindedness. She could obviously forgive me murdering some huge buck as part of the Rambo survival fantasy she was concocting in which she was no doubt going to be saved from a fate worse than death and then ravaged by yours truly.

"Ah, it's not quite like that. They put you in a tree blind and herd a group of farm-raised deer in front of you. You shoot as many as you can, then go back to the ranch-house and drink all night. It's a lot of fun."

"Well!" That had ended the fantasy and her interest in me.

Friday I spent all day at my gym, a small fitness facility just down the road in Vienna run by a 50-something lesbian yoga instructor. No telling just how long wrapping up the Joplin job would take. I don't like going more that two days between weight-lifting sessions, but it might be a week or more before I'd have time to find a gym somewhere. Besides, I like being muscle-fatigued when I fly. Makes it easier to sleep in those cramped little seats.

As always, the worst part of the trip had been clearing airport security at Washington National, lovingly known as Reagan International since the cowboy-actor president died and was deified by the Republican Party. Actually, I think I saw Pat Buchanan standing outside the new multi-billion dollar terminal building once touching a dedication plaque while he bowed his head, then crossed himself before heading inside to take a flight somewhere. Some people carry St. Anthony's medals or rabbits' feet, I figure, so why shouldn't Pat seek Ronnie's protection. Hell, I've heard it said God'll forgive you if you touch your balls when you lie. I don't bother with any of that crap. I know from personal experience, we're all going to die and we don't have any say about when or how. And if there's an after-life that involves punishment for our sins, we're all fucked.

A talisman or religious medal that could get you onto a plane these days without having to deal with the Transportation Security Authority would be nice to have, though. TSA's mission, I am convinced, is to make prospective airline passengers as miserable and uncomfortable as possible prior to departure. There is obviously a TSA office solely devoted to finding obscure, harmless items to prohibit from aircraft and then keeping exactly what those items are a secret so thousands of people unknowingly try to board with their shampoo, toothpaste, nail clippers, digital music players, or whatever else is taboo this week. To add to the stress of random confiscations, there are the random procedures of which items of clothing must be removed prior to passing through the metal detector. Sometimes it's jackets, sometimes shoes and jackets, occasionally belts, glasses, watches. These have to be deposited in plastic bins that are then run past the x-ray on a belt and subsequently dumped out on a table on the other side where everyone who's still stunned by having been screamed at about trying to smuggle peppermint gum onto the flight is now forced to sift through piles of clothes and put their shoes back on standing up. All the while, of course, the semi-literate, grossly obese TSA officers scream random instructions like "No fluids!" or "Shoes only no sandals!" to add to the cacophony.

My favorite was a female TSA officer I saw once when I was boarding a flight to Michigan who must have been 300 pounds minimum—where do they find a uniform for someone like that?—yelling "Matches only no lighters!" A supervisor type waddled up to her and yelled something at her, and she switched to "Lighters only no matches!" Then yet another TSA guy on the other side of the checkpoint waved frantically at her, at which point she started yelling "No match lighters!"

Of course, TSA isn't making us any safer. About six months earlier, in fact, I was drinking in an airport bar in Cleveland between flights returning from a job and got to talking to a guy who turned out to be head of security for one of those puddle-jumper economy airlines. He'd had a bad day and was getting about as wasted as anyone I've ever seen, and I've seen quite a few people tie one on. I've got a soft spot for guys who need to drink away their troubles—I try it myself periodically, although I never get drunk, just belligerent—and I bought him a couple of rounds. In gratitude, he related to me in hushed tones, "Listen, buddy. You should know. About once a month, TSA management picks an airport at random, makes up a phony but realistic looking bomb, like imitation C-4 with a detonator or sticks that look like dynamite wired to an alarm clock, sticks it in a bag and runs it through the checked luggage or walks it past security. So far, the security screeners have missed every one. Every fucking one!"

"You're kidding, of course. They must catch one every once in awhile."

"Believe me or not. I'm not exaggerating." He downed the rest of the Jim Beam in his glass and looked at the bartender for another. "Failure rate so far is 100 percent."

"Well, don't they at least fire somebody when that happens?"

"I'm sure they do. Then they hire somebody else just as incompetent to replace them. I mean, Christ, they pay these people ten bucks an hour. Who ya gonna find with half a brain who's gonna work for that?"

"Still, I'm surprised it doesn't make the news more often, that TSA won't let grandmothers carry bottled water on a plane but allows somebody to walk on with a bomb."

He looked around to make sure no one could overhear. "This is top secret stuff, buddy. Fucking government would kill me if they knew I told you."

"Right." I'd have written him off as a crackpot, except I knew damn well he was correct about that last part.

Anyway, I wasn't concerned I'd have trouble making it through the security checkpoint for my flight to Dallas. I checked one bag containing a few days' clothing and an extra pair of shoes. All I took on board the flight with me was my wallet and watch. Sure, I had the Cedric Dibald driver's license and credit cards visible in the ID section of my wallet and a couple hundred dollars cash stuffed in the open bill section. In the zippered compartment was my Jock Desplanes driver's license, credit cards and $5,000 in hundreds. None of that sets off metal detectors, and TSA doesn't search wallets.

There's no reason to carry anything dangerous or alerting on an airplane. If it turned out I needed something lethal like a gun or machete; well, this is America. I could buy something like that anywhere.

It was after midnight when I pulled into Joplin. Arriving in a city with so many churches in the early a.m. on a Sunday seemed somehow fitting. As I'd expected, there were several chain motels on the outskirts of town. I pulled into a La Quinta. The parking lot was three-quarters full, which surprised me. I hoped I hadn't come right in the middle of some holy-roller fundamentalist convention.

"Got a room available?" The guy behind the counter looked south Asian and wore a name tag that read "Karesh." I couldn't tell if he was Indian or Pakistani—hell, maybe Bangladeshi. The only "Karesh" I'd ever heard of was the Waco cult leader who got killed in '93.

"I have four rooms left. One with a queen and three with doubles. How many?"

"Just one room, thanks."

"No, how many staying in the room?"

"Just me."

He looked up, surprised. "The room is the same price for one or two."

"Yeah, well, it's still just me."

"Okay." He slid a form across the counter. "Fill this out."

I took a ballpoint from a cup on the counter and

started writing, filling in Jock Desplanes' address and vitals. I'd memorized all this beforehand, of course. Pulling out your wallet and copying your name and address from an ID looks pretty suspicious.

"Looks like you're pretty full tonight." I talked while I wrote, like I was just making conversation. It's important to start getting the lay of the land as soon as possible when on a job. If I was going to be running into large tour groups or evangelists on holiday, I'd want to know in advance. "Convention of some kind in town?"

"Convention? Oh, no. Just Saturday night. This is a bit slow, actually. We're usually full on Saturday night." Karesh looked over the form. "Are you here on business?"

"Yes, I am." I'd prepared for this. It's vital to have a story for motel desk clerks. It's not that they really care. They're typically just bored. "Did you want me to fill in all that company information? I can."

"Oh, that's not necessary. How long will you be staying?"

"Not sure, really. At least a couple of nights, maybe longer. Depends on how business goes."

"What business are you in, if you don't mind my asking?"

"I represent a large religious book and software wholesaler."

"Oh." Karesh rolled his eyes. "You've come to the right place, then. May I have your credit card for an imprint?"

"Absolutely." I handed him my Jock Desplanes MasterCard. Whatever spook outfit provided these things to my boss, they all worked. Although he had warned me never to use one for more than a couple of weeks. I had no idea who got the bills.

"So what's the big draw on Saturday nights? People from outside Joplin come spend the night to attend services Sunday morning?"

"You think this is the Mecca of Missouri?" Karesh grinned. "Just locals who need a bed other than the one at home."

"Huh?" I'd been driving too long. It had slowed my mental capacities. "Oh, I get it."

"Yes, but don't worry. They will be in church tomorrow feeling guilty. Joplin is a very Christian city." He slid a key across the counter. "Room 149 is around the back. Have a pleasant night."

"Thanks." I went back to my car and drove to the back of the motel, parking between two very large pick-ups. The room was like hundreds I've stayed in, two double beds, a TV, plastic bucket for ice. I closed the door behind me, turned the security lock, latched the chain, and propped a chair against the door for good measure. Then I took off my clothes, dropped them on the floor, turned out the light and collapsed into bed. It had been a long day.

I finally fell asleep an hour later after the couple in the next room finished banging their headboard against the wall. And, no shit, a loud voice declaimed "Hallelujah!" just before the banging stopped. Joplin is, indeed, a very Christian city.

Sunday was a good day to start an assignment in Joplin. I slept late, finally crawling out of bed around 10:30, took a shower, pulled on jeans, a short-sleeve cotton shirt, Timberland hiking shoes, and strolled out to my car in the now empty parking lot. It was quiet, everyone no doubt in church asking God to forgive them their fornicating ways. I drove around the city for about an hour, then parked at Northpark Mall and set out to explore the town on foot. I like to get the feel of a new city before getting down to business. Joplin seemed like a pleasant enough place, big enough to have plenty of restaurants, movie houses, and bars so nobody gets bored, but not too big. Not like New York or Detroit where you sense people are sick of being forced to live on top of each other. Some of the older buildings were intact and even in use, giving it a little of the feel of those "good old days" people like to reminisce about. With the exception of Northpark, the carbon copy shopping areas spreading like cancer back in Fairfax hadn't made it here, it seemed. Just the American environment the EPA is trying to protect, I figured.

Which made it all the more imperative to find out about Mrs. Gladys Thurington and develop a plan. Whatever caused her to be located in idyllic Middle America, her appearance on my list of targets meant she must be bad news.

I found myself standing in front of an honest-to-god hardware store that wasn't an Ace or Home Depot, the kind of place where hard-working Americans had been buying tools to build this country for generations. There was a sign in the window reading "We Support Our Troops." A feeling of patriotism spread through me like heartburn. I wanted to go in and thank the owner.

Instead, I wandered back to Northpark Mall, cut through the parking lot and found Borderline Books on Bunny Lane just to the east of the shopping center. It was an old two-story wood-frame house that had been converted to a bookstore years before, from the look of it; not the kind of place that attracts lots of customers or has a large staff of sales clerks. Observing Gladys long enough to get a good feel for her habits wouldn't be easy in this environment. Fortunately, I noted a coffee shop directly across the street advertising free Wi-Fi.

The bookstore was closed Sundays, yet another quaint reminder that Joplin was still living in the past. I walked up to look at the books on display in the windows—used books in decent shape, novels I'd never heard of, social commentaries about something called the Weimar Republic. A flyer on the door announced yoga classes every Thursday evening at a nearby gym. I half expected a sign pointing to Alice's Restaurant around the back.

I hiked back to Northpark Mall and went inside. It was open, Sunday notwithstanding. I'd never been in this mall, of course, but I knew I'd find what I was looking for. Malls in Joplin, Springfield, Knoxville, Little Rock are all the same. There was a Radio Shack on the second floor.

Jock Desplanes went in and paid $473.92 cash for an Acer laptop with built in wireless. Tomorrow morning he'd be just another caffeine addict surfing the Web.

I was set up at a table by the window at Missouri Joe's Mocha Cafe by 8:30 a.m., coffee, blueberry muffin and laptop spread out in front of me. The place was more crowded than I'd figured. Actually, I was surprised the place existed at all. Most independent coffee shops went out of business long ago under the crushing wave of Starbucks and Daily Grinds franchises that have washed away the competition. There are always a few hold-outs, though, and this one seemed to have a decent clientele. I was lucky to get the one table with a decent view of the Borderline Books across the street.

Most of the customers were stopping by for coffee on their way to work, an assortment of upper-middle-class men and women in their 30s and 40s, many of them in all probability lawyers or real estate agents. My surveillance Sunday had revealed a neighborhood in transition from single-family housing to nice, older homes converted to small offices, mostly law and real estate offices. Unlike the thousands of Starbucks in the Washington area, Joe's Mocha Cafe wasn't overrun with skinny young girls in shorts, t-shirts and flip-flops. Quite the opposite, four elderly ladies were having coffee and scones at a table in one corner, undoubtedly discussing the finances of living on the pensions of long-buried husbands.

One eye always on the bookstore—it opened at 9:00—I powered up the laptop. I'd made sure to charge the battery the night before only to discover that there was an electric outlet conveniently located by my table. I could sit here all day under the guise of perusing the Internet or writing the great American novel. Or, at least until I got the shakes from too much caffeine.

The Acer wasn't a bad little machine. Since I don't have Internet at home and am not connected at the office, I usually only get a chance to explore the Internet at the library. Not surprisingly, this one had all the same Microsoft Windows software, so I knew to open Internet Explorer. Microsoft has made computers like Holiday Inns, where every room is identical so a blind person can stay there and not trip over the bed. Not being a software engineer or other form of nerd, I appreciate this. From what I've observed, it's only artistic people and social misfits who use Macs—the kind of people I get pissed off just looking at.

Sitting in Joplin, two identities removed from Richard Paladin, Washington wonk, with a brand new computer using a coffee shop's Internet, I figured it was finally safe to see what I could find out about Borderline Books. I Googled the name. Like everyone else in this day and age, they had a website. I opened it.

Classical music blared loudly from the Acer's little speaker. I quickly moved the cursor to the volume control on the task bar and hit mute. Library computers typically have headphones, which I never use because I like all my available senses focused on my surroundings. The music told me the place had some serious attitude. So did the "mission statement" in large, bold italics on the home page.

Borderline Books: Fine Books for Fine People
Chester Dotterling, Prop.

It boasted a "large collection of used and rare books in excellent condition." Its "knowledgeable staff" could advise instantly if a particular title was in stock. Dotterling himself was available to "exhaust book acquisition resources worldwide" for clients seeking an especially rare volume. Apparently Borderline Books was a place for people with too much money and nothing productive to do but pay exorbitantly for literary trophies.

In the bottom right corner of the page I noticed one of those virtual buttons you click for detail. It read "Stocking Personal Libraries." I clicked. A photo of Mrs. Gladys Thurington popped up on my screen.

I think I stopped breathing and reached reflexively

to fold down the computer screen before anyone else could see. For a brief moment I panicked that I had somehow brought the assignment disk and unconsciously loaded it into the floppy drive and displayed it. Calming myself, I glided my hand from the laptop to my coffee and drank a large gulp. That disk was in my safe in Washington. I kicked myself mentally for having lost my composure and took a closer look at the display.

Mrs. Gladys Thurington was Borderline's "home library consultant," available for consultation to help stock the shelves of the well-to-dos' home offices and studies. I read:

So you've finally moved into that beautiful estate home you've worked so hard for. But are you really ready to have friends over for drinks in that elegant library you've fantasized about your whole life? Do you have the books you'll need to properly impress your friends and colleagues with your new social stature? Stocking your library properly isn't just a matter of filling those shelves with old books you've had lying around. Gladys Thurington, our home library consultant, has advised some of Joplin's finest families on books with the correctly-toned leather bindings to match perfectly their library's decor. And she can help you select titles that will add gravitas to your parties and make you the talk of your social circle. Please feel free to call her or drop by the store Monday through Friday from 9:30 to 5:00. And remember, we offer discounts on bulk purchases.

As if on cue, Gladys Thurington walked into Missouri Joe's and ordered an espresso latté to go.

Quickly but as unobtrusively as possible, I redirected the browser to Yahoo.com, hoping no one had noticed my computer displaying Gladys' photo right as she came in. A curious bystander might start wondering why someone would be interested in reading about her on the Internet but then not take the opportunity to speak with her when she dropped in out of nowhere. The last thing I wanted was to give anyone the idea I was stalking her. Because, of course, I was.

She looked a little older in person than the web photo or the passport photo in her file. Yet even though she looked younger in the pictures, they didn't do her justice. Gladys Thurington was a remarkably handsome woman who was maybe pushing 50. Her black hair had just a few flecks of gray, and she kept it short. She was well dressed in a dark blue cotton suit with white blouse, businesslike but summery, and it was modest while revealing enough to suggest that she might be aging but she was still active—maybe golf or tennis on the weekends, a couple of weeknights at a fitness center. Her skin was a pale bronze, like she liked spending time outdoors but was sensible enough to use plenty of sunscreen. I found myself envying Mr. Thurington, whoever he was.

"Busy day ahead, Mrs. Thurington?" The guy behind the register wasn't that much younger than her. I could tell the way he looked at her while he was steaming her milk that he was just a little smitten, himself.

"How many years have I been coming here, Paul, and you still won't call me Gladys?" She gave him a somewhat matronly smile. There was a story of some sort here. I wondered if I'd have time to learn just what it was. "No, not much going on today. Summer's always slow. People seem to stock their libraries in the Fall."

"Yes, ma'am, summers are more about taking the

kids on vacation, I guess. Well, here's your latté. That'll be $3.52." He wasn't looking straight at her any more. She'd embarrassed him. I was getting more and more curious.

"Thank you, Paul. You have a wonderful day." She handed him a five-dollar bill, smiled again and left without bothering to collect her change. He watched her all the way across the street and into the front door of the bookstore.

Since my plan for the morning had been nothing more than putting a pair of eyes on the target just to get an initial gut feel of what I was up against, I decided to pack up the laptop and head out. Hanging out all day watching the bookstore might draw too much attention. I stuffed the laptop, notebook and pen I'd been using into the cheap laptop bag I'd picked up at one of those recreational equipment stores in the mall. I swung the bag over my shoulder and went up to the counter.

"Say, how about a latté to go."

"Sure thing, Mister."

I'm not a latté guy by any means. But since I was going to have to get to know a lot more about Gladys, finding out what her beverage of choice tasted like made sense.

"So, I guess you've got a pretty good location here, a coffee shop right across from a bookstore. Get many customers picking up a book, then coming over here to read for awhile?" It was a long shot, seeing if I could elicit anything about Gladys Thurington out of Paul. Then again, it never hurts to make friendly conversation. I expected to be back in Missouri Joe's a few times over the next week, and there was always the off chance he'd get friendly and let a few interesting tidbits slip.

"Huh?" He was steaming the milk, just like he'd done for Gladys. "Aw, not really. They don't get many people browsing for books over there. It's kind of a specialty book seller."

"Oh, really? What kind of specialty?"

"They sell high-end rare books. I think a lot of their orders come in by phone or over the Internet."

"Too bad. I guess I'm still used to bookstores attracting college students and other people who like to read." Which, I had to admit, is not me.

"Sure, used to be that way, I guess. Nah, we get some folks from the neighborhood and a few customers coming and going from the mall. They're talking about opening a Starbucks in the mall, though. If they do, that'll probably be it for this place."

"Too bad."

"Yeah, I guess. Heck, I don't own the place any more, and I'm not sure I'll miss it that much. I opened up here in 1983, when espresso was still a novelty in the U.S. Business was booming for about ten years. Lots of people back then came in to try 'European coffee' thinking it was really cool and different. Or they wanted exotic beans from Kenya or Jamaica to serve at their dinner parties. I was even roasting for awhile. But business started slacking off in the mid-90s when Starbucks began selling beans and ground coffee in the grocery stores."

"So you sold the place?"

"Yeah, big land speculator in St. Louis came in about seven years back and offered to buy the place. I owned it outright—inherited the house from my folks when they died and turned it into 'Missouri Joe's' when I realized the neighborhood was becoming more commercial than residential—and this guy was looking to acquire properties in the Joplin area. He was thinking long term, waiting for the next commercial building boom here. He leases the place back to me pretty cheap so he doesn't have to worry about keeping it maintained. Hell, it's just a matter of time before he sells it to a developer anyway. And I got enough on the sale to retire, I guess. So let 'em build that Starbucks. That's what people want these days."

"Sounds like you made out alright on the business, though. Still, you must like running the place. I mean, you said you could retire, but here you are."

"Yeah." He looked across the street at the bookshop. "Keeps me occupied, I guess. So what brings you to Joplin, Mister? You don't sound like you're from around here, and I don't remember seeing you in here before."

"I represent a Christian-values publisher of ESL—English as a Second Language—educational materials." Great alias documentation is worthless without a good story to go with it. I don't read newspaper front-page stories much or tune into the nightly news regularly, but I try to spend a full day in the library once every couple of weeks digging through various newspapers from around the country, mostly reading local obituaries. These have a surprising amount of information about prominent people who have passed on. I pay particular attention to professions and life histories to cull realistic-sounding occupations. A year ago, the owner of just such a publishing company in Ogden, Utah had dropped dead of a massive heart attack while vacationing in Nevada, according to the Ogden *Standard-Examiner*, leaving behind a wife and 12 kids. The profile in the Ogden paper went into some detail about his vision of developing a curriculum to teach immigrants English while simultaneously indoctrinating them into fundamentalist Christianity, calling him a 'leading light of Ogden.' Curious to learn more, I had Googled him and his company, learning enough to pass myself off as a sales rep for 'Christian-values ESL materials.'

I also found an article in the *Reno Gazette-Journal* headlined *Utah Man Found at Hooker Ranch Died of Heart Attack*.

"Christian ESL? Well, you got the Christian part right. Joplin's about as Christian as they come. Don't know if there are a lot of ESL programs around here, though."

"Our demographics people say there's a fairly large South Asian population."

"Really? Oh, well sure. We got a large community of Indians here. I mean the ones from India. Not many of the other kind left."

"Yeah, that's what the demographics people told me. They figure it's a growing market."

"They do, huh? Are they aware that Indians grow up speaking English? It used to be a British colony, you know."

I guess sometimes the obvious doesn't hit you until someone else hits you over the head with it. I'd done my homework on Joplin and picked the Christian ESL cover from about a dozen I've pulled together, but it hadn't dawned on me that immigrants from Calcutta wouldn't need English lessons.

"Well, I tried to tell my boss that, but he's got an MBA so he thinks he knows everything." Even a good cover is worthless without occasional seamless bullshitting. I'd gotten good at that over the years. "Hopefully, there are at least some immigrants here who want to learn the local lingo and need converting from heathenism, though. I'd hate to go back empty-handed."

"Hey, that lady who was just in here, Mrs. Thurington; you should talk to her. She does a lot of volunteer work through her church—First Methodist Independent, I think—and I'm pretty sure she's involved with one of those groups who try to help newly arrived immigrants."

"Oh, yeah, I saw you two talking." Meeting Gladys had certain advantages. I could cut down the time needed to get to know her patterns, movements, vulnerabilities a lot faster by talking to her for just a half hour or so. Of course, actually meeting a target prior to carrying out the job has certain inherent dangers, too.

"She's a real nice lady. I'm sure she'd be glad to help you out. I'll warn you though; I think she might be involved with one of those do-gooder groups that tries to help illegal aliens avoid getting deported."

"You don't say. Well, maybe I'll look in on her later in the week."

"Tell her I told you to stop over."

"Thanks."

"Enjoy your latté."

Walking to my car, I found myself feeling better about this assignment. I don't spend a lot of time questioning the selection of clients handed to me. Most of them are pretty obviously enemies of the USA like Mohammed Mohammed or the Community College English Professor in Florida with the poster on his office door denouncing the President as a mass murderer. After watching him for less than a week, I figured I was serving not just my country but also the parents of the half-dozen coeds he was having sex with.

But I'm also aware that the U.S. government can occasionally make mistakes, like misplacing all those WMDs in Iraq. And, certainly at first glance, Gladys Thurington had seemed pretty innocuous to be on my list. Then the coffee shop clerk had said 'illegal aliens' and everything started to fall into place.

I sipped some of the latté from the little slit in the to-go cup and almost spit it out. Coffee should be bold and bitter. This was light and wimpy. I tossed it in a garbage can at the corner and headed to my rental car. Time to drive to her home address, look over her neighborhood and start pulling together a plan.

Chapter V
One Good Killing Deserves Another

IT HAD BEEN A WEEK and I had about as complete a profile of Gladys Thurington as anyone in my line of work would ever need. I'd staked out her arrival at the bookshop from different vantage points on three mornings, confirming that she always stopped by Missouri Joe's on her way in. I'd watched her depart her house twice, backing her 10-year old, impeccably clean and perfectly maintained 4-door Volkswagen Jetta carefully into the street from her driveway before proceeding cautiously under the speed limit to her job. I followed her at a very discrete distance one morning. She assuredly got deep insurance discounts as a safe driver. She came to complete stops at stop signs, waited for lights to turn green and looked both ways even then before proceeding: it was maddening to observe.

She was punctual, too, departing her residence at 8:42 every morning by my watch. And she always took the same route, left at Roosevelt Avenue, right on 7th Street all the way through downtown and past Range Line Road, left on South Northpark to Bunny Lane.

The one evening I took a chance on following her when she left work, Thursday, she headed straight to a fitness center. It was the same address as the Thursday night yoga class posted on the front of the bookstore. I staked out her residence two other evenings; she wasn't home until after 8:00 each night. Clearly she had a full schedule of work and activities, probably mixing fitness and community work just like Paul at Missouri Joe's had indicated.

Not that her life was some perfect suburban dream. Both evenings I staked out her house, her husband, Fred Thurington, came home around 9:45. He was a private practice accountant, yet another rarity hanging on in Joplin while the rest of the accountants in the country were signing up with big international corporations. I looked him up on the Internet, too, using a terminal at a library branch in Joplin's Duquesne neighborhood near the Northpark Mall area—I could have used the laptop at a wireless hotspot, of course, but why risk having a record out there somewhere of one computer looking up both his wife's place of work and his business.

Fred had his own web-page with a list of some of his more prominent Joplin clients. Apparently he was pretty successful. Figuring there was possibly more to him than corporate accounting, I decided to follow him from his office after work on Friday. I guess I was hoping to see him head to a bar and get pissed or drive to the small apartment of some sweet young thing. I was disappointed. He finally emerged from his office at about 9:15 and drove straight home. He just worked late every night.

Saturday proved even less illuminating. I pulled on the running clothes I always carry on trips, parked about three miles from the Thurington residence, and took a slow jog past their house several times. Gladys was working in the yard. That's it. She had on a big sun hat, gardening gloves, khaki slacks and a summery blouse, and spent the morning on her knees planting flowers. I noticed that Fred's car, a silver four-door older model Mercedes, was not in the driveway. After jogging back to my car, I swung by his office on the way back to the La Quinta. The Mercedes was there. Fred was successful because he worked hard. Period.

None of this was making my job any easier. Because she and Fred seemed to be such prominent Joplinians, I couldn't risk a killing that smacked of random, violent crime. Joplin's not New York. The police would immediately suspect a transient and have the entire Missouri highway patrol out in force looking for anyone fleeing the city. Of course, I could catch her coming out of her gym, cold-cock her, shove her into the trunk of my car, drive her out to the middle of nowhere and dump the body someplace where it might take a few days to find her. Still, she'd be reported missing and the cops would take that seriously, given her social standing. Best would be to make it look like suicide, and the best opportunity for that was the hour and 45 minutes she was alone in her house every weeknight before workaholic Fred came home. The easiest way to accomplish this, I figured, would be to let myself into the house shortly before she arrived—picking a suburban lock is child's play if there's no security system, and I hadn't noticed any signs of one—knock her unconscious with a quick rap to the back of the head with a nightstick, something I could easily fashion from a broomstick handle available at any hardware store, drag her into the garage and put her in her VW, then leave her there with the engine running and the garage door closed. Suicide would be believable. Women her age with husbands who never come home do it all the time. The only concern was that she might come to before succumbing to the carbon monoxide.

Method wasn't my problem, however. It was doubt. Much as I kept trying to put it out of my mind, I just couldn't fathom why I was doing Gladys Thurington at all. Maybe Paul was right and she was helping illegal aliens avoid deportation. If so, it was the only thing in her life that wasn't right out of the pages of *Better Homes and Gardens*. Gladys could have been the reincarnation of Barbara Billingsly from *Leave It to Beaver*. Except she didn't have any kids. I guess Fred had been too busy doing other peoples' books to get around to it.

This wasn't my first experience with doubt. Sure, it's best to approach my business with the dispassionate attitude of a technician, focusing on the mechanics of getting the job done and getting away without complications. I'm human, though. Some small part of my brain or soul or conscience or whatever demands that I confirm to some extent that the target is valid. Most of the time this is easy, of course, as with Mohammed Mohammed from the USA-hating UN, or the commie community-college professor.

But there had been that social worker in Detroit. For two weeks I watched her do nothing but counsel troubled youths, drop off meals to elderly invalids, give pep talks to groups of pregnant teens, run an anger management seminar for inmates at the jail. I was beginning to wonder if they'd mixed up my target's address with Mother Teresa's. But after two weeks' surveillance, I followed her on a Friday to, of all places, a mosque. That's when it hit me: she wore a headscarf all the time. Terrorist. For her, I scored four dime bags of Mexican heroin off a local street dealer, let myself into her apartment one evening, tasered her when she came in the door—I've got several tasers stashed away that I bought from an old buddy of mine who works at a police supply outlet in Tennessee—and gave her a shot of about three times what a dedicated addict would shoot up. Detroit cops have enough to do without looking too seriously into a drug overdose.

I decided I was just over-thinking the Gladys Thurington assignment. It was Sunday morning and I knew she was at her church. Rather than spend another pointless day watching her pass herself off as Mrs. Clean, I went to a local gym—not the same one she went to, of course—paid twenty bucks for a day pass, and lifted weights for a couple of hours. There's nothing like bench pressing a couple-hundred pounds or doing curls with some fifty pound dumbbells to restore your sense of purpose. The place was almost empty, too; just me and another guy with a Schwarzenegger build and headphones snaking down to some cheap MP3 player. From across the room I could tell he was blasting Metallica into his eardrums at a volume that could liquefy brain cells. He probably didn't have many of those anyway.

I picked up a six-pack of Miller Genuine Draft on the way back to the La Quinta—thank God Missouri doesn't have alcohol blue laws—and drank myself to sleep watching a televangelist rave about Muslims and Jews and homosexuals. He seemed to think they were all part of some anti-American conspiracy. I drifted off and dreamed about gay terrorists seizing a public library and demanding that the police send in Gladys Thurington to help them restock the shelves with stylish leather-bound volumes.

Monday morning I woke up with a renewed sense of purpose. Today I would stop worrying why Gladys was on the list and come up with a plan to get her checked off it. After showering and pulling on some clothes, I headed to the sad little breakfast buffet in the lobby.

There was plenty of coffee and juice, but despite the fact that it was early—7:00 a.m.—I was forced to choose between several gooey cinnamon rolls and a few of those individual boxes of frosted flakes. The frosted flakes seemed the least bad of bad alternatives.

"Good morning, Mr. Desplanes. How are the Bible sales coming?" It was Karesh. I'd only run into him a couple of times since checking in a week earlier. I was mildly concerned that he remembered me so well. I prefer not to stand out.

"Could be better. You're not interested in buying a few dozen Bibles to have available in the motel, are you?"

"We have all those Gideon Bibles. They are free."

"Yeah, the Gideons aren't doing guys like me any favors. Don't suppose you know anybody looking for some of the more modern editions? We sell several new translations."

"My family is Hindu. Most people I know aren't religious."

"Well, how about you? You Hindu, too?"

"I'm studying at night to become a computer programmer."

"But what about religion?"

"I'm studying at night to become a computer programmer." He grinned.

"Very funny." Actually, I thought it was pretty funny. "But you're making a mistake."

"Oh, are you worried about my soul, Mr. Desplanes?"

"Not at all. It's just there's a lot more money in Christianity than computers these days. Some of those televangelists are really raking it in."

"That is very true. Well, good hunting today, as they

say."

I headed out to my car thinking Karesh was a pretty good kid. I hoped he succeeded with the computer programming and stayed out of trouble. Especially the kind of trouble that could get him on the list of someone like me.

It was a good day to take a fresh look at Gladys with my renewed sense of dispassionate professionalism. She was a target and it was time to start thinking of her as nothing more. I drove to her neighborhood and parked a couple of blocks from her house along the route I now knew she took every weekday. What I was seeking was fresh inspiration, watching her movements and routine on the off chance I'd spot something that I could build into a plan that left her dead with an obvious explanation and no troublesome police inquiry. There was always the fallback of doing the garage suicide later in the week if I didn't find something better. Breaking into her house and waylaying her was pretty risky, though.

She drove past me at precisely 8:43, punctual as ever. I let her get a good 100 yards ahead before pulling in behind her. Keeping a decent distance took patience; she drove precisely 25 mph. At Roosevelt, she stopped—even though there was no stop sign—and looked both ways before making the left turn. Roosevelt to 7th Street was the same, 25 mph and looking both ways at every intersection. One thing was certain, I was not going to be able to fake an accident and make it believable. Gladys gave new meaning to 'defensive driving.'

She caught the red light at Range Line Road. Actually, she was no more than 10 feet from the intersection when the light went yellow, but she stopped anyway. I was three cars back, separated by a Toyota Corolla and a BMW Z4 directly behind her. I saw the Z4 driver throw up his hands in frustration when she stopped.

Crossing traffic on Range Line Road. was pretty light, but when the light went green, she didn't move. My heart literally leapt into my throat. Had she had a stroke or heart attack? Could I be that lucky? Then a red emergency vehicle with siren blaring came speeding through the intersection, alertly noticed by the ever-cautious Gladys. I realized I had my windows up and the AC running—totally out of character—and hadn't heard the damn thing coming. I rolled down my window, impressed by what a remarkably good driver Gladys Thurington really was.

The guy in the Z4 laid on his horn. He'd had enough. Clearly he'd decided Gladys was taking much too long to proceed, now that the emergency vehicle had passed. The sound must have startled her. I didn't have a great vantage, but I'm pretty sure she looked in her rear-view mirror as she pulled slowly into the intersection. It's a natural reaction.

The fire truck that smashed directly into her driver's side door was doing 50 mph at least. The impeccably maintained VW was launched like a goal kick in a soccer match amid a halo of shattered glass. In less than a second the fire truck smashed it into a crumpled mass like you see on the news after a car bombing in Beirut or Baghdad. I'm sure she was killed instantly.

It seemed like an eternity before I started breathing again, but more likely it was just a couple of seconds: I remember gasping as I heard the sound of glass fragments hitting the pavement. Then it got really quiet. I heard a voice from behind me somewhere yelling "Somebody call 911!" I doubted that would be necessary. She'd been hit by a fire truck, for Christ's sake. The place would be crawling with emergency vehicles in no time.

I realized I didn't want to be there when that happened. Fate had done my job for me. No reason to hang around with phony ID to be interviewed by cops looking for witnesses.

The guy in the Z4 came to a similar conclusion about not hanging around, hooking a quick U-turn and hauling ass back the way we came. I decided on the same exit rather than risk crossing the intersection around the trailing end of the fire truck.

I was also curious to follow the Z4 and see where the guy was going, why he'd been in such a rush. I floored it once I got turned around, not wanting to lose sight of him and figuring he'd be making some major speed. I needn't have worried. He'd accelerated fast but topped out at about 40 mph. Then he slowed considerably about five blocks down the road and made a 15 mph right turn. Obviously he was heading to a parallel street to resume his commute.

I had no trouble staying with him. He was a classic bad driver with more car than he could handle. He'd accelerate fast, often squealing his tires, but never exceed the speed limit by more than 5 mph or so. On turns he slowed down more than necessary and still veered into the wrong lane. Even giving him credit for maybe being shaken that he'd basically just killed someone, I had to admit that he was one of those drivers who's simply a danger to himself and others. That he had the money to drive a BMW hot-rod was a crime.

I stayed a lot closer behind him than I had following

Gladys. Frankly, I wasn't worried he'd spot me tailing him. In fact, I didn't care if he did see me. Logically, I should have been grateful. He'd saved me a lot of effort. Hell, I could wait 'til he parked somewhere and leave him a note on his dash: "Thanks a lot!" That'd freak him out.

But I could feel a slow anger building, instead. Sure, I kill people. But I'd feel bad if somebody died for no other reason than that I was acting like a jackass. I'd probably flee the scene, too. Hell, getting away with murder is my profession. But I'd feel bad. I wanted to know if this guy felt bad. I wanted to know if he really had somewhere to be that justified Gladys Thurington having to die. Deep down, I knew; the entire time I trailed him over to 4th Street, back to Range Line Road. where he made a left, and then out of Joplin up 71 to the parking lot of the Carthage Golf Course in Carthage, Missouri, I knew he wasn't on any urgent errand or pressing business. And of course it turned out he just didn't want to miss his tee time.

He pulled in, got out, opened his trunk, pulled out his golf bag and clubs, and headed into the clubhouse. I had to admire that. It's that kind of presence of mind that makes me so good at my job. And he'd pulled this off with no planning whatsoever.

I'm not really sure why I didn't just get back on 71 at that point, head back to the La Quinta, check out, and make my way back to Washington via Dallas. There was nothing holding me in Joplin anymore. Nothing but a perverse curiosity to find out more about Mr. Z4.

I waited in the parking lot about five minutes before going into the clubhouse. Inside I found him with three buddies who could have been his clones: all mid 40s, about 30 pounds overweight, wearing expensive golf slacks, golf shirts, golf caps. The man who'd sent Gladys Thurington to her death was sitting on a bench pulling on his perfectly white golf shoes while his buddies chided him good-naturedly for almost missing tee-off. He finished tying his shoes, looked at his watch, grabbed his golf bag, and the four of them headed to the first tee.

Already I had a lot of information about him. It was Monday and he was playing golf, so he was no working stiff. The Z4 also indicated that, of course, but a lot of people who work for a living buy expensive cars. Working class folks don't sport the bloated faces and fake tans these guys had, though. I was guessing he was a small-business type, maybe a car lot or furniture store inherited from a previous hard-working generation. But not wealthy, by any means. It was a public golf course, after all.

There were not a lot of people at the club. He could have been 15 minutes late and not missed his round of golf. The place was so quiet, I decided to get out of the clubhouse before someone started to wonder what I was doing there at all. I headed back to my rental car, a bit at a loss what to do. I sure hadn't planned to visit Carthage when I'd set out that morning. Nor did I have any interest in playing golf. Golf has always seemed incredibly stupid to me, hitting expensive little white balls with really expensive clubs and paying lots of money in green fees for the privilege. Back in the army, officers had loved golf. They played it whenever they could, while their wives played around with guys like me. Maybe I should have learned to appreciate golf more.

However, as a physically fit and imposing-looking guy, I stood out like a sore thumb hanging around the

Carthage Golf Club. One thing about golf, you don't have to be an athlete to play. From what I've observed over the years, in fact, it seems to be a handicap.

No doubt my Z4 driver would be occupied for several hours, so better to head into Carthage proper and find a watering hole where I could pass the time. I'd stake out the golf club exit later to tail the Z4 back to Joplin. I still didn't have much reason for following the guy around, but I figured I'd planned to spend the whole day doing surveillance anyway, and since he'd taken my target out of the picture, might as well pass the time on him.

Plus I was still looking for some sign of remorse. No one could be as callous as this guy seemed. I sure wouldn't go bowling after a job. At least, not without a respectful time interval.

I found a pancake house in Carthage. The frosted flakes hadn't been much of a breakfast, so I treated myself to buckwheat pancakes, two fried eggs and a side of bacon. No telling when I'd get to eat again. That depended on Mr. Z4.

At about noon I made sure I was positioned across the street from the golf club road exit. I found a shady spot to park and leaned back to settle in. He'd teed off about 10:00, and figuring 3 hours to play 18 holes, it'd be about an hour wait. Getting there early reduced the risk of missing him if he pulled a muscle or something and didn't play the entire course. I dozed on and off for about an hour, nevertheless alert to the one or two cars that pulled out of the club. At 1:00 I roused myself to be more alert. At 2:00 I started to worry that I'd missed him entirely, that he'd left before noon. Then, at 2:30, bingo. The Z4 came up the road and made a left. I counted to 10 and then pulled in behind him. As expected, he got back on 71 headed to Joplin.

His driving was more erratic than before. Not so many tire-squealing accelerations, speed variable between 30 and 55 mph without any logic, some trouble staying in his lane. Obviously he had been four and a half hours in the club because he'd had a few drinks after his golf game. I kept my fingers crossed he didn't pass a cop. If he got arrested for DWI, that'd be the end of that. I wasn't going to hang around while somebody bailed him out of jail.

But he made it all the way back to Joplin, straight down 71 to Zora Street, where he took a left and headed to an auto dealership, Prosperity Nissan/Toyota/Hyundai. He pulled around back. It was a midsize dealership, maybe 100 cars on the lot, all new Korean and Japanese imports.

I pulled into a customer space in front and walked into the showroom. A bored looking salesman at a desk in the back looked up from a copy of *Guns and Ammo*.

"Interested in a new car? I can make you a killer deal today. Inventory reduction." It was a pretty tentative pitch, like he didn't want to commit himself unless I showed some real interest.

"I'm just looking right now. Been thinking about getting one of these high-mileage Jap cars. Thought I might pick up some brochures."

"Help yourself. They're on that display case in the back." He stuck his nose back in his magazine.

I drifted toward the back, stopping to look inside a bright yellow SUV with a $34,996 sticker price and keeping an eye on the door in the back that led to the offices. It opened. In walked the Z4 driver looking none too steady. He took a look around, then half-lurched to the coffee pot where he grabbed a cup into which he emptied the dark remnants from the bottom of the pot.

"You can't go wrong with that XTerra, mister." The bored salesman was suddenly right behind me. "Real off-road power. Comes with a winch and everything. Even gets good gas mileage."

"Seriously?" I turned around and saw that he wasn't looking at me, rather he was watching Mr. Z4 get his coffee. "What do you mean by good?"

"Huh? Oh, 24 mpg highway. It's right there on the sticker." He was still looking toward the back. "Afternoon, Mr. Ruminant."

So now I had a name.

"Afternoon, Karl." Ruminant sort of waved and headed into one of the offices. "Don't let me disturb you. Try to make some sales." The door slammed behind him.

"Twenty-four miles-per-gallon? That's pretty good for a vehicle this size." I was just trying to continue the conversation so I wouldn't seem suspicious, like I had no real reason to be in a car dealership. But Karl had already turned and started back to his desk, obviously ready to start screwing off again now that his boss had disappeared. He stopped and looked back at me, a curious look that said he'd written me off as someone who wasn't there to buy, but he was now wondering if he'd been wrong.

"Sounds too good to be true, doesn't it?"

"Well, honestly, yes."

"It is." He smiled, glanced back toward the office, then winked. "Those mileage numbers on the stickers are bullshit. I think the manufacturers just make them up. I mean, this XTerra is a nice toy if you want to tear around the countryside or drive it along a dry creekbed, but you'll get about 8 miles per gallon doing that. Get it on the highway, maybe 13 or 14. Now, if you want a car that gets good mileage, we've got a couple models on the lot that'll get you 25 city and 45 to 50 highway. You want to test drive one?"

"No, not today. I'm just looking."

"Yeah, I figured. I can usually tell who's here to buy and who's here to look."

"So is that your boss who came in?" I decided to try to buddy up to him. Salesmen usually like to talk, even if they think a sale is unlikely. It's in their nature, I guess. "I guess Monday's must be slow, just you on the showroom and him coming in close to 4:00."

"Monday's are usually pretty slow. But Mr. Ruminant doesn't ever come in before noon. And today's his golf day. He and some of his old frat buddies play every Monday morning. Then they have a few drinks and he comes in here to check on me." He glanced over at me, like he was considering whether I might be a spy for management and then rejecting the idea. "Between you and me, he's in there sleeping it off right now."

"Gee, does he own the place or something?"

"Nah, his dad does."

"Oh. Family business, huh. Surprised it's not named Ruminant Nissan."

Karl laughed. "That's a good one. Actually, the place has changed hands a few times. Bob Ruminant bought it about 20 years back, I guess. Kept the 'Prosperity' name for good luck. He hired me in '91. But he's getting on in years. Pretty much has handed the place over to Lester."

"Who's sleeping it off in his office right now."

"That's right."

"Heartwarming story."

"Hey, keeps him outta my hair. You have a nice day." Karl went back to his desk and his *Guns and Ammo*.

So Lester was really just a pathetic, middle-aged drunk living off his dad. Maybe there was nothing else worth knowing about him and I should let it drop. I got back in my car and drove around for awhile, trying to decide what to do next. Might as well stay one more night in Joplin. It was approaching 4:30, well past check-out time at the La Quinta, so I'd pay through the next day anyway. I spotted a sandwich shop somewhere—I'd been driving aimlessly and had no idea where in Joplin I was—and stopped in, ordering a BLT and coffee after taking a seat at a little Formica-top table in the corner. The sandwich was mostly bread and mayonnaise, the coffee bitter from sitting all day on a burner. I ate the sandwich and sipped the coffee mechanically, staring out the window while my mind just stopped functioning. Shock's a funny thing. It sneaks up on you. The fact that Gadys Thurington was dead and my assignment was over really didn't hit me until right then and there.

"Anything else I can get for ya? Piece of pie, maybe? We got a real good strawberry-rhubarb today." The waitress was the spitting image of the character Flo from the old *Alice* sitcom.

"No thanks. Just the check."

"Okay." She paused, like she needed to keep talking. "Too bad, really. It's Joe's specialty. Joe's the cook. He takes a lot of pride in his pies. Haven't sold a single piece today."

"Really? Slow day, huh?" Monday's must be slow

everywhere in Joplin. People recovering from too much church perhaps.

"Oh, yeah. Big wreck at the intersection over there this morning. Took hours to get it cleared away. Traffic was a mess. Kept the usual lunch crowd away." She'd probably been waiting to tell someone all day. Just my luck.

"Anybody hurt?" Of course I knew the answer already.

"Some lady pulled in front of a fire truck heading to a call. What was left of her car sat right there in front of our parking lot for most of the day. Smashed her to a pulp. Took the EMTs all morning to scrape her out of the car. Pretty grizzly thing to have to watch."

"That's too bad." I didn't point out that she hadn't really been forced to watch. "So what do I owe you?"

"Seven dollars, twenty-six cents. Sure I can't change your mind about that pie?"

"No, sorry." Could she seriously believe anyone would have an appetite for desert after listening to her describe EMTs scraping someone's bloody pulp from a wreck? I tossed a ten on the table and got up. "Keep the change."

"Thanks. You have a nice day."

Walking through the parking lot, I could see now that there were still bits of glass everywhere. A religious or mystical person would no doubt have found meaning in having unthinkingly driven right back to the accident location, probably convincing themselves that it meant they had closed some kind of circle. I'm neither.

But fate or the universe or some force of nature seems to arrange coincidences in such a way to get even the most atheistic among us thinking that they're fulfilling part of a larger plan. I could have just left Joplin the next day and spent the rest of my life feeling stupid and empty that I'd gone to a lot of effort to insert myself temporarily into Gladys' life just to witness her demise in a random event. And I would have left it just like that. Except that on the drive back to the La Quinta, I passed a cheesy-looking strip-club with a big neon sign in front flashing "Exotic Dancers!" in bright orange.

A BMW Z4 was parked right out front.

It took a few moments for my eyes to adjust to the dark, smoky bar. The sign had been somewhat misleading. There was only one woman dancing on a raised platform, enormous breasts bouncing to some old Temptations song. I didn't have to look too closely to see that "exotic" was a stretch, too. She looked to be in her forties, the product of some hard living. Three men sat at little tables by the stage, watching her. I finally made one of them out to be Lester Ruminant. The other two had all the appearance of desk-bound mid-level office types with expanding waistlines and wives they obviously had no urgent desire to get home to.

A short, fat man behind the bar was watching me. Obviously, I'd have to order a drink or leave.

"How about a beer?" I took a seat on one of the bar stools.

"No problem." He continued to stare at me while he drew about 8 ounces of beer into a glass and placed it in front of me. "That'll be eight bucks."

I pulled a ten from my wallet and dropped it on the bar. "Keep it."

"Thanks." His expression was not one of gratitude.

The beer tasted cheap and weak, probably watered down. Of all the bad beers I've had in my life, this might have been the worst. The barman was scowling even more than before, watching with disgust. I downed the rest and set the glass down hard on the bar.

"Want another one?" It was a demand.

I studied the barman for a few seconds. He'd clearly taken a dislike to me as soon as he'd laid eyes on me. Probably just didn't like strangers, like most dogs I'd known as a kid in North Carolina. They snarl, growl and snap at you just because you're unfamiliar. I decided to treat this guy the same way I'd learned to deal with those vicious dogs, snarl right back until he knew I was mean, too.

"Yeah. And a shot of whiskey. Got any whiskey as crappy as this beer?"

He didn't smile, but the scowl softened. "You bet." He poured a shot from a bottle with no label and drew another beer. "This here is the cheapest whiskey they make."

I knocked back the shot without hesitation. It's hard to imagine a licensed distiller would make anything quite so vile.

"That'll be fifteen bucks." He was warming to me, but not enough to let me run a tab. I pulled out two twenties and placed them in front of him.

"How about another shot of that turpentine."

"Don't blame me if you go blind." He poured a larger shot and opened the register to give me my change.

"Keep it." I'd broken the ice. Time to try developing a little rapport. If Lester was a regular, I might be able to get some information. "Give some to the lovely young lady who's entertaining us." That finally got him to smile.

"I've never seen you in here before. You new in town?"

"Just here for a few days on business. So I guess most of your customers are regulars?"

"You could say that." The scowl was creeping back. "Listen, buddy, if you're a cop or working with one of those church groups, you're wasting your time. Our licenses are all paid up and there's nothing going on here except exactly what you see."

"A cop? You think I'm a cop?" I had to stifle a laugh. So he thought I had come in to make a 'lewd and lascivious' bust.

He leaned over the bar and lowered his voice. "Gimme a break. You see those guys over there? Our customers are all just like those guys, out-of-shape losers who can't get laid at home anymore so they come in here, watch Mavis shake her silicon jobs, and kid themselves that they're still in the game. You, however, do not look like an out-of-shape loser, and you come in, check out Mavis and the customers, then head over here to talk to me. Just like a cop."

I had to admit, he'd hit fairly close to home. Like cops and crusaders, I can be bad news. "Sorry to disappoint you, buddy. I'm not a cop and I'm not a spy for the moral majority, either."

"Sure. Whatever you say. You're in town on business. What kind of business?"

"Bible salesman." I gave him a big smile. I didn't bother with the whole religious publishing company front. I didn't want him to believe me, anyway. "Thought this was a church. Figured I'd come in and pray. Oops."

He laughed. I'd finally broken the ice.

"Whatever you say, buddy. Talk about coals to Newcastle."

"So I don't guess I could interest you in a nice leather-bound display volume with an inset for your family tree?" I hoped I couldn't. I certainly didn't have anything like that on me. I took another sip of the wretched whiskey.

"You're serious? You really sell Bibles? I thought that was all on the Internet these days."

"Well, if you really want to buy a Bible, I could probably find one for you." I decided to stop screwing around. I took out my wallet, counted out five more twenties and laid them on the bar, then leaned across and lowered my voice. "Or I could make it worth your while to tell me about the guy sitting all the way to the right over there."

"Ah, fuck you. I should have figured you for some kinda private dick." He glanced over at Lester. "Mr. Ruminant's wife hire you?"

"I can't really say."

"You don't need to. He was in here a month ago more plastered than usual, whining about his wife moving out and filing for divorce." He scowled at me again, looked down at the money on the bar, and picked the twenties up. "For what it's worth, I ain't never seen any indication he's cheating on her."

"Really? Too bad."

"Listen, you can take it from me. He's not screwing anybody else." He looked over at Lester again and smiled. "He's just a pathetic drunk who comes in here to throw money around and feel like a big shot. I've seen hundreds of 'em in my day."

"Well, that's really too bad. Usually there's a bonus if I provide evidence of alienation of affection." This was great news. Lester's wife had moved out and it didn't sound like he was bringing any sweet young things home. He'd be all alone later.

"You can tell Mrs. Ruminant that he didn't stop doing her because he's getting it somewhere else. He's just drinking so much he can't get it up anymore." He picked up the twenties and shoved them in his pocket. "And that's all you're gonna get outta me."

"Appreciate it. And you're sure you don't want that Bible?"

"Didn't I tell you? I'm a fuckin' Hin-doo."

"Well, then, here's to cow worship." I finished the whiskey and downed the beer. It was reaffirming. I knew I'd never drink anything that bad again. "See you around some time."

"Yeah." He watched me leave with the same scowl as before. "And get a new line of work."

"Good advice." And not likely. I headed back to my car, thinking about Lester and his nice life and his rounds of golf and his fancy car and his too much money; thinking about Lester and his busted marriage and his pathetic drunkenness. I'd seen enough of him to be disgusted. Here he'd had all the advantages in life I hadn't, but he'd turned into a loser and I'd become a skilled professional. I wouldn't have given him a second thought, except he'd got in my way, executed my assignment, and gotten away clean just by stupidity and dumb luck. It was galling.

I don't know exactly when it had happened, but I'd decided to kill Lester Ruminant. Hell, I'd come to Joplin to eliminate a threat to the nation's security. Now that I couldn't carry out that assignment, might as well rid Joplin of a drunken menace with a fast car.

Sitting in a car waiting for somebody you're going to follow is the toughest part of surveillance. In old movies, the cop on a stake-out is always smoking a cigarette. Before smoking became the leprosy of the new America, there probably wasn't a cop or FBI man in the country who didn't smoke simply to pass the time waiting for a suspect to come out of a bar at night or get out of bed in the morning. But I don't smoke. It's a nasty habit. All I have to pass the time with is boredom.

Lester left the club at 10:32, which meant I'd been sitting in my car down the street for an hour and forty-five minutes. That's a lot of boredom, but it also gave me the chance to sober up from the cheap liquor and beer chasers. Sure, I can drink all night without getting drunk. But nobody's at their peak performance with too much alcohol in their blood.

Lester definitely left the bar with too much alcohol in his. He stumbled out to the Z4 and took a good five minutes getting it open. Funny, really, because it had electronic locks. He'd push a button on his key, the lights would flash and the horn would make a little beep, then he'd try the door and it was still locked. I half expected him to set off the car alarm. I'd just about given up and decided to get out and help him when he accidentally hit the right button, opened the door, and half-sat half-fell into the driver's seat. Miraculously, he got the car started, backed out onto the road, and swerved away without running into anything and with a minimum of grinding of gears. His driving was even more erratic than after leaving the golf club before. I don't know where Joplin's police usually patrol on Monday nights, but there were obviously none on any of the roads between the strip club and Lester's house. It was only about a ten-block drive. Lester's sense of self-preservation must have made him choose a place that was close to home.

I stayed about fifty yards behind him, worried he might notice my headlights if I was too close, panic thinking I was a cop, try to outrun me and run into a tree or parked car. Winding up bruised and in a drunk tank would be unpleasant, but not sufficient punishment for the callous murder of Gladys Thurington. Not in my book, anyway.

He made it home without incident, although even fifty yards back I could hear his engine over-revving. He made the entire drive in first gear. I breathed a sigh of relief when he took a left turn into the driveway of a nice split-level brick house in a very nice neighborhood. He even remembered to activate the electric garage door opener just in time to narrowly avoid slamming into the door as he pulled into the two-car garage. I noticed there was no other car. Mrs. Ruminant no doubt took it when she left.

I doused my lights and coasted to a stop at the curb across the street. Then I waited. Once he'd gone inside and passed out, I figured, I'd let myself in and come up with a proper way to do the job. I was toying with something creative, like filling the tub, placing him in it, and dropping in a hair dryer. That could look like suicide or stupidity, either of which police would seize on as an easy explanation for the demise of a drunk whose wife had left him.

But Lester didn't get out of his car. I sat watching for half an hour waiting. He didn't move. He'd passed out.

I got out and walked up the driveway, hoping he'd

left the engine running so I could just close the garage door. He'd switched the Z4 off, though. Lester had an instinct for self-preservation. But he was dead to the world, snoring like a chain saw with a dirty fuel line. I walked right up to the driver side door, leaned back against the garage wall, and stared at him for five full minutes. He never moved.

So this would be easy after all. The window on his door was down. I reached in and flipped the little toggle to open the passenger side door, walked around and climbed in.

"Snurfle pflechm." Lester's head shifted. He resumed snoring.

The radio control for the garage door was mounted on the dash. I pressed the button and the door descended.

"Shweeet think." Lester smiled. He was having a dream now.

Leaning over, I reached down with my left hand and gently lifted his left foot by the ankle, then placed the foot on the clutch and pushed.

"Mmmmmmm."

I had a pretty good idea what Lester was dreaming about. There are worse ways to go. With my right hand I turned the key, still sitting in the ignition, and cranked the engine. It started without a problem. Lester obviously had regular tune-ups. I slowly moved my right hand from the ignition to the gear-shift and placed the car in neutral. Then I eased my left hand away from Lester's left ankle, gently pulled away from him, got out and closed the passenger door as quietly as possible. Lester shifted once more, farted, and kept snoring.

The door leading from the garage to the house was

unlocked. I went from room to room like a burglar, silently making sure no one else was there. The place was a sty. Mrs. Ruminant must have been gone for awhile. In the bedroom, I found a picture of the two of them looking young and happy and ready for life together. She had been quite a looker, I had to admit. But Lester was a handsome, fit guy in the picture, so it must have been taken years before. I wondered if there was much money for Mrs. Ruminant to get on with her life. Lester had all the trappings of affluence, but that can be misleading. So many people look like they've got loads of money but all they have is loads of debt.

I figured I'd hang around for about an hour to make sure Lester didn't wake up. By then, he never would. There was a large plasma TV in the living room, maybe a 60 inch model. I checked that all the curtains were closed, found the remote and switched it on. Lester had cable. I sat down in a big leather comfy chair and surfed, scrolling through endless advertisements for laundry detergent, hair coloring, men's and women's colognes, disposable diapers, deodorants. One of the channels that runs old movies was showing *Casablanca*. A panicked Peter Lorre was pleading with Bogart to help him just as the cops came in and plugged him. Bogey was impassive. I'd seen the movie many times, but it's just so great I sat back to enjoy it again. It's reassuring to see someone else so capable of dealing with death without getting all emotional about it. I watched through the part where Bogey shoots the Nazi and the French cop decides to let him get away with it. Inspiring. I switched it off. The rest, the tearful farewell and Bogey and the frog walking off into the dusk is just too sappy.

Grabbing a dish-towel from the kitchen, I went back

to the door to the garage, put the towel over my face, and eased it open to take a look. The Z4 was still purring. Lester was sitting in the driver's seat like before, dead to the world. But now, he really was.

I let myself out the front door, locking it behind me and glancing both ways down the street to make sure no one was around. It was a bit past midnight. The suburbanites were all safely tucked away in their beds. I walked back to my car and drove away without looking back.

Things felt right. I'd come to Joplin to do a job, and in the end I'd pretty much carried it out the way I'd originally planned, right down to the fake garage suicide. That it had proved so easy just reinforced what I've come to believe over the years, that killing someone isn't really that unnatural. We're all headed to death one way or another. Sometimes I provide a more abrupt transition than might otherwise be expected. But all too often, as with Lester, I'm just providing that last little push in the direction they've been heading for years.

I slept soundly and dreamlessly back at the La Quinta. I was looking forward to heading home.

Chapter VI
Betrayal

MOST PEOPLE never experience the satisfaction that comes with real accomplishment, but that's what I was basking in the entire flight back to D.C. I'd carried out my assignment—with a little help from old Lady Luck—and dished out some justice to boot. Even changing my flight to head home a few days early had proved no problem, although I had to pay a $75 charge. What did I care? It's the taxpayers' money.

I'd checked out of the La Quinta the morning after Lester Ruminant's last night on earth, but instead of heading straight out of town, I stopped one last time at Missouri Joe's to see how Paul was handling Gladys Thurington's death. I needn't have bothered. It was closed. Paul obviously had gotten the news and was too grief-stricken to open up. He'd carried a torch for her all those years without saying a word. Now that she was gone, I doubted he'd find a reason to keep Missouri Joe's going. I'd never know how Fred Thurington handled it. Maybe he'd just work even longer hours at his accounting practice. Of one thing I was certain: Gladys would be missed a lot more than Lester.

For me, of course, it was two successes: an enemy of the USA removed from my list and a drunk-driving menace eliminated from the streets of Joplin. I wouldn't mention Lester Ruminant in my report when I got back, though. Some good deeds have to be their own reward. On the drive back, I even stopped at the Oklahoma-Texas border, got out of my car, and spent a few moments in respectful silence. That's also where I said good-bye to Jock Desplanes, shoving his driver's license and credit cards into the laptop bag with the Acer and flinging it out into the middle of the Red River.

I didn't celebrate until the plane lifted off from DFW. Then I splurged and bought a can of beer when the stewardess came by with the drink cart.

My flight landed 15 minutes ahead of schedule at 4:37 in the afternoon. I grabbed my bag and hopped the metro, making a roundabout journey home via the Yellow Line to Mt. Vernon Station, backtracking one stop on a Green Line train to Gallery Place-Chinatown, Red Line to Metro Center—a complex maze of escalators and ramps—where I could catch an Orange Line train out to Fairfax. It was rush hour, so the Orange Line was packed. I waited on the platform while people forced their way onto two trains bulging with passengers, finally boarding the third train that was only about two-thirds full. Metro Center to Fairfax was a forty-five minute ride, giving me plenty of time to get a good look at the other passengers, see if anyone was paying too much attention to me.

Fairfax is the end of the line. I waited until everyone else exited, then got off and headed to the turnstile. I'd made sure to buy a fare-card that was twenty-five cents light, meaning the turnstile rejected it when I tried to leave the station. This afforded me the opportunity to curse, retrieve the card, turn around and reverse course to the add-fare machine, looking around as I did to make sure no one else was loitering suspiciously. Topping off my fare-card, I exited successfully and headed out to the street. From there I walked a zig-zag route to my apartment. Arriving back in Washington as

Cedric Dibald, I wanted to make certain no one was following me when I returned to my Richard Paladin residence. It's always a temptation to relax and get sloppy at the end of an assignment. I never give in to that temptation.

Finally arriving back at my apartment, I checked my mailbox and retrieved the week and a half accumulation of crap that was stuffed inside. Amazingly, Richard Paladin, who had only existed for a couple of years, received an impressive amount of mail from companies desperate to extend him credit. In the accumulated mail were five pre-approved credit card offers, an offer from a local car dealership for a no-money-down loan on a new car, and a letter from a mortgage broker inviting me to refinance the house loan I didn't have. I tore up the mortgage and auto loan offers and tossed them in the trash, then put the credit card come-ons in a drawer where I've collected about two-dozen of them. I figure a time will come when Richard Paladin will disappear, and before that happens, I'm going to fill out maybe ten of the applications and max out the cash advance limit on all of them.

Not that I need the money. I've been rounding my expenses up very generously for quite awhile. When I get reimbursed, I take the money in cash and store it in an old Bubba's Burgers box in my freezer. And, at the end of assignments when I'm using phony IDs, I'll often get cash from a couple of ATMs with the alias credit cards before disposing of them. That money goes in the Bubba's Burgers box, too. Arriving back from Joplin, I put the extra cash I was still carrying with the Bubba's stash and did a quick count: it was about $20,000. Some people might consider this unethical. I figure it's justifiable compensation for the fact that I'm probably not going to be able to collect Richard Paladin's pension and social security.

It was a little after seven. I sat down at my tiny kitchen table with a pair of scissors and cut the Cedric Dibald cards into little pieces, placing them in a plastic storage bag. Then I collected my Richard Paladin wallet, shoved that and the plastic bag in my pants pockets, and headed back to the Metro station. Hopefully, my office would be empty and I'd have plenty of time to write up the Joplin trip. The hell with Riffelbach's admonition to avoid working evenings for awhile. Getting this assignment wrapped up would feel good. And I could toss Cedric Dibald's remains into a dumpster near Union Station.

The office was empty when I got there. I checked the parking lot before going in, too, making sure Sharon's car wasn't there. I hadn't told anyone when I'd be back, so I figured it was unlikely she'd be waiting for me. But it never hurts to be sure.

I unlocked the front door, switched on the lights and headed to my office. My EPA outpost is in one of the last federal office spaces without an array of electronic locks and identification systems. Most of the federal government is now locked down like a maximum security prison; getting into an office means swiping IDs at numerous turnstiles, remembering passcodes and combinations to enter bank-vault-like doors, hell, maybe even getting pricked on the finger for a DNA sample. Of course, then you find out that the cheap plywood door by the loading dock hasn't been locked for twenty years. But maybe that was just in that Federal Building in Mississippi, where it had proved very handy when I'd had to sneak in after hours to plant a small explosive under the desk of an IRS supervisor. That America's enemies had infiltrated the IRS came as no surprise to me. I didn't worry about making that look like suicide, either. The list of people wanting to kill IRS agents is long and starts with various militia groups scattered around the country. The local police and FBI would still be pursuing leads on that case for decades, looking for some UNABOMBER type.

I switched on the light in my office and noticed immediately a manila folder sitting in my inbox. I don't get a lot of inner-office mail. In fact, I couldn't remember the last time I found something in my inbox. I flipped it open. Inside was a neatly typed report, maybe a dozen pages or more. I read the title. *Kyoto Protocol Public Relations Initiative: Quarterly Report.* Sharon had left me a copy just like she'd promised. Later, I'd give it a read and try to figure out what it had to do with me and how I could be program manager of something I knew nothing about.

But first I went to work writing up the verification that Gladys Thurington was no longer a problem. To be honest, I'd have felt funny if I'd had to write a report implying that I had played some part in her death, yet it'd be bad form as a professional to reveal that an assignment had been completed while I did nothing but question my orders. Fortunately, the entire report was nothing but lies anyway—euphemisms, I should say—and my boss would just assume I'd done what I was supposed to.

I inserted a blank disk and pressed "save," then spun open my safe while the aging floppy drive whirred with a kind of resignation. Making a mental note to suggest to my boss that it might be time to start looking for a new PC, I pulled open the top drawer to the safe and noticed a new assignment disk inside. That and the Kyoto report would give me something to look over later while I enjoyed a few cans of Miller Genuine Draft. The floppy drive had finally gone silent. I popped the disk out, put it in the safe, retrieved the new assignment disk and Kyoto report and placed them both in an old government-issue leather portfolio I'd liberated from the store-room. Then I turned out the lights, locked up the office and headed home. Before I left, though, I dropped by my bosses office, wrote "See ya later. R.P." on a little yellow sticky note and affixed it to his computer screen. Assuming he got the note, I figured I'd see him tomorrow at the Wafle Shop.

I stopped by Dan's for a quick beer on the way home. It had been almost two weeks. Sometimes I worry I'll come back to town after an assignment and find an Olive Garden where his bar used to be. But he was still there, plopping a cold draft Budweiser on the bar in front of me.

"Haven't seen you for awhile. Where you been?"

"Business trip. Just got back today."

"Where to this time?"

"Checking air quality in Rochester," I lied. It sounded like something an EPA employee would do.

"I thought the EPA had stopped checking air quality."

"Nah, we still check."

"So how was it?"

"Rochester? It's a pit."

"I mean the air quality."

"What do you think? Is the air actually getting better anywhere?"

"I guess not." Dan went back to unloading glasses

from the dishwasher under the bar, wiping then down and lining them up on the shelf behind him. "Must be frustrating for you."

"Frustrating?" Here he was again, trying to make conversation about my job.

"Yeah. I mean, I figure a guy like you goes to work for the EPA because you care about the environment. And from what I read, the EPA's been pretty much out to lunch under this administration." He was looking pretty serious. Maybe some of the old do-gooder Dan Stigler of Indian Affairs was still lurking around inside Dan the bartender. That would not be a positive development, in my book.

"Sure, I like doing my part. I also like earning a paycheck and kicking back after work with a good beer. I sure don't bring my job home and worry about it." That much was true, anyway.

"Then what's in the case there?" He pointed to the leather portfolio. "Looks to me like you're bringing work home tonight."

"Just some paperwork. Nothing earth-shattering." He was leading up to something.

"Okay, whatever you say. It's just, I know some people who are concerned about where things are headed. Thought you might be interested in meeting some of them. Maybe offer some friendly advice about where they might target their efforts to get this country back on the right track."

I was at a complete loss for words. For one thing, I had no idea what the fuck he was talking about. And when he said 'target,' alarm bells went off in my head. The only meaning 'target' has for me is a silhouette in the cross-hairs of a high-powered rifle scope. Was it possible he had figured out what I really do? I stared dumbly back at him.

"Well, think it over. You always know where to find me."

I finished my beer and dropped ten bucks on the bar. "Dan, you're beginning to worry me. You're not becoming some kind of activist, are you?"

"Hey, we all gotta breathe the same air."

"Well, here's some advice, then. You want to improve air quality? Put up a no smoking sign." I walked out. Maybe it was time to find a new bar.

Back at my apartment, I popped the top on a can of Miller and pulled out the Kyoto Protocol report. It was deadly boring. The first five pages discussed polling statistics. From what I could make out, it appeared that most Americans didn't have a clue what the Kyoto Protocol was. I didn't see where that was anything to be concerned about. Before I went to work at the EPA, I'd have assumed it was something we made the Japs sign at the end of the Second World War. I only knew about it now because I'd been told to reference it as cover for my assignment write-ups, so I had looked it up in Wikipedia just so I wouldn't look stupid if anyone ever brought it up.

In fact, according to the numbers in the report, of the thirty some-odd percent who actually had an inkling what Kyoto was all about, most thought it was a stupid waste of time and effort that, if implemented, would cost Americans jobs and money. Which is exactly what the President of the United States had concluded. So why all the concern? Why a Kyoto Protocol Public Relations Initiative?

Turns out, though, that among the minority of the minority who support Kyoto, there's a vocal group of activists writing letters, getting petitions signed, and generally making nuisances of themselves to try to pressure the U.S. into changing its policy. Somebody senior in the administration thought this was a problem and had ordered the EPA to devise a plan to counter the efforts of these activists. And that was the Kyoto Protocol Public Relations Initiative. The report concluded, in fact, that the initiative was making great progress.

Certainly the report was successfully boring me to tears. If I actually had a job working on something so bureaucratic, so utterly without any significance in this world filled with terrorists and nuclear-missile wielding rogue dictators, I'd probably have thrown myself in front of a speeding Orange Line train.

And yet, on the last page, there I was. The report listed four names integral to the project: two senior EPA suits I'd never heard of; my boss, the Project Administrator; and last but not least, Program Manager, Richard Paladin. I felt a headache coming on, so I grabbed another Miller. Tomorrow at the Wafle Shop I would ask my boss what he was trying to pull. Cover is one thing, but this just seemed to call undue attention to me. At the very least, he should have discussed it with me, warned me just in case someone asked me about it. Like Sharon had.

I shoved the report back in the portfolio and pulled out the assignment disk. Looking over a new assignment was what I needed to clear my head before hitting the rack. I didn't want to think about public opinion surveys, greenhouse gasses, idiotic political/environmental summit meetings. *Just give me somebody who needs killing.*

I powered up the laptop, inserted the disk, and loaded the file. A photo and name popped up on the

screen.
I stared in disbelief.
It was Dan Stigler.

I didn't sleep that night, just sat drinking beer and staring at Dan's picture on the screen. At first I was numb. My mind couldn't make sense of it. Dan Stigler. How could I kill Dan Stigler? I knew him, for Christ's sake. This had to be a mistake. No way Dan Stigler was a terrorist or spy. No way.

But I kept remembering him nosing around about my job, asking if I was "frustrated" by current policy. His comments about getting the country "back on the right track" took on new meaning for me.

Then it started spreading over me, the feeling of betrayal. It had been awhile since I'd felt it, years since Cpl. James Fucking Trasker had been detailed to do yard work on the officers' quarters; seen me arrive one Saturday shortly after Captain Seward Monroe left for his weekly round of golf; seen me leave two hours later literally unwrapping the negligee-clad Mrs. Monroe from my neck; gone running to Captain Monroe to rat me out. So Dan Stigler turned out to be the same kind of traitorous piece of shit. All this time I had been buying his beer, laughing at his jokes, *liking* the guy, only to learn he was the fucking enemy.

My assignments had always been strangers. I handled them dispassionately, professionally. That's the secret to success in my line of work. When people are close to you, everything changes. Emotions take over. You stop thinking about consequences and just use your fists on the little shit until he stops blubbering for you to stop. Then you get court-martialed for assault and kicked out of the army. After the court, the Corps

Commander lets you know that he holds you personally responsible for Captain Monroe being unable to forgive his poor, lonely wife for screwing an enlisted scum; that he blames you for Captain Monroe emptying the magazine of his service issue .45 into his poor, lonely wife and then popping in a fresh magazine to blow his own brains out; that he'd like to see you hang but can't legally do anything more than have you cashiered.

Richard Paladin could not afford to get emotional. I'd have to deal with the anger, get past it and start thinking and acting professionally. The smart thing, in fact, would be to tell my boss that I knew the man and couldn't pull off the job without a real risk of getting caught and exposing the entire secret program. Surely he would understand the bigger picture, realize the need not to blow me on one job so I could keep working on the larger list. I'd reason with him, try to talk him into assigning Stigler to someone else.

It was six in the morning. No point trying to sleep. I decided the best thing to do was go to my gym and sweat out all the emotional baggage. Exercise is purifying, and not just in the sense of sweating out a night's alcohol consumption. I'd be a lot better prepared to meet with my boss after working out, just like working out in Joplin had cleared my head to take a fresh look at the target there. I threw some exercise clothes into my backpack and headed out the door.

Pris, the lesbian yoga instructor and owner of Alternative Fitness, had just opened up and was stretching when I arrived. I get along great with Pris. She admires my dedication to fitness and likes the fact that I don't care that she wants to have sex with other women. And I really don't care. I like Pris. Liked her immediately the first time I tried her gym.

"So what are your fitness goals?" She'd been taking down my personal information on an application form. Unlike other places I'd tried, she wanted more than a credit card to let me on the premises. And she asked the question with a definite sense of disdain, like she was really getting sick of hearing "I'd like to lose fifty pounds before my high school reunion next month."

"I'm just trying to stay physically strong enough to snap someone's neck if they fuck with me." I'm not sure why I was so blunt. Instinct, maybe.

She looked up, like she was trying to decide if I was joking. I didn't smile. "Okay. Let me show you around the place. I think you'll find everything you need." I've gotten to know Pris pretty well since then. She wouldn't hesitate to snap someone's neck if they fucked with her, either.

When I first moved to Fairfax, I tried out several of the large chain gyms—Gold's, Bally, etc.—and I have to admit that all of them had decent equipment, including plenty of free weights, bench press racks, dumbbells and everything necessary for the kind of strength conditioning someone in my profession needs. Each one even had a group of regular weight lifters who weren't bad to work out with, willing to spot each other on the bench or toss a medicine ball around every once in a while. But the chains also have juice bars, clothing shops, and, worst of all, periodic social evenings. I got real sick real fast of all the twenty-somethings of both sexes who might as well have been wearing nametags labeled "Hi I'm Fred/John/Linda/Aurora I Work Out Why Don't We Fuck?" I don't go to the gym because I'm looking for a sex partner.

Of course, I stumbled into a couple of gay men's gyms during my search. They're actually better than the heterosexual meat markets because gays tend to take fitness more seriously. But that's about the only difference. The gay clients are just as focused on looking good so someone will find them sexually desirable.

But Pris's place was perfect. Most of her business was teaching flexibility to chubby housewives, but she had an excellent weight room in the back. I think she liked the camaraderie of pumping iron. She was pretty damn strong herself, routinely bench-pressing 200 pounds, for example. She'd have been good at my job.

Actually, I don't try to set any lifting records. I'm not trying to develop a Charles Atlas physique. The one year I played football in high school, I was a free safety, the guy who's fast enough to chase someone down and then strong enough to knock the crap out of them. I thought I was pretty good at it.

My coach thought I was a "mean kid with an attitude problem." At least, that's what he said when he kicked me off the team after I broke our quarterback's nose running a safety blitz in practice.

I waved hello to Pris and slipped into the little locker room in the back to change. There were only three lockers and one shower stall for men, reflecting Pris' mostly female clientele. At least, I assume the women's locker room is bigger to accommodate the 20-25 women she attracts most mornings for yoga and stretching. Like I mentioned, they are mostly flabby housewives, but there are always a few lookers. I've been tempted sometimes to sign up in order to try making the acquaintance of some lonely lady with a husband who works too hard or plays golf every

Saturday. I never have, though. Not that I'm not like every other man, willing to repeat the same mistake over and over in the quest to get laid. But I'm pretty sure Pris runs the gym and yoga classes with exactly the same motivation, and I'm betting she would not look favorably on any competition.

Once changed, I grabbed a treadmill for a fifteen minute relaxed jog. I warm up rather than stretch before lifting weights. You can damage muscle tissue by straining it when it's cold, so raising the body's core temperature is the best way to prepare for a heavy workout and avoid injury. I learned this the hard way in the army. Military training made me strong, sure, but I always had a strained muscle or nagging pain somewhere. This was the case with pretty much everyone in my platoon, despite the fact that we all stretched religiously because our sergeant demanded it. Of course, we told ourselves the constant pain was good, that it was making us stronger, tougher. We all took steroids, too.

Then one Saturday in the early afternoon, I was drinking in a bar and some woman fitness guru was on the television talking about techniques to strengthen muscles without injury. The basic tenet of her program was core fitness, strengthening the stomach and back muscles, then progressing to the extremities, the arms and legs. And she absolutely opposed stretching before exercising. I had to admit, whatever she was doing, she looked damned good. The only reason the bar had her program on in the first place was because she and the other women working out with her were hot looking babes sweating in skin-tight outfits. Quite a few of us from the base stopped by just to have a few beers and imagine pumping iron—or something else—with some of them.

But I got interested in the message. Hell, I couldn't see anything wrong with getting strong without being in constant pain. I decided to find out more, checking out the base library—my first real experience with a library—to see what I could learn about various theories of fitness training. There wasn't much, but in addition to the basic manuals published by the army, I found some interesting articles in several *Men's Health* magazines. Soon I was reading everything I could find, absorbing magazines on running, weight-lifting, backpacking, and just about any sports journal with occasional articles from fitness trainers and even doctors. I guess I've become something of an expert in the field. Certainly I'm the fittest guy I know.

Devouring all that information on the human body told me I could probably have done better in school if I'd given a shit. Like my mother said once in a rare lucid moment, "You could make something of yourself, Kyle. You're not really dumb. You just got a bad attitude." Maybe my coach was right.

Nicely warmed up with just a light sweat, I loaded 150 pounds on the weight bench for some bench presses. I always start light, then work up in 20 pound increments to 250. After that I usually take a similar approach to squats, although with more weight. Mostly I work on upper body with some leg strengthening thrown in.

"Good morning, Richard." Pris had finished stretching.

"Morning. Where are all the housewives today?" The place was emptier than usual.

"I cancelled today. Everybody seems to be off on vacation with their hubbies and kids. I needed the break anyway. Was getting sick of the constant bitching about how I push them too hard."

"Hell, Pris, you do push them too hard. I've seen you working them out. I sure wouldn't sign up for those torture classes you offer."

"Right." She smiled. Pris was really very attractive. Sure, she was 15 years older than me, but I'd have been interested if she'd been hetero—or even bi-sexual. "Mr. Rock Fucking Solid afraid of aerobics classes."

"Aw, I don't push myself that much. You know me better than that."

"Well, I'd kill to have muscles like you've got. It's total bullshit that men build muscle so easy while us women work our asses off and never get as strong. Fucking testosterone. It's not fair."

"Geeze, Pris, you bench as much as me."

"Not quite. 'Course I'm old enough to be your mother."

"Older sister, maybe."

"So when are you gonna quit wasting time with that government job you don't seem to go to very often and come work for me as a trainer? I get lots of inquiries from some of the husbands of my yoga students about setting up some evening sessions so they can lose some of their guts and not feel so lousy about themselves. You could make some good money. Hell, you could keep your day job and just do two or three evenings a week."

"I travel a lot. Besides, I'm not certified to be a fitness trainer."

"I could certify you."

"Spending my evenings watching a bunch of middle-aged guys sweat and give themselves hernias is not my idea of a good time."

"Can't say I blame you. They'd probably whine as much as their wives." I was up to 250 on the bench. Pris moved into position to spot me. "So, broken any good necks lately?"

"Not recently." I've never actually broken anyone's neck. "How about you?"

"Came close last week."

"Really? What, some customer behind on their dues?"

"Shit, if I killed everyone that owed me money, I'd be a serial murderer. Nah, some creep tried to jump me last Thursday night. I was out running on the WO&D."

"You're kidding. Mugger?"

"Nah, just some kinda perve. Jumped out of a bush. Had a knife."

"What did you do?"

"What do you think I did? He came up from behind and grabbed me, so I twisted out of the hold just like I teach my housewives in self-defense class, kneed him in the groin, grabbed the hand with the knife and spun him into a judo hold, then broke his fucking arm."

"Guess he picked the wrong jogger." Pris is nothing but muscle and sinew. What kind of idiot would try to jump her?

"Got that right. I had my cell so I called the cops. Took 'em twenty minutes to get there and arrest him."

"He didn't try to get away?"

"Nah, not with a broken arm. And I mean a clean break, too. I think bone was sticking through the skin. He cried like a baby until the cops got there. Kept saying 'You broke my arm' over and over. Big fucking pussy."

"So who was he? Vagrant? Illegal immigrant?"

"Hey, watch it with that kinda talk. You don't want to come off as a racist or something." She grinned. "Actually, turns out he was some mid-level policy analyst for a right-wing think tank. Go figure."

"The cops ID'ed him and told you who he was?"

"Nope. He had one of those badges you see on all federal employees and contractors. Except his was for some outfit called Project for American Morality."

"He was wearing his badge when he attacked you?"

"Nah, it was in the back pocket of his pants."

"Pris, you didn't search the guy after you broke his arm, did you?"

"Sure I did. Wanted to know who the bastard was. Cops are thinking he's the guy who's been attacking women along the WO&D for a couple of years."

It took me a minute. Sometimes I'm slow. "And how long have you been running the trail at night hoping this guy would make the mistake of attacking you?"

"About six months." Maybe Pris and I had more in common than I'd figured. "You know, you should try pushing to 300. You handle that weight pretty easily. I'm betting you could get up around 500 pounds if you let me spot you more often and work you to muscle failure."

"No way. I don't want to carry the extra muscle. Being strong is great, but not to the point it slows you down."

"Sure. 'Cause you want to be able to run that guy down before you snap his neck. I get it."

"Listen, I'm not the one who's out playing vigilante at night." If I were, though, I wouldn't mind having Pris watch my back. I wondered how she'd react if I told her what I really did for a living. She probably wouldn't approve. But if I told her I was organizing a group to beat the crap out of sexists or homophobes, I'm betting she'd have joined right up.

I worked out for about two hours. Sweating cleared out most of the alcohol and toxins, and shooting the breeze with Pris cleared my head. It was still early, so instead of showering at the gym, I shoved my clothes in my bag and went back to my apartment. There was plenty of time to shower there and throw on some decent clothes before taking the long, indirect drive to the Wafle Shop. Today I'd have a substantive conversation with my boss, whether he wanted one or not.

He arrived five minutes after me, like always. We exchanged the usual paroles. He ordered his spinach salad and sparkling water. I got my usual eggs, bacon, pancakes and coffee. But before he had a chance to start into the Nationals or some other mundane topic, I looked straight at him and dove right in.

"We need to talk."

"Really?" He arched an eyebrow and sighed. "Some problem with the last client? I was wondering why you were away so long. It seemed a simple enough job."

"Simple?"

"Sure. It's not like you were up against a Green Beret or anything. Older woman in a sleepy little town like Joplin? I figured that'd be child's play for you."

I was surprised. This was the first time he'd given any indication of actually having read the assignment files. Given the numerous non-discussions we'd had at the Wafle Shop, I'd always assumed he just passed on assignments with only a cursory glance—if he even looked at all. But he'd at least read enough to know

Gladys' age and location.

"Sleepy towns require more planning, not less. Cops there have less to do. They focus pretty fast when something happens to one of their prominent citizens."

"I hope you're not telling me you attracted the attention of the police. That would be very unfortunate."

"No, everything went smoothly, because I took my time and arranged everything carefully." Hopefully he wasn't interested enough to start checking obit notices in local papers to make sure I was doing my job. He might wonder how I'd arranged an accident with a fire truck. "Gladys isn't a problem any more."

He arched both eyebrows and sighed deeper. "Must I remind you that it is never a good idea to say the name of a client at these meetings?"

"Sorry." That had been stupid. Nothing tied us to Gladys Thurington except her file, and that was compartmented to very few people. But mentioning her in conversation; well, even the FBI could probably correlate a conversation about 'something happening' to someone named 'Gladys' with the recent death of Gladys Thurington by means of a simple Google search. If they were listening, that is. That was unlikely, unless: "Nobody's been nosing around asking questions about what I do, have they?"

"No. But I see no reason to take risks."

"Right." I wondered how careful he was, whether he took the same precautions as I did to make sure he wasn't followed to these meetings. I glanced around but couldn't see anything out of the ordinary. Not that you can ever tell when a wino is a wino and when he's a cop on stake-out. "Anyway, I don't want to talk about Joplin." He grimaced. "I want to talk about the next client."

Our food arrived. We waited until the waiter retreated out of earshot. Then he began picking at his salad with his fork.

"I don't know what there would be to discuss. It's another straightforward job."

"Except I know the guy."

He paused, put down his fork, looked up at me. "What do you mean? You've seen him somewhere before?"

"Come on, he runs a bar five blocks from my apartment. I've been in there dozens of times."

"Okay. So what's the problem? Seems to me you should have all the information you need. No need for this 'casing' work you think is so essential. No need to screw around for a week and a half."

"Yeah, and no way to walk away after the job with nobody being able to make a connection to me. You must see that's a problem."

"Make it look like an accident or something. That's what you're good at."

"Wouldn't it just be easier to assign him to someone else, someone who doesn't know him, doesn't live in the same town with him?"

He stopped eating and looked up again, but he was staring at nothing, a reflective look in his eyes like he was weighing what to say.

"Someone else? Do you have someone in mind?"

"What? No, of course not. I just assume you have other people like me working this project. There are thousands of . . . clients . . . in the file. You can't expect I'll do them all. Not in one lifetime."

"This is not a topic I'm authorized to discuss with you."

"Sure. I know I can't know about other compartmented programs. I'm just saying ship this file to one of them."

"Sorry. That's not an option at this time."

It had never occurred to me that I might be the only person working this project. Honestly, I hadn't thought about it much. I'd been satisfied to go from assignment to assignment and leave the bigger picture to others, satisfied to do what I was told and draw my paycheck. Now I started to wonder.

"Then how about we put Da . . . this guy's file on hold for awhile and just move on to the next one. We can always come back to him later."

"That's not an option either."

"Why not? We've got plenty of other clients to choose from."

His expression went ice cold. I'd never seen him show any emotion before. He shifted into hate with surprising ease.

"He is the worst of the worst. Every day he's out there, he's a threat to everything this country stands for." He leaned forward and looked me in the eye. "You'll have to trust me on this. He is the most dangerous person in our files."

"You're gonna have to give me more than that. I'm telling you, I know the guy. He's just an ex-civil servant running a bar." The thought that Dan Stigler was some dangerous terrorist seemed ludicrous. It occurred to me that my boss had snapped.

"I can't give you the details. You don't have a need to know." He sat back, assessing just how much of a problem I was going to be on this one. "But I can tell you this. He is not just a soldier for our enemies. He's an organizer. A key player in the conspiracy to end our way of life."

And then it all fell into place. Dan's questioning me about my work, asking me if I was frustrated, talking about the 'group' he was pulling together, wondering if I could give him advice on 'targets.' Dan Stigler really was a terrorist. That had to be it. The feeling of betrayal started creeping into my gut again. All those nights he'd served me beers, made small talk, acted like my friend. I'd actually come close to letting my guard down with him. Any terrorist slick enough to make me drop my guard really was too dangerous to let live.

"Okay. I get it. Consider it done."

He picked up his fork and went back to his salad. I started in on my pancakes. No point in letting them get cold.

"Was there anything else?"

"Uh, yeah, in fact." I'd almost forgotten. "The Kyoto Protocol Public Relations Initiative."

He laughed. Another first. "You seriously want to talk about the KPPRI?" He actually said 'Kip-Ree.' Government wonks love to turn acronyms into idiotic words.

"Well, as the program manager, wouldn't it be natural for me to discuss it with the project administrator?" I looked for a reaction. My sarcasm didn't phase him.

"So you've seen the report. What do you think?" The hate was gone from his eyes now, replaced by a kind of puppy curiosity. He seemed earnestly interested in my opinion of his paper. I wondered if he remembered that he had never told me I was project manager.

"I think it's a bit awkward when Sharon asks me about something I've never fucking heard of and then find out I'm supposed to be intimately involved with."

"Well, you are. Intimately involved, that is."

"Are you nuts? I read the report. I'm not a pollster, remember? And I'm not out giving presentations to persuade people to support the government's environmental policy."

He went quiet again, giving me another of those distant stares. I guess he was organizing his thoughts to make sure the explanation he was about to give me was just right, the way a mother will pause before telling her kid where babies come from or why daddy's going to live somewhere else from now on.

"I know we've talked about these issues before, but I can understand your confusion. You remember, of course, my telling you that our program is so secret, it can't even be laid out explicitly in your after action reports."

"Sure."

"Or in your accounting."

"Right. I understand all that."

"But we have to get the money to pay for all this from somewhere. And since there is no line item in anyone's budget laying out the kind of work you do, that means the money comes in with the same sort of euphemistic language we use to account for it. You remember our discussion of 'euphemisms,' I hope."

"Of course, I remember. I'm not stupid." He was irritating me, talking to me like I was a child. I'd had more than enough of that crap from officers in the army. "What does any of that have to do with my name showing up in this fucking KPPRI report?"

"Calm down, okay? And watch your language. There's a mother with her child over there." He nodded toward a table on the other side of the patio.

Some housewife with a stroller was nibbling on a fruit salad. I doubt her infant was offended by my profanity. "Maybe I made a mistake, listing you on that report. But you do recall, I hope, that the policy documents you're using as cover for these assignments are Kyoto Protocol policy memoranda. Right?"

"Yeah. But that's just so if anybody ever gets hold of one of them, they won't be able to figure out what we're doing."

"Sure. But I didn't just pick the Kyoto cover at random, you know. The money comes from the KPPRI fund. We use the Kyoto language in our reports and accounting so it matches up with the language in the KPPRI allocation. And since I've got you claiming money under KPPRI, I thought it might look good to give you a substantive position in the KPPRI report. Understand?"

"I guess so." I had to admit, it made some sense. "But you could have warned me before you gave it to Sharon to type up. She already wonders what I do that is so disconnected from everything else going on in the office. Now she's wondering how I'm not even in the loop on programs I'm supposed to be managing. We can only push the incompetent loser cover so far, you know."

"You're right. I should have told you what I was doing. I apologize." The apology should have made me feel better, but it smacked of manipulation, like something they teach in management seminars on how to control problem employees. "Tell you what, you leave Sharon to me. I'll have a talk with her."

"I don't think that'll be necessary. Now that I've read the report, I'll just read up some on Kyoto and try not to sound so stupid around her. If you talk to her, she'll get even more suspicious, wonder why I raised the issue with you at all."

"Well, I'm just concerned that she's getting so curious about you." He was sopping up the left-over salad dressing on his plate with a piece of bread, considering. "I could fire her."

"Now I know you're joking." I hoped he was. "She's the best employee in the office, hard working, smart, stays late when you need her to do crap like type up that KPPRI report at the last minute."

He didn't respond.

"She's civil service, too." I was sounding like her union rep now. "You can't just fire her out of the blue. It takes years to establish a poor performance track record. And even if you could cite evidence she wasn't doing her job, you'd have to give her opportunities to seek counseling, go to training, all that bullshit that the civil service has to protect its own. Otherwise she'll just appeal it up the management chain, and then the IG will come snooping around and we'll all be in trouble."

I realized I really didn't want him to fire Sharon. I liked her. There haven't been that many people in my life I can say that about.

"You don't need to worry about any of that. All that documentation you mentioned is already in her file. I can make a case to fire her anytime."

That caught me by surprise. "How is that possible? Like I said, she's the best employee you've got. And she's only been in the job six months."

"That's right."

"So how does she come to have such a lousy personnel file?"

"I wrote a very damning mid-year performance review and substituted it for the good one I actually showed her and got her to sign. And I copied her signature onto the mid-year evaluation and onto several memoranda detailing specific performance deficiencies."

"W-why would you do that?" I found myself wondering what he was arranging for me behind my back.

"Oh, a few years back I had a real problem employee, young woman right out of college, degree in chemistry. She wasn't much of a worker, but I didn't think much about it during her two-year probationary period. At the end of her probation, I recommended she be let go. I called her into my office for a long chat and explained to her that her production during the probationary period had been pretty abysmal. She even sat across from me and agreed that the job had been a lot more than she'd expected, that she'd felt pretty overwhelmed at times. We shook hands and she left, no hard feelings."

"So what does that have to do with Sharon?"

"Well, the little bitch-chemist then went to my boss and accused me of sexual harassment. Said I made crass sexual jokes in the office all the time and that she had complained to me, so I was trying to get her fired in retaliation."

"Had she?"

"Had she what?"

"Actually complained about you making crass sexual jokes?"

"That had nothing to do with the reasons I recommended she be let go."

"Oh. Sure."

"Anyway, she was transferred to another office and I had to attend several sexual harassment seminars.

Delayed my next promotion by two years."

"Too bad."

"And it's all because I hadn't documented her performance sufficiently to get her fired. If I had just given her poor performance evaluations consistently over time, management would have sided with me." He took a bite of the salad-dressing saturated bread. "So I told myself then that I'd make sure I never have a similar problem with any women working for me again. Any one of them gives me any trouble, I've made sure their file won't help them."

"I see." Indeed, I did. He really was a scary bastard. Maybe that shouldn't have surprised me, given what he had me doing. "Listen, that's great to know, just in case Sharon gets to be too much trouble. But, for now, why don't you just let me handle the problem? I think I can deal with her."

"I don't know."

"Look, if I'm wrong, you can always fire her later."

"True." He thought about it. "Okay. You deal with it for now."

"Thanks."

"I'd better be getting back." He produced his wallet from his jacket, took out two twenties and set them on the table. "This should cover lunch. You pay the check when the waiter comes back."

I watched him walk away, wondering whether I should warn Sharon that she should transfer to another office.

Chapter VII
A Little Rest and Relaxation

I PULLED ON a decent pair of slacks, tie, dark jacket, and went to the office early the next morning trying to look a little more professional than usual. Office professional, that is. I didn't have a lot to do at the office other than pick up a couple of alias packets on the off chance I might need them. But I did have one important agenda item.

Sharon came in a few minutes before 9:00. I heard her arrive, humming some happy tune she had probably been listening to on her car radio. She dropped her oversize shoulder-bag on her desk, keys and change and other mysterious items clanking around inside. I heard her sit, switch on her computer, rummage around in a drawer. I counted slowly to 10—didn't want her to think I'd been waiting for her—and walked out of my office to her desk. Her back was to me.

"Good morning, Sharon."

She jumped, gasped, spun around in her chair, put her hand to over her heart.

"Goodness, Mr. Paladin! You scared me out of my shoes. What are you doing here this early, sneaking up behind me?"

"Sorry, Sharon. I thought you'd have noticed I was here. My light's on. I didn't mean to startle you."

"That's okay. You just surprised me, that's all." She looked rattled. "Why, since I started here, I don't believe you have ever come in to work ahead of me."

"Hmm. You might be right. I never thought about

it." I knew damned well she was right.

"So what's the special occasion?"

"Well, I came in late the other night after getting back into town and picked up the copy of the KPPRI to go over at home." I made sure to say 'KIP-REE' so I'd sound like I knew what I was talking about. "Looked really good. I could tell you fixed a couple of sentences. I wanted to thank you for making me a copy."

"You're welcome." She cocked her head. A quizzical look came over her. "So you suddenly remember that you're running that program?"

"Aw, I was just pulling your leg. Figured you believe I just sit in my office when I'm here reading the newspaper and were wondering how I could be managing something like KPPRI. So I decided to have some fun with you."

"Then you really are the program manager?"

"Sure. What, you think I don't have anything to work on?"

"It's crossed my mind." She gave me a dead serious look for about 15 seconds. Then she laughed. "I'm just joking, Mr. Paladin. I'm sure you have lots of important projects. It's just you never talk to me about your work. Naturally, I've been curious, you traveling so much. But I can understand KPPRI keeping you out of the office a lot."

"Hey, that's the nature of public outreach." 'Outreach' was a term I'd gleaned from the report. I wasn't too sure what it meant. Until reading KPPRI, I hadn't even known it was really a word.

"Still, I'm a little surprised."

"That I'm program manager?"

"No, that you're in public relations. You don't seem

like the public relations type."

"I don't?" I decided to flirt a bit, that it was time to get close to Sharon, see if I could deflect her curiosity into interest of another sort. I sat on a corner of her desk and leaned ever so slightly toward her. "Just what 'type' do I seem like?"

She leaned ever so slightly back. "Well, I have a friend who's an ATF agent. I know a few of his colleagues at ATF. You seem more that type."

"You think I'd be more suited to law enforcement?"

"Maybe, maybe not." She leaned toward me, reached up, put her hand on my bicep and squeezed. "But you look like you enjoy time in the gym a lot more than time in the office."

"I just don't like to let myself go. I'm health conscious."

"If you say so."

"What, you think it's odd, trying to stay healthy?"

"Of course not, Mr. Paladin." There was a sparkle in her brown eyes. "Like Mr. Millpond down the hall. He runs every day at lunch, does 10Ks every so often, even plans on doing the Marine Corps Marathon. Says he wants to keep his heart healthy so he'll live a long time. Makes perfect sense."

"Absolutely."

"Of course, he doesn't go to the gym to lift weights, build big muscles like you do."

"Everybody's got their own ideas of fitness."

"Right, like my ATF friends. They're in the gym all the time like you, building big biceps and forearms."

"Hey, I run, too, you know."

"Sure, like my ATF guys."

"It's just trying to be all-around fit."

"Uh huh."

"Nothing wrong with that."

"Nothing at all." She leaned back again. "But my ATF friends don't work out because they want to keep their hearts healthy."

I knew what she was driving at, but I decided to play along. "I'll bite. Why do they do all the weightlifting, then?"

"Because they want to be ready in case they have to wrestle someone to the ground."

"Is that what you think I'm preparing for?"

"Maybe."

"Then I guess I'm overdoing it." I winked at her.

"Whatever do you mean?"

"Well, the only person I'm interested in wrestling to the ground is you." I paused ever so briefly for effect. She didn't say anything, but I could tell she was breathing heavier. "And I'm betting I wouldn't need to be a circus strongman for that."

"I might surprise you." She turned her chair back facing her computer. "I have work to do this morning, Mr. Paladin. And I suspect you do, too."

"I get the message, Sharon. I'll stop harassing you." I stood up and started back to my office, then stopped as if I'd just thought of something. "Why don't we do lunch sometime?"

"Lunch?"

"Yeah. You know. What people do during the lunch hour."

"I don't think that would be appropriate."

"No? You're sure?"

"Absolutely."

I turned to leave.

"Dinner." She said it without looking up from her computer. At first I wasn't sure I'd heard right.

"Dinner?"

"Yes, dinner. Tomorrow night. Unless you have plans. Tomorrow's Friday, you know."

"I don't have plans."

"And if you did, you'd cancel them." She was enjoying herself. "You pick the place. I'll meet you there."

"Friday's fine. It's a date. You like steak?"

"I love steak."

"Know where Chester's is up on Capitol Hill?"

"Yes I do."

"How about 8:00?"

"How about 7:00? I get hungry early."

"Okay. I'll make a reservation." I'd picked Chester's because I knew it was only a few blocks from her apartment. And I wasn't just being considerate, thinking that it would be convenient for her to get there; I was strictly thinking about after dinner, starting to convince myself that getting to know Sharon a lot better might not be all that stupid. Guy's do this, by the way. They rationalize all the time that they're making an intelligent decision about a woman, as if it wasn't just hormones overriding reason.

"Now go to your office and let me get some work done."

I obeyed.

I didn't get any work done. It wasn't that I was excited to have a date, although it had been quite awhile. Truth is I just didn't have anything to do. I needed to come up with a plan to deal with Dan Stigler, but I'd already decided to put that out of my mind until next week. It would be a tricky job, so I deserved a little R and R in advance. I had high hopes Sharon would be just the R and R I needed.

I collected several back issues of the *Washington Post* that had been stacked by the coffee pot and spent the rest of the morning catching up on the news. As always, I focused on obituaries, looking for interesting stories I could adapt to covers. There wasn't a lot for me; almost all the recent deaths turned out to be pretty mainstream people.

The *Post* mixes memorial notices in with the obituaries; a few lines from family or friends in remembrance of someone who'd passed away the previous year, or on the anniversary of a death even further in the past. Usually, there's a photo. Scanning the photos for the Washington area gives the impression that people who die in D.C. are either very old or very young. I suspect that's the case in most big American cities. If you can just make it past your early twenties without getting killed in a drive-by or dying in a car accident, you've got a decent chance of living a long life.

Sometimes I come across a detailed obituary that provides inspiration for my line of work, like the attractive young American Petroleum Institute policy analyst who skidded her bicycle on wet pavement and plowed straight into a garbage truck. Apparently she slammed head-first into the truck's rear the way a cornerback puts his helmet into the back of a wide receiver—except she wasn't wearing a helmet. I'd have difficulty reproducing that with a client, though.

Mostly, obits provide little in the way of information on manner of death—with the exception of the endless varieties of cancer that kill people. I wish I had a formula for cancer.

Close to noon, I looked up Chester's in the phone

book and called. They had no problem taking a reservation for two the next night; tables for two are fairly easy even at the best restaurants, since they're motivated to cram in two more paying customers at all times. It had been quite a while since I'd eaten at a decent place. A good steak and decent whiskey might be just the appetizer I needed, assuming Sharon proved a willing main course.

It flashed through my mind again that this might be a mistake. Common sense said starting something with Sharon would only make a deteriorating situation even worse, get her asking more questions, trying harder to find out what I was all about. As if I would suddenly pay attention to common sense regarding a woman.

I'd wasted as much time in the office as I could without going stir crazy. The walls were starting to close in on me. I shoved three of the alias packages into my backpack and headed out, stopping briefly at Sharon's desk.

"Got meetings out of the office all afternoon and all day tomorrow."

"Public relations, no doubt." Sharon rolled her eyes, but she smiled while she rolled them.

"You bet. See you tomorrow night."

"I'll be there."

With no social plans until Friday evening and no desire to do anything productive, I decided to spend the afternoon hiking from Union Station through the Capitol Mall and into Virginia. From the office to my apartment is only about 15 miles: I hadn't ruled out just walking the whole way. It was hot and humid, meaning I'd work up a good sweat. Since I'd worn fairly nice office attire for the day, I wasn't ideally dressed for it.

But I never care if I sweat through a shirt. Growing up in North Carolina gets you used to it.

The Mall was fairly empty, despite being the middle of the tourist season. By mid-afternoon, the hordes of corn-fed mid-westerners with their overweight children had long abandoned seeing the nation's monuments and decamped to air conditioned shopping centers for blended beverages and t-shirt shopping. The only other people along the hard-packed dirt path paralleling Constitution Ave. were a few derelicts and a couple of military-looking types in USMC sweats out for a jog. I figured them to be officers on Pentagon duty, out to prove to themselves they weren't getting soft. They had smooth, lean muscles; not the big blocky builds of ordinary grunts. Officers never have to lug around 100 pound rucksacks or fifty-caliber machine guns.

I stopped at the Lincoln Monument to pay my respects, then hiked out to Constitution and past the Kennedy Center toward Georgetown. The memorials to the two fallen Presidents have special meaning for me: John Wilkes Booth and Lee Harvey Oswald are exactly the kind of amateurs who give my profession a bad name. Taking out a client is something that should be done quickly and efficiently in a back alley or in their garage. The goal is eliminating an enemy and living to continue the fight, not getting the attention of a large audience so you can yell *Sic Semper Tyrannus* or some other bullshit. Booth and Oswald were just grandstanders, in my book.

I made my way to Georgetown and bought a bottle of water in a CVS Pharmacy. It was still early, not yet 4:00. Too early for the mobs of drunken university students cruising the shooter bars. I don't go to Georgetown often. Lots of Washington's very powerful people own multi-million dollar townhomes there. I read somewhere once that they fought successfully to block a Metro station even though the Orange Line runs underneath M street right through the neighborhood. Didn't want the riff-raff who ride the subway to have easy access to the place. I'd never had to do a job in Georgetown, but I didn't figure the absence of a subway station would be too much of an impediment. I made my way down M Street to the Key Bridge and crossed into Virginia.

I had planned to catch the Orange Line in Rosslyn and ride to Fairfax. I'd been walking for a couple of hours and didn't really need any more exercise. Halfway across the bridge, I changed my mind. There was a scruffy looking guy—late 20s, stringy hair about 10 inches too long, jeans, sneakers, ratty baseball cap—about 100 feet behind me. I'd noticed him earlier hanging around outside the CVS. It was possible he had coincidentally just decided to walk into Virginia the same as me, but I doubted it. I don't believe in coincidence.

Instead, I kept walking, right through Rosslyn, up Wilson Boulevard to Courthouse Metro and on to Clarendon, two small business and shopping hubs that have sprung up along the Orange Line corridor. I maintained a brisk pace, punctuated every so often by turning into a strip shopping center to check out something in a store window. He stayed with me, always about 100 feet behind. At Clarendon, I went into a Starbucks and ordered a Frappuccino. He hung out across the street, trying to look inconspicuous.

I figured he was too obvious to be a well-trained professional like FBI or Secret Service. It was possible, of course, that I'd screwed up on a job somewhere and been made by some terrorist group that was now surveying me for the best time and place to kill me. But that didn't seem too likely. I hadn't screwed up any jobs. Sucking on my Frappuccino through the big green straw and watching him out of the corner of my eye, I decided he was in all likelihood just a petty crook looking for an opportunity to mug me. I had worn nice business attire that day, after all. Obviously I looked like someone worth robbing.

I could have lost him easily, ducked through stores with multiple entrances; entered a crowded Metro stop, pushed my way through the rush-hour gaggle on the platform, left by the opposite exit while he struggled to follow; any of a number of tricks that would have convinced him to drop me and look for another mark. But I needed to be sure he was just a mugger. I exited the Starbucks with my best oblivious to the world expression, hiked up Clarendon Blvd. about a block, and then turned off into a residential area with fewer pedestrians. I cut through a park to a row of townhomes, made a right just beyond the first one, turned around and stopped.

He rounded the corner ten seconds later and froze.

"Something I can do for you?" I said it real friendly.

"Uh . . . " His eyes were darting around. But he wasn't panicked. I think he was just checking to see if there was anyone else in the vicinity. Nobody likes witnesses.

"You've been following me since Georgetown. I just thought I'd save us both any more exertion and find out what it is you're after."

He'd had his right hand in his jeans pocket the whole time. He produced a switchblade and snapped it open. I doubt he noticed me breathing a huge sigh of relief.

"Yeah, your wallet, dude. And that backpack you're carrying. I don't want to have to cut you."

"I'm sure you don't." I let the backpack strap slide off my shoulder, hefted it and tossed it gently in his direction. He wasn't a complete amateur. He didn't reach for it. He just glanced briefly at it.

I grabbed the knife hand with my left and pulled, placed my right on his shoulder and pushed, spinning him nicely so that I had a hammerlock on his neck while I pulled his right arm up tight and high against his back.

"You might want to drop that knife before I get mad."

He dropped it.

I shoved him up against the wall of the townhome, putting additional pressure with my knee shoved into his butt. Now he could worry about whether I was going to strangle him, snap his arm, or just crush his balls. I let him consider those options for a minute.

"Now tell me why you were following me."

"Lemme go. I can't breathe."

"If you don't tell me, I'll break your arm." I put more tension on the arm for emphasis. I got a sudden flash of Pris doing the same thing to the think-tank stalker, wondered if she'd enjoyed it as much as I was enjoying this.

"Christ, man, that fucking hurts."

"Then tell me why you were following me all the way from Georgetown."

"I just wanted your cash and credit cards. What else?"

I was pretty convinced he was telling the truth. But not certain. "Who told you to follow me?"

"Nobody. Are you fucking nuts? Do I look like a cop or a spy?"

"Actually, you look exactly like a cop or spy trying not to look like a cop or spy."

"Jesus, you are crazy. Lemme go, man. I'm real sorry I bothered you, okay?"

"Oh, you don't know how sorry I can make you." Actually, I was beginning to feel sorry for him. As criminals go, he was pretty pathetic. But I had to make absolutely certain that's all he was. "So let me ask you, you ever hear of the Department of Homeland Security?"

"What?"

"Homeland Security. Heard of it?"

"Yeah, man, everybody's heard of them."

"Any idea what they do to terrorists? I'll tell you. They lock them up in dark little cells no one knows about and throw away the key." I tightened my hold on his neck. "Or should I say we lock them up. 'Cause that's who I am and that's what I'm gonna do with you. Right after I break your arm."

"I'm not a fucking terrorist. I just wanted to rob you, got it? Jesus, call the cops. I got a record. They'll tell you."

He'd convinced me. But I wasn't going to call the cops. "All right, I believe you. You're nobody. So I should just kill you so you don't rob somebody else, like some old lady."

"Please don't kill me." He rasped the words, barely audible, either from terror or the choke-hold I had on him. It was almost comic.

"Maybe I won't kill you. On one condition."

"Sure. Name it."

"If I decide to let you go . . . and I still haven't

decided... I want you to run away from here as fast as you possibly can, and I want you to keep running until you're in another state or another country. I don't ever want to see you again. You think you can do that for me?"

"Yeah."

"You're sure?"

"Aw, please, man. I'm sure. You won't ever see me. I promise."

I released the choke-hold, let go of his arm, relaxed my knee and stepped back, all so quickly he stumbled a bit. There's always a chance, when you release someone from a death grip, that they'll do something stupid like spin around and try to fight. I'd immediately assumed a judo stance, ready to thrust my right palm all the way through his sternum if he hadn't had enough. But he just stood there with his back to me for a few beats, still in shock, unable to move.

"I told you to run," I whispered.

He took off like an Olympic sprinter. If he's smart, he didn't stop until he'd crossed the Canadian border.

I picked up the knife. It was a cheap piece of crap, probably made in China. I dropped it in a dumpster behind a Cheesecake Factory just around the corner from the Clarendon Metro station and headed west on Wilson. I'd decided to walk the remaining 7 or 8 miles home. I felt that good.

Chester's was packed. I got there half an hour early—it's rude to make a woman wait for you—and took a seat at the bar. They didn't serve Miller or Budweiser, of course. Most everybody was drinking vodka martinis. Maybe James Bond can pull off sipping out of a martini glass and still look tough, but most guys just look silly. I ordered a black and tan. That's about as sophisticated as I get.

Sharon arrived at ten of. She was dressed to the nines, slinky black dress cut low, thin gold chain with a small gold cross draped around her neck to draw your eyes down. She was carrying a tiny black handbag that had maybe enough room for a driver's license and lipstick and nothing else. She looked a little nervous, scanning the restaurant and bar like she wasn't sure I'd really show up. I waved. A look of relief came over her, followed by a big smile.

"You look fabulous, Sharon."

"Why, thank you, Mr. Paladin." She might have blushed, but between the bar's dim lights and her milk chocolate skin, it was hard to tell.

"Place is packed tonight, but I made a reservation for 7:00, and they said they'd come get me when the table's ready." I stood so she could sit on the stool I'd been occupying. "How about a drink while we wait?"

"That sounds nice. What are you having?"

"Black and tan." I nodded to my glass on the bar.

"I like those. But I think I'll have a martini tonight."

I motioned to the waitress behind the bar. "My friend'll have a martini."

"Vodka?"

Sharon interjected, "No, gin. Bombay Sapphire if you've got it. With an olive." She obviously knew her martinis.

I added "shaken, not stirred," but the waitress just looked at me like I was from Mars. People are idiots.

"So, did I miss anything at the office today?"

"You didn't ask me out to talk about work, I hope." Her martini arrived. She picked it up and sipped, spinning to and fro on the barstool like a little kid. Like

I said, men look silly holding a martini glass. But it makes a gorgeous woman like Sharon look very sexy. "But no, you didn't miss anything. Except me."

I reached past her to grab my black and tan, brushing her shoulder. "I always miss you when I'm not there, doll."

She laughed. "Doll? Gee, Mr. Paladin, where did you pick that one up? One of those old Bogart movies?"

I flushed. It's probably exactly where I'd heard it. But Sam Spade always got the girl, and some things are timeless. "You could do worse than Bogie, shweetheart."

"Yes, but I'll settle for you tonight, if that's okay."

"You got no choice. You even look at someone else; well, I get jealous."

"Ooh, big muscles and a cave-man ego. Just my type."

The headwaiter was waving at me. We picked up our drinks and headed into the restaurant. I pulled Sharon's chair out for her when we got to the table, laying it on as thick as I could.

Our waiter was exactly what one would expect in a high-end steak joint on Capitol Hill, mid-twenties college type looking smug in his black pants, black vest, black tie and white shirt. He handed us menus and recited the evening's specials like he was in a big hurry to get back to the kitchen and finish a chapter in his business administration textbook.

" . . . may I bring you an appetizer?"

"Hang on." I'd had enough. This was just one snooty waiter too many. "I lost you at the blackened swordfish. What'd that come with?"

"Uh, the swordfish?" He was flustered. I suspect he

had memorized the list without really thinking he might have to recall specific items. "Oh, yes, that comes with a side of white asparagus."

"And you said something about venison?"

"Venison? Oh, right. It's a venison ragout served in a bread bowl."

"Ragout?"

"Stew." He sighed, like the weight of the world was on his shoulders.

"And the salads? They went by so fast, I completely missed them."

No shit, he rolled his eyes. I guess he wasn't counting on my tip to pay his tuition. "Okay, there's a spinach basil salad with a hot mustard vinaigrette . . . "

"Ooh, I'm allergic to spinach." Not really.

" . . . a traditional Caesar . . . "

"Traditional? How so?"

" . . . er, it's the chef's interpretation of the traditional Caesar . . . "

"So it's not really traditional."

He stopped and shot me an exasperated glare, like he could tell I was trying to goad him into taking a swing at me. Sharon jumped in and saved him.

"I think I'd just like a plain garden salad to start. And some wine. Should we get a bottle?" She looked at me with sparkling eyes that said 'Behave yourself.'

"Sure. Two garden salads. And why don't you choose the wine, Sharon. I'm sure I'll like anything you pick."

"Okay. I'm assuming you're having steak." I nodded. "So a red, then."

"Sounds good to me."

She batted her long eyebrows at the waiter and smiled. "Do you recommend a nice Merlot?"

"Yes, ma'am. We have a very good Italian Merlot, a '99 Alighieri that stands up quite well to red meat."

"That sounds perfect. Thanks."

He headed back to the kitchen, no doubt wondering why such a nice lady was having dinner with a jerk like me.

"You are a bad man, Mr. Paladin." She said it with a smile. I think she was looking forward to finding out just how bad I could be.

"Ah, waiter's like that give me the creeps. They're all working their way through college and figure the rest of us are a bunch of rubes."

"Interesting. You don't like college kids?"

"Not much."

"Must have made it tough."

"What?"

"Getting that advanced degree in environmental science that's on your resumé."

I should read my personnel file sometime. It's funny, but I'm very cautious to prepare myself when I do jobs in alias, like the Gladys Thurington assignment. But I've been lax learning all the details my boss put in the Richard Paladin file. I guess it's because I never really kill anyone as Richard Paladin.

"Ah, you've caught me, Sharon. I confess. I made all that stuff up. I don't have any college degrees. Never even finished high school. In fact, I'll let you in on the biggest secret of all." I leaned across the table to whisper. She leaned in close, too. "I can't read or write, either."

"You're illiterate?"

"Nah, Southern Baptist. But I still can't read."

"Now I know you're bullshitting me."

"Really? What gave me away?"

"No way you're Southern Baptist, Mr. Paladin." She was right. I'm not. At least, I hadn't been for a long time.

The waiter arrived with the wine and glasses. He pulled the cork with a professional flourish and poured a little drop in my glass for me to taste.

"She's the wine expert, son. Better to let her decide."

He rolled his eyes again, but switched the glasses. I decided to have some more fun with him.

"I'm surprised you don't recognize her."

"Excuse me?"

"Ms. DeLoris. I'm surprised you don't recognize her."

"I'm sorry." He looked at Sharon, confused. "Do I know you?"

"Son, this is Phoebe Deloris, the famous rhythm and blues singer from Quebec. She's in town doing a show at Wolf Trap. You should get out more."

"Sorry, Ms. DeLoris. Welcome to Chester's." He looked suspicious, like there was an ever-so-slight inkling in his head that I was having him on. Of course, if he actually listened to his customers, he'd have known I was bullshitting him. I'd already used Sharon's real first name in front of him.

"She's just having dinner with me because she's interviewing me for a job."

"Oh, well, that's nice. Are you a musician, too?"

"Nah, gigolo."

"The wine is fine. Very good in fact." Sharon's look this time said 'stop.' Maybe my common sense was trying to get my subconscious to torpedo this thing right from the start, I don't know. More likely the animal part of my brain was goading me to insert sex into the conversation. The waiter poured the wine and left.

"Leave the poor waiter alone, Mr. Paladin. He is much too young to be exposed to your adult sense of humor."

"Okay, Sharon. I promise. On one condition."

"What?"

"That you stop calling me 'Mr. Paladin' and start calling me Richard."

She smiled again. Sharon's got a real nice smile, one a guy could get lost in.

"All right, Richard. It's a nice name. Suits you."

"Sounds nice when you say it." I couldn't very well ask her to call me Kyle.

We didn't talk for awhile, just sipped wine and exchanged meaningful glances. I was starting to forget why I had made the date in the first place. What I'd had in mind, actually, waiting for her to arrive the morning before, was taking her to lunch and warning her about our mutual boss. But then she'd made it dinner and Friday night and, well, my hormones kicked in and I started acting like a teenager on prom night. Sitting there taking in her dreamy eyes and luscious skin, I knew damned well that sleeping with her would be about the stupidest thing I could do. Sharon is just not the kind of woman I could jump in the sack with once; she'd have me coming back for more. Much as I wanted to make the leap right then and there, a torrid affair with the office manager was not something Richard Paladin could pull off. She'd be asking too many questions, questions he . . . I couldn't answer.

Of course, it did occur to me that I could have sex with her and then tell my boss to go ahead with his plan to fire her.

"So what's going on behind that very serious expression, Mr. . . . Richard?"

"Just wondering what a smart, beautiful lady like you is doing wasting her life in a low-paying government job, not to mention wasting a perfectly good Friday evening on a date with a mid-level government bureaucrat like me."

"I bet you say that to all the girls." She swirled the wine in her glass. "Maybe I'm just curious."

"About how the government really works?"

"Have you always been such a tease? Of course it's you I'm curious about."

"Ah, come on, Sharon. You've seen my file. EPA'd fire me in a heartbeat if they could. But I've got too much tenure, so they shipped me out of sight. Not that I'm complaining. I get paid. And I met you."

"Right. Dust-up with your previous supervisor. Gave you a bad evaluation. You wrote that rebuttal. Not a good career move. Your file's pretty detailed."

"Uh huh. Very sad story." I was developing a new appreciation for Riffelbach. Apparently he was quite the creative writer.

"Which division was that again?"

"What?'

"The division you worked in before getting transferred to our place."

"Water quality." Maybe I hadn't memorized my file, but my boss had filled me in on the rough outline of what he'd put in there to backstop me.

"So was he right?"

"Who? Right about what?"

"Your previous boss. Was he right that you're not a team player?" Obviously she'd read my file pretty thoroughly. I was tempted to remind her that her responsibility was to maintain the files, not memorize them.

"Hey, let's not talk about all that, Sharon. That's water under the bridge."

"Polluted water?"

"Very funny. I just don't see much point in dwelling on the past."

"So what do you dwell on, then?"

"Planet Earth. How about you?"

The waiter returned with an order pad. I was thankful for the respite from the third degree. It was Sharon's out-of-control curiosity I needed to get under control. As she ordered a rib-eye, rare, with baked potato and shallots, I tried to think of a convincing lie that I could use to co-opt her into silence. Maybe tell her I was living under a phony identity, was on the run from the law for a crime I didn't commit, something like that. But it sounded an awful lot like an episode from *The Fugitive*. I'd watched re-runs of that show growing up and thought it was pretty cool that Richard Kimble got to drift around the country, solve people's stupid problems, and then move on without having to get permanently entangled in their lives.

"And you sir? What will you be having?"

"Porterhouse, medium rare."

He jotted down my order and left without comment.

"Well, you must be hungry." Obviously, Sharon felt the need to comment. "Porterhouse. That's basically two steaks served as one."

"It's all protein. That Chet Atkins diet, you know."

She frowned. "Dr. Atkins first name was Chet? I didn't know that."

She was serious. I had to laugh. "It's a joke, hon. You're supposed to laugh that I'm such a rube, I confused Dr. Atkins with Chet Atkins."

"Who's Chet Atkins?"

"The Nashville guitarist? You've never heard of him?"

"Sorry." She made a face. "Where I grew up, we didn't listen to country and western much."

"Yeah, I guess not. It's all I ever heard on the radio as a kid."

"In Connecticut?"

I just sat there, dumbstruck. Sharon had definitely missed her calling; she could have worked for the East German secret police ferreting out spies. In less than an hour, she'd gotten me to stumble all over my phony file. Pulling off an alias is pretty simple with the ordinary yokels I met routinely in my work, but Sharon was no ordinary yokel.

"Well, it was rural Connecticut, after all."

She stared back. Then a smile crept slowly across her face. She almost laughed.

"So, are we going to drink this wine or play twenty questions all night?" I picked up my glass and waited. She did the same.

"I think drinking is definitely in order. It is, after all, a very good Italian Merlot."

Our steaks arrived. They were quite good. Cooking a big slab of red meat properly is an art, and the chef at Chester's had mastered it. I don't eat steak all that often. Too much of it too often and I feel sluggish, so I tend to stick with grilled chicken and broiled fish except on rare occasions, like celebrating a particularly tough job pulled off . . . or having dinner with a delicious woman. Next time I decide to treat myself, I may well go back to Chester's.

Now that she'd had enough of interrogating me, we made small talk, mostly about her. She'd grown up in Maryland, just outside the District. Her parents still lived there, in the same house they'd lived in for forty years. They were solid working class; her father retired after a career with the Potomac Electric Power Company, PEPCO. Her mother had been an elementary school teacher and still substituted occasionally. Sharon was their only child.

"I'll admit, they spoiled me."

"Looks to me like you turned out okay."

She'd taken a degree in English at the University of Maryland. It's just down the road in College Park, so she'd been able to stay at home right through graduation. All in all, she described the kind of stable and happy home life I'd always figured only existed on television. After graduation, she'd immediately taken a civil service job with the EPA as a secretary, rising to Office Manager with the transfer to the outpost where we worked.

By the time we'd finished our steaks, we'd hit that zone in a perfect evening where we both just felt very comfortable, enjoying each others' company without feeling any pressure to ask more questions or show off more details of our lives. The waiter brought dessert menus, but she declined . . .

"I've already eaten more tonight than I usually eat in a week!"

. . . but she readily accepted my suggestion of an after dinner drink . . .

"Ooh, a nice brandy sounds good."

. . . which she sipped ever so slowly while her eyes became warmer and more inviting. I don't think I'd ever felt so at ease with a woman. I didn't even get mad when the waiter dropped the check on the table without asking if we wanted anything else. I just counted out eleven twenties to cover the $181.73 tab. He didn't deserve a big tip, but I didn't want Sharon thinking I was cheap.

"Should I get the waiter to call us a cab?"

"I only live a few blocks from here, Richard."

"Then how about I walk you home?"

"Mmmm. That sounds nice."

We strolled arm in arm like newlyweds, hardly talking, just enjoying the evening and, well, pretty loopy on all the red meat and alcohol. Not that I wasn't keeping an alert eye peeled all the time for trouble; Washington's not the safest place to wander through at night. But the streets were quiet.

"So you haven't told me," I said, squeezing her hand, "how a smart, gorgeous gal like you hasn't snagged some successful lawyer or executive to take you away from all this."

"Guess I've been too busy living my own life. Until now." She smiled up at me.

"Not even an old college flame still pining for you, always seeking you out to sweep you off your feet at those Terp homecomings?"

"Twerp homecomings? Is that what it's like when all you environmental engineers get together to rehash your college days?"

I laughed. "Right. We see who's got the biggest pocket protector. But I said 'terps,' not 'twerps'."

"I think you've had too much to drink. You're not making much sense." She stopped, turned into me and put her arms around me, looked up into my eyes. "But this is my building."

"That wasn't far at all."

"So what do you think?" She asked it softly. "I'm pretty sure, Richard, that we should say goodnight. It's been a wonderful evening."

"Yes, it has. I'm sorry it has to end."

She laid her head against my chest. "Me, too."

What Sharon really wanted, of course, was for me to suggest ever so softly that I should come upstairs just for a minute. We could maybe have another drink, talk just a bit more. She wanted me to take charge, sit close to her on the couch, take her in my arms, ignore her when she worried we were getting in over our heads, complicating our lives at the office. She wanted me to take her upstairs, pull off her clothes and make love to her like nothing else in this world mattered except us. I wanted that, too. I wanted her more than I've ever wanted any woman in my life.

I put my hand under her chin, lifted her head, and kissed her soft and long. She kissed me back. When I finally stopped kissing her, her face was all glow and submission.

"Sharon, I would like nothing more than to come upstairs right now."

"I want that too, Richard."

"But I think you're right. We can have something, you and me. But I think it'll have more chance to be meaningful if we take it slow."

She looked surprised, disappointed. "You sure?"

"No, but I'm pretty sure."

"Well, if you think that's best." She pulled ever so slightly away. I could tell she was feeling rejected. If I walked away, I'd have a harder time in future getting her into bed.

"Yes, I do." I kissed her again, lightly. "But I want to do this again, soon. I'll be out of the office most of next week. When I get back, let's have dinner together."

"All right." She sounded doubtful. "Good night."

"Goodnight, Sharon." I gave her a peck on the cheek, turned, and walked away. It was close to midnight. If I hurried, I could catch the subway to Fairfax before the system shut down for the night.

I suddenly had a lot to think about. Sharon didn't seem to have a clue that the University of Maryland's mascot was the terrapin, or terp. Maybe she wasn't into sports; hell, I'm a guy; I pick up information like the mascot of a local college basketball powerhouse by osmosis. But I don't think it's possible to attend a university for four years without knowing the school mascot. Her whole story, laid out so elegantly over dinner, was probably as phony as mine. All of a sudden the months of flirting, teasing, and curiosity no longer seemed so innocent. Like I said, I don't have a lot of common sense where women are concerned. But I know better than to get naked with someone who's spinning an alias back at me.

Doubt can be a killer, I've found. It creeps in and undermines your confidence just when you should be trusting your gut instinct. I didn't sleep that night, doubting the whole time whether I'd made too much of what could have been an innocent slip. Sharon and I had both been drinking, after all. Maybe she just hadn't heard me right. Or maybe I'd really slurred my speech and said 'twerp.' An inner voice kept telling me I'd let stupid paranoia stop me from a night of awesome sex. Of course, that voice was probably just the hormone-driven beast that lives inside all males. Nevertheless, it finally nagged me into getting into my car at 7:30

Saturday morning and driving back to Sharon's. The entire drive I kept going over what to say, all variants of how stupid I had been, how I had to have her right then and there. Hormones make you stupid.

Instinct, however, can be a life-saver. It had stopped me more than once; from stepping on that coral snake when I was twelve, from getting involved with Joe Sprague's militia buddies. It stopped me that morning, persuaded me to park a block and a half down the street from her building, kept me from running right up to her apartment, got me to adjust the rear view mirror so I had a view of her front door. It made me sit there for close to an hour, just watching. I pulled on a baseball cap and sunglasses I keep in the car.

At 9:00, she came out of the door to her building, did a quick glance up and down the street, then started walking at a brisk pace in my direction. I ducked down and kept still, hoping she didn't see me. She walked past briskly on the other side of the street, heading in the direction of the Capitol Mall. Two blocks up, she crossed the street, glancing quickly back in the direction she'd come from, and headed down a side street. I waited five seconds, started my car, and cruised slowly up to where she'd turned, just in time to see her make a right on a street paralleling the one she lived on.

I played a hunch, drove up 8 blocks, made a left, drove two blocks, made a right, and parked. Sure enough, she appeared about a minute later, now walking up a parallel street two blocks over from her building. As I watched her in my rear view mirror, she made another left, glanced back in the direction she'd come from, and disappeared to where I was sure she would again turn right on a parallel street.

I knew better than to try to follow her. She was doing the same thing I do all the time, making sure she wasn't being followed. She'd spot me in a heartbeat if I tried to stay on her. One thing was certain. Sharon was a pro.

Traffic was fairly light, so I had no trouble getting out of Sharon's neighborhood quickly. There was no point hanging around and risking bumping into her. I cut over to the Mall and made straight for the Constitution Bridge back into Virginia. Driving was therapeutic, forcing me to focus on traffic, avoid all the gawking tourists driving their SUVs slowly and erratically, glance periodically in the rear-view mirror to make sure I wasn't being tailed. It kept my mind off the unexpected complication of Sharon not being what I'd always thought, a harmless yet attractive office colleague. Not that I could just ignore the issue and move on. But I needed to clear my head.

Passing Rosslyn, I took 66 into Arlington, exited Glebe Road and backtracked to the Arlington Library. Backtracking increases your chances of spotting a tail. I suspected Sharon was doing a bit of backtracking at that very instant. There are only two kinds of people who worry about being followed; criminals and spies. Well, and government killers like me, I guess, although some people might classify that in the spy category. I couldn't believe Sharon was a crook, so that left spy. And as far as I knew, the only person in our office worth spying on was me. Still, it didn't make any sense. In the six months since Sharon had started her job, I hadn't picked up anybody following me, hadn't experienced any complications with my assignments. If I was being investigated, somebody had been content to let me take care of more than two dozen clients during that time. So who had planted her in the office, and why?

The library is where I go instinctively when I have questions. Anonymous Internet access has proven to be integral to my research on clients. Pulling into the library parking lot, though, I realized I didn't even know what to search for. Sure, I could Google Sharon Denovo, but what were the odds that was her real name? All I'd learn is how carefully her employer—whoever that might be—had backstopped her story.

I sat in my car for awhile, blanking about what to do. The parking lot was almost full, not because Arlingtonians are any more literate than other people, but because the library abuts a large park with six tennis courts, a basketball court, and a baseball diamond. The tennis courts seemed to be the hub of activity, every court occupied. Two older guys, maybe early 50s, were playing singles on the court closest to me. It was quite a contrast, really. One guy was trim, fairly fit, and a pretty good tennis player. The other guy was about 40 pounds overweight and beet red from the exertion. I decided to sit back and watch.

Amazingly, the fat guy was winning: his approach to tennis was simple, just stick the racquet in front of the ball and try to get it back over the net as best he could. The athletic guy, on the other hand, wanted to crush every shot. He'd hit two or three pretty impressive rallies, then invariably hit the ball too long. When he served, he'd pound his first serve about 120 mph and miss the service line by a foot, then drop in a lame second serve, crush a couple of the fat guy's loopy returns, then again hit one beyond the base line. It was inspirational to watch, a real David and Goliath struggle, except for the fact that this particular David looked like he might drop dead of a heart attack at any moment.

Goliath played yet another point with three killer forehands right at fatso—who deftly rebounded them back to him—then crushed the fourth forehand five inches long.

"Out." Fatso was so out of breath he could barely talk.

"Are you fucking blind?" Suddenly Jock-o was as red-faced as Fatso. He punctuated 'fucking' by hurling his racquet into the chain-link fence surrounding the court. It was a perfect strike, missing the harmless chain-mesh and striking one of the solid metal fence poles head on, cracking the racquet in three places.

The two of them stood silently for a minute, staring at the smashed racquet. Then Jock-o walked to the side of the court, picked up his tennis bag, and headed for the exit.

The show was over. There's an IHOP a couple of blocks from the library. I decided I could use some breakfast and needed to stretch my legs a bit. It was a nice day, sunny but not blazingly hot like it had been Thursday. As I skirted the library and meandered toward the IHOP, I found myself envying Sharon, out enjoying the day but with a real operational purpose that, I know, can make life seem worth living.

And then I saw her, as if I'd conjured her out of nowhere by thinking about her. She was a half block away on the other side of the street, walking in my direction. I ducked behind a tree, hoping she hadn't seen me. But I needn't have worried. She made a right at the next corner, peering yet again behind her as she turned, obviously still focused on making sure no one was following her, not really looking for someone in front of her.

I figured she's come from the Metro station near the IHOP, having made her way out by subway to Virginia and then backtracking on foot, just like I had done earlier in my car. She'd been at this for a couple of hours. There was a good chance that wherever she was going, whatever she was doing that she didn't want anyone following her, she was almost there. I took a chance and headed to the corner where she'd turned, peeking out from behind a building to see if I could pick her up. She was a block and a half away, walking briskly. I waited, all but one eye hidden behind the building. She went left two blocks up, again scanning quickly for a tail. I paralleled to the next intersection, running to get ahead of her, peered out again from another building just in time to see her appear two blocks away, cross the street, make a left, and duck into a coffee shop.

Maybe I don't believe in coincidence, but I definitely believe in luck. It's bailed me out plenty in my life. Hell, most people don't think they're lucky because they don't recognize good fortune when it hits them right between the eyes. Not me. Luck had landed me right where I needed to be to see what Sharon was up to. This was the time to stop worrying about being seen and just walk right to that coffee shop and look in the window. Not doing that would be spitting in Lady Luck's face.

A block up, I realized I wouldn't even need to cross the street. From half a block away, I could see through the window that she was sitting at a table for two across from a man. His back was to me, so I couldn't make out much about him. But I could see they were having a fairly serious conversation.

I retreated a block back to where I'd watched her go in and waited, guessing their meeting wouldn't last more than twenty minutes or so. A coffee shop is a great place to meet, but not for anything too long. It attracts attention if two people hang out for an hour or so in a place most people just pop in and out of. The two of them probably did not want to attract attention.

Fifteen minutes later, she left, fortunately heading away from where I was staked out. I let her go, waited. A minute after that, the man exited and headed in the opposite direction. He was about mid-40s, tall and lanky—I made him at 6'1" and 180 pounds—dressed casually, like for a Saturday in the mall with his kids. He made a right at the first street, glancing around just like Sharon. I had a hunch I knew where he was headed, crossed my fingers and trotted straight back to the library, setting up across the street from the entrance.

I'd beaten him there by two minutes; he'd lost time meandering, looking for surveillance. But no one spots a tail who's not tailing them. I'd guessed right. He entered the library. I waited, figuring he wasn't going there to read. Sure enough, ten minutes later, he came out with a woman and a twelve-or thirteen year old girl carrying an armful of books. So he'd brought the wife and daughter to the library on a Saturday morning and then ducked out to make his meeting. Nice cover. Very professional.

Whoever Sharon really was, she had a control officer.

Chapter VIII
On Target

FINDING OUT Sharon was some kind of spy meant the smart thing to do would be to cool it operationally for awhile, at least until I figured out who she worked for and what she was after. There was no sign any of my previous jobs had been compromised, after all, so just stopping could very well leave them in the dark about the real nature of the program I was managing. But I'm a soldier in an ongoing war against America's enemies. I couldn't very well declare a unilateral cease fire.

Ike wouldn't have cancelled D-Day just because he got word the Germans were planning to put up a fight.

In fact, knowing as I now did that Dan Stigler was the 'worst of the worst,' I figured there was an added imperative to move against him before Sharon and whatever she represented got in the way. I'd taken out enough PFCs and pawns: the chance to eliminate an enemy general was just too important to start getting risk-averse. Besides, the Stigler assignment wouldn't be easy, meaning I'd have to spend at least a week observing his every move to concoct a plan of attack. During that week surveying Dan, I'd have plenty of opportunity to sniff out anyone who might be surveying me. If things really looked too hot, I could abort and inform my boss. I hadn't dismissed the possibility that Sharon's people were just bureaucratic rivals in some spook-related turf war. It's common knowledge, after all, that government agencies hate each other more than any external enemy. Hell, in the army, I always saw a lot more action in bar fights with marines and sailors than I did against terrorists.

Maybe I should have gone right to my boss anyway. Just going ahead with the job was taking on a lot. But that phony evaluation in my file was right on about one thing: I'm not a team player.

I started Monday morning fresh, pulling on my running clothes and throwing street clothes and shoes in a backpack. A five mile jog with a backpack is nothing compared to some of the 20 mile hikes with full equipment I used to do in the army. Ending my jog at Pris' gym meant I got in a good upper-body work-out as well while checking through the large front window for anyone hanging around, waiting for me to come out. I showered, put on my street clothes, dumped the sweaty workout stuff in the backpack, and hopped a bus to my first stop, the large mall at Tyson's Corner. My plan was to spend several hours on foot to draw out any person or persons who might be keeping tabs on me.

The mall wasn't crowded; it was Monday morning, after all. I hadn't been there too often, so I stopped right by the entrance to examine the large chart of store locations. I scrutinized the list of stores, like I was having trouble finding what I wanted. What I was actually doing was checking to see if anyone came through the mall entrance behind me. Three people entered; well, actually, four. One was a woman, mid-twenties, with an infant in a stroller. Right behind her was an older woman, not unattractive, well-dressed with a nice leather purse. After her came a beefy guy in jeans, green t-shirt, work shoes and gimme cap. The women looked like perfectly ordinary mall shoppers.

The guy had every appearance of a normal Joe running a quick errand. Appearances can be deceiving.

I took the stairs up to the second floor and wandered slowly to Victoria's Secret, went in and headed to the back of the store, ducking in behind a lingerie display so I wouldn't be visible to someone waiting outside. If someone was following me, maybe they'd get curious and come in to see what I was doing.

"May I help you?" A well-dressed saleswoman appeared from nowhere. She looked slightly amused. Men go to Victoria's Secret all the time, of course, mostly to buy gifts for their wives. Her expression said she was expecting me to start acting embarrassed.

"Yeah, thanks. I'm looking for a gift but I'm not real sure what I'm looking for, to be honest."

"We have some very nice terry cloth robes up front. They're quite attractive and really highlight a woman's shape, but they're also very comfortable and practical. Great for wearing around the house in the morning. I'll bet your wife would really enjoy one."

"I'm not married. It's actually for a friend of mine from work." I winked at her. "We finally went out on a date for the first time Friday. Thought I'd get her a gift to surprise her at work today."

"Oh. We do carry a nice line of perfumes."

"Yeah, that'd be nice." I reached out and plucked a sheer two-piece negligee from the rack. "Actually, I was thinking of something to kinda let her know where I'd like things to go."

She blushed. The smile vanished. I could read disapproval in her eyes. Who could blame her? What kind of classless jerk buys a woman sexy lingerie after one date? But I was having fun. If someone had wandered into the store to see what I was doing, they'd hear me in the back obviously shopping for something sexy to give their colleague Sharon.

"That item is nice." She nodded to the piece I was holding. "But we have some really attractive items in the same vein just over here." She turned to the rack behind me. Obviously, her disapproval wasn't going to stop her making a sale. Moral relativism is rampant in this world.

I took a few steps out from behind the rack as if to get a better look at the display she had indicated. Actually, I was just confirming that the store was still empty except for the two of us. My act was a waste of time. There was no audience.

"Yeah, those are really sexy." I stopped, feigned a look of concern. "But, you know, maybe this isn't really appropriate. I mean, we've only gone out once."

"Well, sir, that might be a consideration. Although you know the lady better than me."

"Ah, you're right. It's a bad move at this point. I think I'll get her some chocolates at the Godiva store instead. Thanks anyway."

"Anytime."

"We're going out again this weekend. Maybe I'll come back Saturday. You gonna be working here then?"

"Uh, well, yes, I'll be working the evening shift Saturday."

"That'd be great. You've been so helpful."

"We always welcome your business. Let me get you my card." She walked back to the counter, plucked a business card from a drawer, came back and handed it to me with a real sweet smile.

"Okay . . . " I looked down at the card, " . . . Doris. That's a nice name."

"Thank you." She blushed again, but this time the smile came back.

"I'll look for you next time." I left with the thought crossing my mind that I could come back Saturday, tell her a sob story about getting stood up by that colleague I'd been pining after all these years, and persuade her to have dinner and who knows what else with me. You never know.

Exiting on the opposite side of the mall from where I'd come in, I headed to the bus stop in the parking lot. I didn't care what bus I caught, although I let two come and go before boarding the third and dropping the maximum fare in the change box. It turned out to be the 2C headed south on Gallows Road. There's a big multi-theater cinema at Merrifield where Gallows intersects Rt. 29. I got off and walked up the street and through the parking lot to the ticket booth. Again, I seemed to be clean, but I figured I couldn't be too cautious. Above the ticket seller's booth was a large signboard with movie titles and starting times. I bought a ticket to something called *Hellboy* because it was slated to begin in 10 minutes and sounded like a motorcycle movie. Before heading into the theater to find a seat, I picked up a box of popcorn and coke at the concessions stand, glancing back to the entrance to see if anyone came in behind me. Three acne-faced teenage boys came in; that was it.

Hellboy turned out to be a truly stupid movie. The plot revolves around some Satan-like figure who's had cosmetic surgery to remove his horns and joined the fight against evil. What follows is a lot of pointless violence. The teenagers loved it. They yelled "fucking awesome!" every time something blew up or someone was killed. I watched for an hour and left mid-movie through the side exit that empties out directly into the parking lot. I wasn't disturbed that the movie was so bad. I just wanted to see if anyone else left the theater in mid-movie, too. Fifteen minutes watching that exit door from across the parking lot finally convinced me I was not being followed.

About a half mile up 29 I stopped in a Bolivian chicken joint and had lunch. Someday I'm gonna visit Bolivia. They have mastered roasted chicken and black beans. They must like to eat a lot of it, too. My waitress weighed 250 minimum.

Well-fed and surveillance free, it was time to meander back to Fairfax. Figuring out the best way to kill Dan Stigler was something I'd decided I could do face to face.

It was a little after 3:30 in the afternoon when I walked into Dan's, but there were already two overweight rednecks drinking at the bar. Since discovering Dan's, I'd thought of it as my haven from the TGIFication of northern Virginia. In reality, it was a haven for the dwindling community of good old boys slowly being squeezed out of the area by real estate agents, building contractors, and county commissioners conspiring to replace the housing stock left over from the 1950s with more expensive planned communities occupied by two-income white collar families servicing larger mortgages, paying higher property taxes, and dropping money at pricy retail outlets and upscale restaurants. The nearest WalMart is about five miles west of Fairfax, meaning the guys sitting in Dan's that Monday afternoon got a not so subtle reminder every Saturday when they loaded the wife and kids into the pick-up to go shopping at the only place they could afford that life would be easier if they'd just sell out and move to the hinterland. That and the escalating property taxes throughout the Washington area were the main reason the redneck population was dwindling.

At Dan's, beer was still cheap so they could afford to get drunk and bitch about working miserable blue collar jobs for not much money and going home to wives who were sick of dealing with kids and having their redneck husbands come home drunk every night. That and griping about overpaid athletes playing like bums—but whose games the rednecks at Joe's watched religiously—pretty much dominated conversation any busy evening at Dan's. Life gets tougher for rednecks every year. I don't have a lot of sympathy. I'm from the same roots, but I don't sit around and cry in my Budweiser about it.

Dan was at the other end of the bar talking to one of the two early drinkers, a bloated looking guy with a gut the size of a beach ball, and didn't notice me come in at first. I took a seat at the bar and waited for him to look up.

"If you get a moment there, Dan, how about a beer?"

"Well, lookie here. The return of the prodigal son." He seemed happy to see me. I had to remind myself that he had no idea anything had changed. "I was beginning to think you'd found another watering hole."

"Nah, no place else waters the beer down as good as you, Dan." I grinned, like I was glad to see him, too.

"Hey, that's pure Budweiser, son." He set the glass firmly in front of me. "Watering that down would be a crime."

"Got that right. So how you been?"

"I'm okay. Just the usual crap. Got a letter from the

city council last week. They're threatening to rezone this place again."

"What? I didn't know there was talk of rezoning."

"Sure, they've been discussing it for a couple of years. Some of our finer Fairfax citizens seem to think the grocery store next door is an eyesore. And there's been a vocal crowd complaining about me at City Hall for quite awhile."

"What's their complaint?"

"They say establishments like mine encourage public drunkenness."

"Aw, that's bullshit."

"Yeah, you know it and I know it. What's really going on is a couple of developers have their eyes on this cite to knock down my place and the grocery store and build one of those apartment/shopping/restaurant complexes. They organize these citizens groups to lobby the council about improving the community, but it's really just about making a bunch of money. What else is new?"

"Fuck 'em. There's too many fucking Barnes and Noble clusters in Fairfax already."

"Ain't that the truth? But where the hell have you been? Off on another EPA boondoggle?"

"Had to take a trip out west."

"For what."

"Water purity study."

"Really? Whereabouts?"

"Death Valley."

"You're not serious."

"Dead serious."

"There's no water in Death Valley."

"Hey, you know this administration doesn't let us inspect water purity anyplace where there's water anymore. Too much risk we might find some big corporation pouring toxins into drinking reservoirs and try to make them stop."

He stared for a moment. I think he almost believed me. Then he laughed. "You are such a bullshitter. Someday I'm going to get you to tell me what it is you really do."

"You know, Dan, someday I just might."

I spent the better part of the evening drinking Budweiser there at the bar, nibbling peanuts and pretzels, bantering with Dan and some of the other customers about nothing. It had been quite awhile since I'd had the chance just to hang out with ordinary folk. The two rednecks turned out to be not so bad. Their names were Red and Dylan and they'd lived in Fairfax their whole lives, even attending Fairfax High School together in the early 70s. Red told me he played tackle for the football team and didn't get along with Dylan back then "'cause he was smokin' dope all the time."

"Yeah, I was a big-time stoner back then." These days Dylan was just a big-time beer guzzler. "Red didn't think much of us stoners. If he'd been old enough, he'd have voted for Nixon."

"Nixon was a great president." Obviously Red still didn't see eye-to-eye with Dylan on politics.

Dylan's father had been a local plumber. After high school, he worked for his dad for a few years and then took over the business. Red blew out his knee his senior year, worked construction jobs for awhile, and eventually hired on with Dylan and learned the trade. The two of them made a pretty good living repairing the cheap commodes and fixtures installed by developers in the mini-mansions and townhouses that now dominated formerly blue-collar Fairfax.

"They build those places with the cheapest stuff they can find, then sell 'em for a million bucks. Takes about a year for the plumbing to crap out. Me and Red got as much work as we want." I had a pretty good idea just how much work that was from the fact that the two of them had started drinking at Dan's early in the afternoon. "Lotsa well-paid college graduates . . . " —actually, he said something more like *gra-jee-yates*—" . . . in this town who don't know how to replace the float in a toilet tank."

"Developers and big building contractors are making big money ruining this town, in my opinion." Dan didn't like developers and building contractors much. In fact, he didn't seem to like businessmen of any variety, at least not the ones who made a lot of money. I had to admit, a lot of what he said made sense. Not liking big shots is a time-honored tradition where I was raised. But there's a line you can't cross: commies bad mouth corporations, too. Knowing what I now knew about Dan put a whole new light on comments like that.

"It's the damn Democrats is what it is." Red spat that out with particular venom. "Always raisin' taxes. That's what's ruinin' this place. Nobody can pay the taxes so they're all movin' out, sellin' to the people who blow down the houses and build big mega-manshits."

"Manshits? Red, you're drunk." Dylan was calling the kettle black.

"Yeah, Red. And you don't know what you're talking about anyway. It's your property taxes that keep going up. They're set by the county board. The board's Republican." I half expected Dan to pull out Mao's little red book and start waving it. He was just getting warmed up. "Politicians are screwing us all. We elect them, then corporations bribe them to pass laws cutting corporate taxes and giving corporations *carte blanche* to rip us all off, then we go back and elect the same corrupt politicians. Ask Paladin there. He works for the government. He knows what I mean."

"You work for the government?" Dylan eyed me suspiciously. "You ain't a narc or somethin', are ya?"

"Fuck, no." I took a big swig of my beer. "Don't ask me about any of this crap. I'm a working stiff just like you. I'm not like Dan. I don't know no fancy French like *carte blanche*. What is that anyway, Dan? Some credit card the government issues to big corporations so they can charge us taxpayers direct?"

That got Dan to laugh. Red and Dylan just nodded knowingly. I'm sure they now believe all corporations have direct access to the Federal budget via their *Carte Blanche* cards.

"I apologize, guys. Who the hell brought up politics, anyway? It's just I get mad sometimes, what with the council trying to shut me down these days." I have to say, Dan seemed upset. "So how are the Redskins gonna do this year?"

Red: "They are gonna be fuckin' awesome!"

Dylan: "Man, you're an idiot."

The conversation turned to who was going to be quarterback, how much money the latest draft pick was getting, all the stupid football drivel that drunk guys all over America argue about. I couldn't stay interested. I used to love football, loved to watch guys lay violent hits on each other, loved to see a big running back bowl over a safety or see a middle linebacker almost take a quarterback's head off on a blitz. I don't have time for it anymore. The Patriots winning the Super Bowl just doesn't seem very important now that I know how many bad people are out there trying to destroy the country.

Anyway, I was always a Cowboys fan.

I spent the better part of the evening there, drinking beer, listening to the drunken banter of Red and Dylan, watching Dan. He was pretty distracted the whole time, not up to his usual wisecracking, hardly busting my ass at all. I guess the prospect of losing his life's work to urban renewal was getting to him. Not that he seemed to be feeling sorry for himself or anything. It was pretty sad, though. Even I had to admit that.

I left with a pretty good idea how I'd proceed.

Mid-morning the next day I drove to Dan's house and parked just around the corner. His address had been in the file, of course. Not surprisingly, he lived in one of Fairfax's few remaining 1950s era neighborhoods about a mile from his bar. I had a good view of his driveway, but he'd really have to be paying attention to see me. I had on my baseball cap and sunglasses, and a clipboard on the seat next to me. If anybody asked me what I was doing, I was prepared to tell them I was with the city doing a traffic survey. Anybody got too nosy, I'd just drive away and come back the next day in a rental. But nobody asked. People see something suspicious these days, they just look the other way and hope they don't get involved. Lucky for me, too. Makes my profession a lot easier.

Dan backed out of his driveway at 11:00 and drove away in his beat-up twenty-year-old Subaru wagon. He was headed to his bar to open up for the lunch crowd who prefer a blue-collar liquid lunch. I'm betting Red and Dylan dropped by periodically between jobs.

I waited exactly ten minutes, picked up the clipboard to look semi-official, then walked to his front door and let myself in. He lived in a tired-looking brick rambler with a front door lock that any teenager could have opened with a bobby pin. Honestly, I don't know why most people bother to lock their doors.

The place was empty, as I'd expected. Dan's wife left him five years back. All those years he'd been burning the midnight oil at his bar, turns out she'd been carrying on with a married guy across the street who ran a drywall company. After the guy's wife died of ovarian cancer, he'd decided to relocate to Mississippi. He took Dan's wife with him. Dan told me all this late one night when I was the only customer. He hadn't seemed too bothered by it.

"We never had any kids. I guess she just got bored being alone all the time. Hell, I'm glad she found some guy who makes a good enough living to take care of her. Don't know what I'd have done if she'd wanted alimony and the house."

I'd expected to find the place a mess. Men whose wives abandon them generally live like slobs—Lester Ruminant's house had been a sty. But Dan was the exception. The place was neat and clean, all the dishes washed and put away in cabinets and cupboards, dirty clothes in a hamper in the bedroom, clean clothes neatly folded in drawers or hanging in the closet. Of course, he maintained his bar with the same meticulousness, so I shouldn't have been surprised. It was possible, I surmised, that his wife left him as much as anything else because he was such a neat freak. I'd have trouble getting along with someone who rolls his pairs of socks after washing them.

He didn't have a lot of possessions. There was a TV

with rabbit ears and no cable and a stereo that looked like he'd had it since the 70s. Lining a bookshelf were actual vinyl records. I flipped through them. A museum would have been envious. He actually owned a copy of the Beatles' White Album with the original cover, the John and Yoko in the nude cover, from before it was the "White" album. I wondered how much that would be worth on E-bay.

Procol Harum's first album was sitting on the turntable. I switched on the stereo and listened to *Whiter Shade of Pale* while I searched the rest of the house. It didn't take long to find what I was looking for. I flipped through a stack of mail on a kitchen counter—a few bills, mortgage refinance offers, a bank statement. Toward the bottom was an envelope from Fairfax City. I pulled out the letter advising Dan of the impending rezoning order and stuck it behind the papers on my clipboard, then set the envelope carefully back where I'd found it. Before I left, I switched off the stereo and turntable.

The most curious thing about Dan's house was what I didn't find there. He'd had no magazines of any kind, no mail from any organizations soliciting donations, no books other than a collection of Penguin Classics, nothing at all that might tell you about his political leanings or sexual proclivities. A man who runs a blue-collar bar, I'd expect to find a copy of *Playboy* or *Hustler* lying around. Having heard him express his concerns about air quality and the environment, I was surprised not to come across a newsletter or something from, say, the Sierra Club or Greenpeace.

I've broken into a few houses in my time. Every one of them had a wealth of materials that told you something about the occupant. Dan's told me he liked to listen to old records and read old books. But what Dan's house also told me was that Dan didn't want someone to be able to break into his house and find out what sorts of things he was really involved in. Only people with secrets have houses that clean.

One thing continued to puzzle me: Dan's comment the previous week about wanting to introduce me to some "people concerned about where things are headed." As best I could figure, Dan spent about 14 hours a day in his bar, and having just explored his house, it was clear he didn't entertain there a lot. The only possibility that I could see was on weekends. Ever since I'd been stopping off at Dan's, he'd had a law student tending bar on the weekends. The aspiring ambulance chaser worked some day job during the week, attended night classes, and helped out at Dan's on weekends to make a few extra bucks. Saturday nights were usually busy, so he and Dan manned the bar together. But Dan often left him on his own during the day and occasionally even Sunday evenings. If Dan was meeting with fellow conspirators or managing a cell of terrorists, it had to be during those times he didn't have to be at the bar.

It's always a good idea to fill in as many details in a client's world as possible before executing the job. That reduces the likelihood of some loose end unraveling a seemingly perfect plan designed to leave the local police with a body and a nice, neat explanation. Sometimes, in fact, those extra details provide the ideal plan of attack. I'd had a client in Lexington, Kentucky, for example, a psychiatrist who specialized in suicidal patients, and I'd gone into the job with a working hypothesis that faked suicide would work because his job was so depressing. But something made me hold off a few days, wait for the weekend to see how he spent his leisure time. Lo and behold, he decided to drive to an isolated cliff face that weekend and do a little solo rock climbing. He was pretty expert at it, carefully making his way from one handhold to another, feeling for crevices with his climbing-shoe clad feet. But rock-climbing is a dangerous sport, even for experts. It's especially dangerous when someone drives up the nearby forest service maintenance road to the summit and drops a boulder on you when you're clinging precariously to the side of a cliff only 50 feet or so from the top.

So as much as I hated delay—particularly since my boss had implied I'd screwed around too long on the Gladys Thurington job—I decided it was best to hold off until I could watch Dan over the weekend, maybe get an idea who his co-conspirators were. I'd have to find some way to occupy myself for the rest of the week.

Chapter IX
Kyle Takes a Road Trip

WEDNESDAY MORNING I trekked into the office. I didn't even bother to check for someone tailing me, although at Union Station I stopped off at a little gift shop, browsed for a minute, and bought a goofy looking stuffed frog, the kind you get for your toddler or dog. Nobody seemed to be hanging around outside. It still didn't make sense, but whatever Sharon and company were up to, it didn't seem to involve watching me.

At the office, I walked right up to Sharon's desk. She feigned surprise.

"Well, look who decided to come to work."

"Had some time between meetings this morning and thought I'd bring you a present." I set the stuffed toy on her desk.

"A stuffed frog? Is that supposed to mean something?"

"It's a toad, actually. If you kiss it, maybe it'll turn into a prince." I grinned. "Since that obviously didn't work with me."

She smiled. Not much at first, but it developed.

"Thanks. I'll keep it here at my desk to remind me of you."

"Hey, I called you Saturday morning. Guess you were out. Thought you'd be sleeping it off. You must be able to hold your liquor better than me."

"Sorry I missed you." She looked sincere. "I went to the gym. I like to get in a good work-out on

Saturdays. Sweat out the poisons, you know."

"Mmmm. Now that's something I'd like to see, you working up a good sweat."

"Well, you should have called back. I went straight home afterwards, took a shower, and just lounged around in my bathrobe all day." I had thought Sharon would be mad, still feeling the sting of rejection. Again, I'd misjudged her. She was secure in herself, confident. Her smile was telling me that if I was too dumb or cautious to jump into bed with her on the first date, then that was my problem, not hers. Confidence is very sexy in a woman.

She was also a very good liar. That's something else I can appreciate.

"Anyway, I called to tell you what a great time I had."

"I had a real nice time too, Richard." She should have left it at that. "But I'm kind of embarrassed."

"What? What do you have to be embarrassed about? I thought we had a great evening together."

"Except I had a little too much to drink."

"Me, too. I hope you're not trying to tell me that nice, long kiss was just the alcohol."

"Oh, no. That was all me."

"Good, because I'm counting on another one."

"We'll see about that. If you behave yourself better in the restaurant next time." So at least she wasn't giving me the brush off. "But I'm embarrassed because I was so tipsy, your little joke about me being a terp just went right in one ear and out the other."

"Huh? Oh, that. I figured I must have been so in the bag I couldn't talk straight. Was afraid you thought I was calling all your friends twerps."

"Maybe some of them are. Anyway, I just realized

later that you must have thought it was really strange, me going to the University of Maryland and not knowing what you were talking about." She was still smiling, but now her eyes were serious. She was watching me, assessing whether I was buying her explanation.

"Hey, I just figured you were distracted by my obvious sex appeal." Her eyes lightened a bit.

"Anyway, now you know better than to let me drink so much."

"Hah. Now I know to make sure I get you a second martini before dinner." I arched an eyebrow mischievously. "Maybe a third."

I could read relief in her eyes. She'd obviously been sweating her cover mistake for days. And that's why she wasn't pouting about being rebuffed. She'd been more concerned about plugging that hole in her alias the next time she saw me. But it's a mistake to try to fix a slip like that. People who aren't lying about who they are don't need to explain minor oddities in their behavior. I'd have just moved on, acted dumb if it had come up again. Still, it was a nice try. I might even have bought it, if I hadn't spotted her making that clandestine meeting the next day.

"Unfortunately, you're going to have to wait awhile for another chance to ply me with liquor. My cousin called Monday and invited me up to New York for a visit this weekend. We're going to see *The Producers*."

"Your cousin, huh. Should I be jealous?"

"I don't think you need to be jealous of her."

"Just make sure you don't meet some skinny artistic dude in one of those New York nightclubs and fall for him."

"And why not?"

"'Cause I'd have to go up there and break his neck. And I don't like going to New York. It's not my kind of town."

"I'll keep that in mind."

"Anyway, I've got meetings the rest of the week, and then I've got some stuff to catch up on this weekend."

"No doubt all your KPPRI paperwork?"

"It's a demanding job, but somebody's got to do it. Just keep next weekend open."

"Is that an order?"

"Please?"

"Well, if you're going to beg, I guess I'll have to say yes. I hate to see a man cry."

"As if you haven't left a trail of sobbing broken hearts in your wake."

"Absolutely. They don't call me devil-woman for nothing."

I laughed and headed toward my office, figuring to read the paper for awhile. Out of the corner of my eye, I noticed a large electrical cord running down the hall to Riffelbach's office. That seemed strange.

"Hey, Sharon, cleaning crew in today? I thought they came after close of business."

"That's a couple of phone technicians. Been some problems with the phone service recently."

I walked toward his office and peered in. Two guys dressed like what seemed to be phone workers were at his desk, looking at the underside of his phone. The electrical cord I'd noticed ran to an industrial-looking computer sitting on the floor. The two guys stopped what they were doing and stared back at me.

"Gee, when did you get so nosy?" Sharon had followed me.

"I'm the curious type. Riffelbach decided to leave

until they're finished?"

"He's not in today. He called this morning, said he got word late last night that he needed to attend an all-day policy meeting at headquarters."

"Lucky for him these guys showed up on a day he's not around."

"Lucky for them, too. I'm sure phone technicians prefer not having someone look over their shoulder while they're working."

"Okay, I get the point. I'll leave them alone." It was odd that Sharon was suddenly so concerned that they have unmonitored access to his office. "They planning to fix my phone, too?"

"Is it broken?"

"Don't know. You said there have been problems with the phone service."

"His phone service." She nodded toward the boss's office. Then she smiled, a forced smile, like she didn't want me to see how concerned she was that I was asking questions. "I didn't know you ever used your phone, anyway."

"Of course I do, Sharon. I used it just last Thursday to make a reservation for two at Chester's." I winked at her. Better that she believed I wasn't at all suspicious.

"Then I guess it works."

"Yeah, lucky for me. Well, I'll leave them to it and go wait in my office for the President to call, now that I know he can."

"Very funny."

It all made sense now. Sharon and her friends were investigating Riffelbach. They must have been investigating him for months, since before Sharon had been assigned there. I had no idea what they were looking for, but it was possible that it had nothing to do with me.

Possible, yeah. But I had a bad feeling. I'd covered my tracks just fine since signing on with the EPA. Now I found myself wondering if my boss was as competent.

I needed to clear my head and get a fresh perspective. All of a sudden there were too many unknowns occupying my thoughts. Just who did Sharon work for? Why was my boss under investigation? Was I under suspicion because Riffelbach had slipped up? Nagging questions can be toxic, building up in your system like lead poisoning or bad liquor. Most of the time, a good workout is all I need to sweat out normal stress and get back on track. Pumping a little iron at Pris's gym wasn't going to cut it this time, though.

I slipped out of the office at lunch and headed back to my apartment. There were two cans of beer in the refrigerator. I popped the top on one and threw the other in a rucksack with some clothes and toiletries. Getting out of town seemed the best way to get a fresh perspective on everything. It had been a long time since I'd been to North Carolina. Breathing a little countrified air would do me a world of good.

Of course, I also knew an old army buddy who owned a gun shop just outside of Kannapolis. He made a pretty good living selling high-powered deer rifles to the state's enthusiastic hunters. And if he knew you, he always had a decent selection of hand-guns on offer. He'd sell you one without registering it, too. For a price.

I was beginning to think I'd feel a lot more at ease with a reassuringly untraceable piece tucked into the waistband of my trousers.

It was a nice afternoon for a drive, sunny and hot. After gassing up, I headed west on 66 to the US 29 exit, then turned south. Kannapolis is on 29, so it's just a matter of following what's really a back road for eight hours or so. In this age of interstate highways, most people are in too much of a hurry to make a long trip on a road like 29. They stay on the interstates so they never have to slow down for small towns. I like the small towns. Every so often you come across a beat up old diner or some mom and pop pie shop left over from the days when town squares were the centers of the communities that made up America. These places are becoming increasingly rare, even on back roads. More and more what you see are refurbished McDonalds and WalMarts. Towns that still have real town squares; well, those are the towns that are being abandoned for nearby cookie-cutter developments surrounding new shopping areas with Barnes and Noble, Starbucks, Applebees, and various other stores that give people the illusion that their lives are getting better. Of course there's always a WalMart nearby where these people can actually afford to buy clothes, groceries, and cheap electronics from China.

I figured I'd drive until 9:00 or so and find a motel to crash. That would put me an hour or so from Kannapolis, where I could stop by my buddy's shop, pick up what I needed, and then drive straight back to the Washington area. I wanted to be back in town by Friday night, giving me time to prepare for a weekend of surveying Dan. And the drive would help clear my mind of distractions to decide if I was actually going to proceed with the assignment.

Two hours south of Washington I hit

Charlottesville, home of the University of Virginia and God knows what else. I don't drive through often, but I always seem to hit the town at rush hour, and the traffic is worse every time. Charlottesville looks like a very prosperous place. Newer and bigger homes are spreading along 29 in both directions. But they never seem to improve the roads, so traffic just gets worse. Virginians are an odd bunch when it comes to roads. They bitch constantly about traffic, but any politician who even mentions raising taxes to actually widen a few highways or build some extra avenues to access the ever-growing suburbs is committing political suicide.

Eventually I cleared the Charlottesville area, drove for a couple of hours and pulled into a Knights Inn along the road. It was pretty run down, only a couple of beat-up pick-up trucks in the parking lot. The office was empty when I entered. After a few minutes, an Asian guy emerged from a door behind the desk. I could see a small apartment off the office where I guess he lived. He pulled a registration form from under the counter and slid it toward me.

"Just fill in your name and give me a credit card."

"I'll pay cash in advance. Gonna leave early tomorrow."

"Even better. Just leave the key on the counter on your way out. The room with tax is $42.95."

I gave him $45 and filled in 'Eric Rudolph' on the registration card while he got my change. It's a joke I'd learned from Joe Sprague. He used to sign in as Rudolph every time he got a room at a cheap motel—usually when he was with a hooker or somebody else's wife—figuring to confuse the FBI agents working the Rudolph case. Probably wasn't as funny anymore, since Rudolph had been arrested about a year earlier.

An ancient candy machine was just outside my room. I dropped in some coins and, to my amazement, it worked. I hadn't eaten much the whole day, so I splurged and bought two Snickers bars and a package of peanut-butter crackers. I still had the can of beer in my rucksack. Back in my room, I shoved a chair up against the door, sprawled on the bed with my dinner and switched on the TV.

O'Reilly Factor was on Fox News. He was berating some guy who was opposed to the war in Iraq. O'Reilly's a real horse's ass. He likes to say "sir" all the time while insulting someone, as in, "You, sir, are a traitor." I guess he figures it's more polite that way. His guest was an annoying twit, of course. The guy kept trying to interject that we were killing lots of innocent civilians in Iraq, but O'Reilly wouldn't let him finish a sentence. I could care less about Iraqi civilians myself. If you don't want to get killed by the U.S. military, don't live in a country that pisses us off, I say. Still, I can't stand O'Reilly's snotty, condescending bullying. He gets pacifists on his show and yells at them because they're such easy marks. Anybody ever talked to me that way, I'd punch their lights out. He looks soft, too. Push him around a little, I bet he'd cry.

I don't dream that often, but I always seem to have them after drinking beer and watching TV in a motel room. That night I dreamed O'Reilly came into Dan Stigler's place and started mouthing off about liberals and traitors. Red and Dylan were there. Red kept nodding his head in agreement, saying "Amen" and "Hallelujah," but Dylan got pissed, started arguing. He got into a heated exchange with O'Reilly about Nixon. Every time Dylan would try to say something, O'Reilly would cut him off and yell "Nixon was a great president!" Finally Dylan grabbed the baseball bat Dan keeps behind the bar and split O'Reilly's skull in two.

I woke up with a headache. Too much sugar and a beer on an empty stomach. I left the motel, pulled into a McDonalds a couple miles down the road and ate an Egg McMuffin, washing it down with an acidic cup of coffee. That's about as American as it gets, I figured, going to sleep with Fox News on the TV and starting the next day at McDonalds for breakfast. All that was left was getting to Kannapolis and buying a gun. I pulled back onto 29 and sped on through rural North Carolina. An hour later I was there.

Kannapolis, like many small towns in America, is a place that's best days are fading in the rear-view mirror. It had been a textile manufacturing center for over a hundred years—named for James William Cannon, founder of the Cannon Mills Corporation—and was the corporate headquarters of the Pillowtex corporation after it bought out Cannon Mills. Allegedly, the first towel ever made in the United States was manufactured in Kannapolis. Pillowtex filed for Chapter 11 in 2000 and closed for good in 2003. The company had employed a large portion of the local population making pillows, mattress pads, and other bedding materials. I guess Americans don't sleep on American made pillows any more. Kannapolitans no longer get paid to make them, that's for sure.

I'd been to Kannapolis more than a few times over the years, always to visit Fielding's Sport and Hunt. Graham Fielding had been in the same unit as me and Joe Sprague, mustering out a couple of years after us. He'd gotten an honorable discharge, though. In fact, I'd been surprised he quit the army. Graham was smart: he hadn't joined the army out of high school like me and Joe; he'd finished college and even got a Master's degree in, of all things, philosophy. He used to quote Nietzsche all the time and introduced Joe to Oswald What's-His-Name's *Decline of the West*, which may have sewn the seeds for the decline of Joe Sprague. Graham was a tough son-of-a-bitch, picking up a black belt in karate during his spare time in graduate school. He'd excelled at everything in the army; hand-to-hand combat, weapons of all kinds, ten-mile runs through swamps with full pack, drills. The army loved him, too, trying repeatedly to make him an officer. He just kept refusing. He hated officers. It's the one thing we had in common.

I figured that's why he left. A guy as smart and skilled as Graham can only take orders from half-wits for so long. Still, opening a gun shop in rural North Carolina was surprising for someone with his brains. He wasn't given much to explanations, though. All he ever said to me on the subject was, "Nobody's ever gonna go hungry selling guns in this country."

Graham's place was a good 15 miles south of Kannapolis in an isolated stretch of woods. He'd cleared an area around back and set up a small shooting range. I pulled into the gravel parking lot in front a little after ten that morning. There were only two other cars, the 1970s vintage Toyota Land Cruiser Graham had owned since high school and a Cadillac Escalade I didn't recognize.

A buzzer sounded when I opened the door, a security device so no one could sneak in while Graham was in the back. I happened to know it was unnecessary. Graham was very security conscious. In addition to the light sensor he had on the gate to alert him whenever a car pulled into the parking lot, Graham had three security cameras covering the entrance, parking lot, and shooting range out back. A couple of years back he'd shown me the expensive lock-down switch he'd had installed. If he didn't like someone's looks, he could seal the place tighter than a bank vault.

Graham was behind the counter showing an AR-15 to a tall guy wearing jeans, fancy boots, white cowboy shirt and matching white cowboy hat. The customer could have passed for Kenny Rogers, except he looked to be in his late 40s. He glanced back at me when I walked in, then turned back to continue inspecting the assault rifle lying on the counter. Graham never looked up.

"Be with you in a minute, buddy."

"No rush. I'll just look around some." I didn't want to interrupt a sale, and my business is best handled when no other customers are around.

Basically two kinds of merchandise are on display at Fielding's; high-caliber rifles for serious hunters looking to bring down a buck with one shot, and military model assault rifles for gun enthusiasts with Rambo complexes. The military models aren't fully functional, of course. Fully automatic weapons are illegal, even in North Carolina. Which is what Graham was explaining to Tex Ritter.

"Can't you sell me the model with full rock 'n roll?"

"Not if I want to keep my license. What are you hunting that you want full auto, anyway?"

"This is for home protection."

"Home protection." Graham spat the words out like they were a bad chaw of tobacco. "Mister, the best thing I can sell you to defend yourself if somebody breaks into your home is that Winchester .12 gauge pump on the wall behind you. Any punk kicks in your door, he'll wet himself at the sound of you pumping a buckshot cartridge into the chamber."

"I got a shotgun already. I was thinking of something with a little more punch, something that can penetrate body armor."

"Body armor?" Graham grinned. "Must be some well-outfitted burglars working your neck of the woods. Still, anybody comes at me with a bullet-proof vest, he's gonna get a mouthful of double-ought buck unless he's wearing a helmet with a face-plate. But you are right that this AR-15 with a Teflon round will punch a hole through most commercial body armor. Still don't know why you want to be able to empty the magazine into the poor sum-bitch."

"What if there are several of them?"

"You worried about the Rooskies invading or the ATF?"

"A man can't be too careful."

"Tell you what. You buy this AR-15, I'll tell you the web site that'll show you how to restore it to full military operation."

"Really? That's on the web?"

"Sure is. Easy to do, too. A kid could do it."

"Well, okay. I'll take it."

"Great. Just fill this out." Graham pulled a form from under the counter. Tex glanced over the form, a pained look forming on his face.

"Christ, I really got to give you all this information? This used to be a free country."

"This is just for the warranty. This gun gives you any problems, manufacturer'll fix it or replace it, no charge."

"Oh, okay. Great." He picked up a pen from the

counter and started filling in the form.

"Cash or credit card?"

"Visa."

"Perfect. That'll be one-thousand three hundred ninety-five dollars, plus tax."

Tex stopped writing, looked up. "I thought the price was twelve-ninety-five?"

"You want the web site or not?"

"Oh." Tex took out his wallet, dropped his credit card on the counter and resumed writing. He finished filling out the form, then signed the credit card receipt. Graham boxed up the rifle and wrote something on a piece of paper, presumably the web address. He slid the box and paper across the counter, then produced two boxes of 5.56 mm cartridges and placed them on the AR-15 box.

"Here's some ammo to get you started."

"These got that Teflon coating?"

"No can do. You gotta mail order those. Web site there'll tell you about that, too."

"Great. Thanks a lot."

"Good shooting."

Tex left with his arms full, looking like a kid with a new video game. Graham watched him out the door, then looked down below the counter where I knew he kept the video monitor, waiting until Tex had left the parking lot before saying anything.

"Excuse me, mister." He was still staring at the monitor as I walked up to the counter. "You think you should have explained to that guy that he'd need something that fires a NATO 7.62 round to penetrate any body armor that's not total crap?"

Graham looked up slowly and smiled. "Kyle, where the hell have you been? I haven't seen you for ages."

We shook hands, the firm handshake of old friends glad to see each other. With his left, he reached down and flipped the lock-down switch. We wouldn't be disturbed.

"Been keeping myself busy. How about you? Thought you'd have re-upped by now."

"Not likely. I see no reason to get my ass shot off in Iraq so some West Pointer can make Colonel." Graham's good-ol'-boy accent was gone. "Besides, I'm serving my country right here, arming the local population for the coming apocalypse."

"Not arming them all that well, as far as I can see. That AR-15 you sold that guy is a piece of junk. It'll jam up on him before he empties a single magazine."

"Trust me, that guy will hardly ever fire that piece. He'll hang it on a wall somewhere and admire it, maybe pull it down every once in awhile just to hold it. Did you see his boots? Spotless. Anybody who keeps his boots that clean isn't going to muss up his brand new assault rifle by actually firing it."

"You really didn't make him fill out a registration form?"

"Why bother. He gave me all the information I need on this bogus warranty form, and he paid with a credit card, so I can pull all his information off that. I'll register it for him and he'll never know the difference. People around here are suspicious of the government, so if they thought I was making them register, I'd lose a lot of sales."

I grimaced in mock horror. "You haven't registered anything I've bought, have you, Graham?"

"The last thing I want is a record that I sell guns to low-lifes like you." He walked out from behind the counter and headed to the back of the store. I followed him into his office. It was pretty Spartan; roll-top desk and a refrigerator. "Want a beer?"

"Has the sun come up yet?"

He tossed me a can of Bud, pulled out another for himself and popped the top.

"So what exactly are you doing these days, Kyle? I got a letter from Joe Sprague a couple months back. He said he hasn't heard a word from you in three years."

"Damn, I completely forgot to send him a 'get out of prison' card."

Graham sipped his beer thoughtfully. "He wasn't exactly the smartest guy in our outfit, was he? But I never figured him for some kind of Christian terrorist."

"He fell in with a bad crowd. Started screwing a church-going woman."

"Never a good idea, I say."

"Yeah, but you're the one who got him reading all that narcistic philosophy."

"Nihilistic, Kyle. Hey, I could tell he was the kind who needed something to believe in. I figured nihilism was as good as anything else."

"I thought nihilism basically means nothingness?"

"So you were listening all those times Joe and I talked."

"Sure. It was very entertaining seeing how worked up you could get him. Man, he followed you around like a lost puppy. He quoted you all the time."

"Well, I'm sure I never told him to be an idiot and start blowing up Planned Parenthood clinics. And I know damned well I never told him to get caught."

"Like you said, he wasn't exactly smart."

"Well, here's to Joe." He raised his can. "Maybe they'll let him out some day."

I raised my can and took a long drink. "I don't plan on being anywhere nearby when that day comes."

"So what brings you to Kannapolis? Wait, don't tell me, let me guess." He closed his eyes and touched his fingers to his forehead. "I know. You've decided to buy a small farm here, raise goats and get into the organic goat cheese market."

"Not even close, Graham. Nah, I figured I'd swing through here and stick up a local gun shop, then head for Vegas with the cash."

"Bad idea, Kyle. Everybody pays with credit cards these days. Gun shops just don't hold that much cash."

"Too bad."

"Besides, the only gun shop owner in these parts is ex-special forces and I hear he's a tough customer."

"Guess I'll have to go with plan B, then."

"And that would be . . . ?"

"I was thinking of adding to my handgun collection." It was time to get to business.

"No shit." He drank some more beer. "Seems to me you must have a few by now."

"Ah, I keep losin' 'em."

"That's not good, you know. Better make sure you get one that won't come back to haunt you if it winds up in the wrong place."

"Something untraceable would be nice."

"Hard to do. But almost as good would be, say, one that traces back to a police property room somewhere in Kansas or Idaho."

"That'd work." I never had figured out how a philosophy-major special-forces type got plugged into a national black market buying guns off corrupt police departments. I didn't care, really. Why look a gift horse in the mouth?

"What'd you have in mind. Compact .38? I've got a few of those. Got a couple of .44 magnums, too, if you're looking to put a big, nasty hole in some . . . thing."

"I was hoping for something smaller. A .22 automatic would be perfect."

He gave me a look of real appreciation. "Christ, Kyle, have you joined up with Mossad or something? That's their trademark."

"I'm planning on doing some hiking around Cumberland Gap. Lotta rattlesnakes. No need to carry a huge cannon."

"Sure. Yeah, you were always a good shot. Guess you can still hit a rattlesnake with a popgun like a .22. That's about all it'd be good for. I've got just the one. Nice little automatic, perfect for a woman's handbag, 10-round magazine."

"Great." He got up and went to a heavy metal door at the back of his office and started to unlock it. "And, Graham, a box of soft-point hollow-tips, too."

"Just in case you run into some jealous husband out there in the woods?"

"Bears."

"You kill a bear with a .22, you'll make history."

"I assure you, Graham, even a bear dies when you pump ten dum-dums into its vitals."

He disappeared into the back room for five minutes, then came out, locked the door behind him, and placed a nice little flat-black metal Bersa Thunder on the desk with a box of cartridges. "Nice piece. Picked it up for a couple hundred. I'll let you have it for three."

I took out my wallet and laid four-hundred in fifties on the desk. "Put the extra in the memorial fund." It was an old unit joke. The fund was for all of us to get drunk if one of us got killed.

"Just watch your back." Graham's eyes were deadly serious. "And for damned sure don't go and get some officer promoted."

"I'll be careful. I always am."

"Got time for another beer before you head back to wherever it is you're hiding out these days?"

"Sure. Aren't you worried you'll miss a customer, though, while we're locked up in here drinking?"

"I can afford it. Business is good."

"I thought the economy was bad. That many people around here can afford a new deer rifle?"

"Nah, most of my sales are assault rifles to guys like the one that was in here this morning." He grabbed two more beers from the refrigerator. "Best be careful around here these days, Kyle. Half the state is armed better than the 82nd Airborne."

"What, they worried that with the U.S. Army tied down in Iraq, Mexico's gonna invade?" I finished my first can of beer and popped the top on the fresh one.

"Actually, I think most of them are convinced they're going to discover some of their neighbors are al Qa'ida sleeper agents. Or homosexuals. Take your pick."

"I guess they figure they'll be ready if the gays rise up and revolt."

"You can laugh if you want, but people are afraid. They keep hearing on the news that there are terrorists everywhere and they're worried that the government is run by greedy bastards who are leaving them defenseless while they send the army to steal the oil from Iraq."

"Christ, Graham, you turned into one of those Iraq-war protestors or something?"

"You know me better than that." He laughed. "I'm just telling you what I hear people say when they come in to buy guns."

"Well, they've got every right to protect themselves."

"Damn straight. Government's sure not going to protect them."

"Aw, that's unfair, Graham. Government's fighting terrorists here just like in Iraq."

"Really?" He gave me a hard look. "So when did you start trusting the government, Kyle?"

I'd slipped up. Graham didn't know Richard Paladin. I could see he was concerned, wondering what he was hearing from his old buddy Kyle, the dishonorably discharged malcontent who used to say the only scum worse than officers were politicians. Not that I didn't still believe that.

"I'm just saying that there's probably stuff the government's doing against terrorists here at home that we don't necessarily know about."

He stared for a long time. "You're not working for the Feds, are you?"

"You gone nuts, Graham? You think the FBI would hire me with my record?"

"I was actually thinking of the ATF. Specifically, the 'firearms' part."

One stupid comment and I'd gotten Graham thinking I was setting him up on a weapons trafficking charge. Something about being back in North Carolina makes me careless. The air must bring out the redneck in me. If I didn't nip this in the bud, I'd have to find another place to buy the tools of my trade.

"Ah, you got me, Graham." I raised my hands in surrender. "Yeah, I'm in here for the ATF. They're gonna bust you."

"You better be shitting me, Kyle."

"They don't care about you selling guns, though."

"You don't say." A smile cracked his expression. He was familiar with my sense of humor.

I held up the can of Bud. "You got a license to serve alcohol?"

"Only to assholes. Want another one?"

"No thanks. I better hit the road. I got a long drive and I want to be back by tomorrow."

"Sure. Big weekend of bear hunting ahead, no doubt."

"I'll get one stuffed and send it to you." I gathered up the Bersa and cartridges. Graham walked out to the counter and flipped off the lockdown switch. There was an awkward silence. One thing you don't learn in the army is how to say goodbye to someone you've bunked with, bivouacked with, gotten drunk with. Admitting you'll miss someone if you never see them again is just too damned hard.

"Don't speed going back through Kannapolis. Cops have been setting up speed traps to raise revenue since the pillow factory closed. They particularly like to nail people with Virginia plates."

"I'll keep that in mind. And if you send Sprague a Christmas card, tell him you saw me and I said he's a dumbass."

"Will do."

The drive back was uneventful until just south of Manassas. Taking Graham's advice, I had obeyed the speed limit in Kannapolis. Charlottesville at early afternoon was an easy transit with no traffic congestion at all. I sailed right through Culpepper thinking I'd be back in Fairfax with time to pick up a six-pack and some Chinese take-out, eat an early dinner and get a good night's sleep. Right at that moment I noticed the ugly dark clouds moving to intersect my route from the southeast. At first, I sped up, figuring I was only a little over an hour from my apartment and thinking I could beat the storm. Lighting lit the sky ahead of me, followed five seconds later by a thunderous boom. I was too close to home to pull over and wait for the storm to pass, but the torrential downpour that erupted slowed me to a crawl that washed away my illusion of an early night.

I made it back to Fairfax around eleven, stopping at a 24 hour Safeway for a twelve-pack of Miller Genuine Draft and a TV dinner—Mexican enchiladas, refried beans and rice. The rain had slowed to a steady drizzle, but the drive had drained me pretty good. Food and a few beers and then I'd sleep sound. The road trip to clear my head hadn't really worked; most of the drive I'd been going back and forth on the current assignment, weighing risks and benefits, reaching no conclusion. Then nature sent a sign, a thunderstorm almost as impressive as the one I'd hit on the way to Joplin, on the way to Gladys Thurington.

Dan Stigler was going to die.

Chapter X
Death of a Barman

WHAT I'D ASSUMED was a passing summer thunderstorm Thursday night turned out to be a stalled low pressure system that brought wet and miserable weather for several days. Not that I mind a little rain. Friday morning I got up early and did my five-mile run to the university and back, pushing myself extra hard and remembering that time in basic training when we'd been sent out on bivouac in a category 3 hurricane, everyone in the unit shivering all night thinking we were going to drown in swollen creeks or die of hypothermia. Everyone except Graham, of course. It hadn't fazed him.

"Christ, Graham, are you human?" I had to shout to be heard, even though Graham was six inches away from me. We were sitting in a foot of water at the bottom of a foxhole while the wind snapped limbs off trees and sent them crashing down around us. He'd clipped his flashlight to his tunic and was reading a paperback under his poncho.

"Always remember, Kyle, no matter how deep a shit-hole someone puts you in, you choose where to put your mind."

"What the fuck are you reading?"

"Xenophon. Life of Cyrus. Now shut up. I'm trying to concentrate."

I couldn't tune out the world like Graham. But I had learned something on that bivouac. No matter how cold and miserable you are, you can gut it out. And the colder and wetter and muddier things get; well, a hot shower and warm rack just feel that much better afterwards. I actually caught myself smiling as I sprinted through the rain back to my apartment.

The hot shower was almost sexual. I didn't jump into my rack, though. My body was warm and primed for more exercise. This was a morning for Pris's and serious weight-lifting. I was a fighter in training, an athlete boosting his confidence before a big game. Pumping a little iron reminds me that there's very little in this world I can't handle.

By Saturday morning the weather had deteriorated to a constant drizzle punctuated by five minute showers of hard, heavy drops beating a tattoo on the roof of my car. I'd gotten up early, driven north of I66 to Vienna, then cut east toward the Beltway. Bad weather and an early Saturday start make spotting a tail child's play. Sure, it's harder to see through the rain into the car behind you, but the only car that's going to be behind you is somebody too stupid to stay out of the rain or too curious about what you're up to. In an hour I could tell I was clean.

I switched on the radio for a weather update. There'd been a few reports of flooding and I wanted to be alert to conditions. Nothing fucks up a morning of carefully planned surveillance like running into a flooded road and realizing you're cut off from the target. Flooding had indeed gotten worse, but mostly in the district and Maryland suburbs. Hopefully, I'd be in Virginia all day. Northern Virginia floods less than the district because the county governments actually fix drainage lines and clear debris from creeks and streams occasionally. It floods less than Washington's Maryland suburbs because northern Virginia is not yet entirely paved over with shopping areas and large townhouse developments. That's changing rapidly, though.

I pulled up a half block down the street from Dan's house around 8:30, parked, and settled in. The rain was steady, so I didn't have to worry about people out for a Saturday morning stroll wondering why I was sitting in my car. It didn't matter anyway: I didn't have to wait long. Fifteen minutes later Dan backed his Subaru out of the driveway and headed down the street right past me. I started my motor as he passed, watching him in the rear view mirror. He made a right a block away. Quickly I pulled into a driveway across the street, backed into the street headed in the opposite direction from how I'd parked, and raced to the intersection to follow. After the turn I could see him at a stop sign two blocks up. I slowed, letting him pull away before I closed to about a block behind him. My plan was to stay on him, even if it looked like he was taking the kind of precautions I always do to make sure he wasn't being followed. I'd keep my distance, make it as hard as possible for him to spot me. But I wasn't going to lose him.

Following him proved pretty easy. He was a cautious driver, but nothing like Gladys Thurington. He kept to the speed limit, not really making any aggressive moves. But he didn't seem to be driving extra slow, which is a sure sign someone is looking in the rear view mirror to check out possible trailing vehicles. He drove like a guy out on a Saturday morning errand. I was somewhat concerned when he started following basically the same route I'd taken earlier, winding through Fairfax to 123, turning north past 66 into Vienna. It's eerie, driving along a particular road trying to make out trailing surveillance, then following someone else down the same road trying not to be spotted. If he'd made the turn east toward the Beltway, I'd have had to be more cautious. But he didn't.

He stayed on 123 all the way through Oakton, past the golf club north of Vienna, through the Tyson's Corner area. *It's too early for him to be going to the mall,* I thought. He drove right past Tyson's Shopping Center, continued on 123 under 495, on past the Dulles Access road. He was heading straight for something, that was certain. I began to doubt he was up to anything at all except some harmless errand. He passed a large development of multi-million dollar townhomes and stayed maddeningly straight on 123 into McLean. *Christ, the CIA's about 2 miles up on the left. Surely he's not headed there.*

He made a left into McLean Central Park just beyond the intersection with Old Dominion Drive, catching me off guard. I started to follow him in, thought better of it, turned into the parking lot of J. Gilbert's restaurant across the street and shut off my engine. I grabbed a poncho I'd thrown on the back seat earlier, jumped out of the car and ran across the street, slipping the poncho on as I raced to get behind some trees. I could see Dan getting out of his car. He was wearing a bright red Gortex jacket that made him stand out like a human tomato. I kept my distance but stayed within visual range of him as he headed into the park and took a path past the tennis courts into a wooded area stretching north-north-east.

In the year I'd come to know Dan, I'd learned plenty about him, including that for all he ran a blue-collar bar, he had a bit of tree hugger in him. But taking a nature walk on a soggy, rainy Saturday morning put him in a whole new league, in my book. And that's exactly what he seemed to be doing. Walking slowly, looking up into the trees—as if any birds would be fool enough to be out in this weather—stopping to pick up the occasional stone, study it, toss it back down to the ground. After half an hour he was a mile deep in the woods and I was beginning to feel like a complete fool, ducking from tree to tree, peering through branches to keep his red beacon jacket in sight. A crazy thought came into my head that I should stop shadowing him and just head up to him and ask him what the fuck he was doing walking in the woods on a day like this. He stopped at a little wooden footbridge and I almost did exactly that.

Except when he stopped, he looked quickly behind him, then glanced from side to side. I pressed as close to the tree I was behind as possible, hoping my military green poncho was good camouflage in the rain. He did a slow 360, obviously reassuring himself no one else was in the area. I found myself hoping he was just planning to take a leak. Instead, he laid down on the footbridge, reached underneath, and pulled out a black package. Standing back up, he produced a rolled up shopping bag from inside his jacket—one of those grocery totes people buy these days so they can feel good about not using throw-away plastic bags—dropped the package into it, and then headed back in the direction of his car, shopping bag in hand.

I followed cautiously, staying in the trees. I didn't need to catch up to him, but I did need to get in position to see which way he went when he got back to his car. He walked directly back to the Subaru and climbed in, tossing the package on the passenger seat beside him. He pulled onto 123 headed back the way he'd come. As far as I could tell, the only time he bothered to make sure he wasn't being watched was right at the footbridge. Whatever was in that package, he hadn't wanted anyone to see him collect it. But he was being damned incautious otherwise. He was either a rank amateur or supremely over-confident.

I wasn't going to get sloppy, though. I waited five minutes to let him get well on his way before crossing back to my car. With any luck I could catch him, assuming he was headed back to Fairfax. Tossing the wet poncho on the back seat, I pulled onto 123 in pursuit, exceeding the speed limit by about 10 mph and crossing my fingers that, like before, he wasn't. I spotted him 100 yards ahead of me about the time we crossed back under the Beltway and slowed again to maintain distance. We retraced the route past the golf course, Vienna, Oakton, under 66 to Fairfax.

The logical thing would have been for him to go back to his house to inspect whatever it was he had retrieved from the dead drop. Cash, secret documents, drugs; I'm betting most people would have gone somewhere to make sure the package contained what they were expecting. Dan was full of surprises. Back in Fairfax, he made straight for his bar, parking right out front. Again, I turned into a parking lot across the street. This time I could see him without leaving my car. He got out and headed in to open up. He wasn't carrying the shopping bag. Apparently he wasn't all that concerned someone might steal it. That level of nonchalance indicated to me that he picked up packages like this routinely.

I waited across the street. Dan probably was just setting up to hand over to his law-student bartender for the slow Saturday afternoon crowd. I passed the time speculating about what was in the package. Drugs didn't seem likely. I couldn't see Dan as some kind of pusher. Cash made more sense for a terrorist ringleader; money to buy guns or explosives. Then again, most people wouldn't leave a bundle of cash sitting on the front seat of their car. It didn't make a lot of sense.

The weekend bartender showed up at 11:00. Fifteen minutes later, Dan came out, got in his car and drove away. I followed, again maintaining a distance of about 100 yards. He headed back to 123, but this time turned south. The rain slacked off so I dropped further back, about 150 yards, following him past the university toward Burke Lake. I wondered if he was heading to Burke Lake Park to service another dead drop, but then he made an abrupt left. I had to speed up to keep from losing him, following closer as he cut through another of northern Virginia's mini-mansion developments. A couple of times I cursed, plowing through foot-deep standing water, hoping he didn't notice me setting off a tidal wave behind him. Developers apparently don't find it necessary to install adequate drainage when they're covering once vacant grass fields with dozens of 4,000 square foot houses.

He didn't notice me. He just kept driving another two blocks and pulled into a fairly new community center. I pulled over to the curb and parked in front of a three story monstrosity with a for sale sign in front. It struck me that the houses in this area were obscenely large, the kind of places tree huggers rail against. Was it possible, I wondered, that Dan was planning some kind of terrorist strike out here in suburbia, lashing out at the mindless development that he saw not just despoiling the environment but even directly threatening his livelihood at Dan's Bar? That package he'd picked up wasn't overly large, but it was big enough to hold a sizeable quantity of C-4 or Semtex. As I watched, though, he parked at the community center and went inside, again leaving the package in the car.

I had to know why he had come. Following him into the community center was risky. On the other hand, taking risks is part of my job. If Dan was planning to blow something up today, I damned well better find out. I waited ten minutes to make sure he wasn't coming right back out, then pulled into the community center lot and parked as far away from his Subaru as possible. I dashed across the lot to the entrance, not directly to the glass doors but off to the side a bit, hoping to get a look inside without being too visible. Just inside was an empty foyer leading to several larger rooms in the back. I decided to chance it, walked inside as quietly as possible. Directly ahead was an open door. I could hear someone inside speaking. I walked slowly forward until I could see a bit inside. There were about thirty folding chairs set up in neat little rows with maybe ten people sitting, listening attentively to a woman speaking at a podium. I made out the back of Dan's head, nodding agreement periodically to whatever she was saying.

"You here for the meeting?" A woman had come out of a side office. I'd been so focused on Dan I hadn't noticed.

"What meeting?"

"Keep Fairfax Green."

"Excuse me?"

"The Keep Fairfax Green committee. They arranged today's presentation by Laurie Verdoyer." I gave her a blank stare. "The environmentalist. She's giving a talk about organizing local campaigns to get the EPA to start doing its job."

"You don't say."

"Go on in. There's plenty of room."

"No thanks. I just came in to take a leak. Where's the bathroom?"

"Public restroom entrances are outside." She gave me a disapproving look. She could pull it off, too. She was about fifty and very matronly. "Back through the front and go to the right."

"Thanks. Appreciate it."

I wondered if I should look up Laurie Verdoyer and tell her I knew of one EPA employee who was damned sure about to start doing his job.

The meeting lasted over an hour. I know because I waited the whole time in my car, parked back on a side street with a view of the community center parking lot. It was imperative that I stayed on Dan now so I could try to find a chance to see what was in the package. I could have broken into his car and looked, of course, but that risked someone seeing me and calling a cop. And I didn't want Dan to come out and find the package opened or missing. Alerting him that he was being followed would only complicate the task at hand.

Sitting there waiting, I had plenty of time to add things up. It was pretty clear now that the Keep Fairfax Green committee was the group Dan had mentioned to me. It was also clear that Dan was more than just some concerned citizen. People who engage in clandestine behavior fall into two, and only two, categories: good guys and bad guys. I knew where I fit. And if I was fighting America's enemies for the EPA, it was pretty obvious which group Dan Stigler, anti-EPA activist retrieving black packages hidden in public parks, represented. After doing the job, I'd report all this to my boss; orally, of course. We might have to open a whole new file on this Keep Fairfax Green outfit; maybe even add Laurie Verdoyer to our list.

I wondered about the wisdom of killing Dan directly, though. Sure, that was the quickest way to disrupt his organization, but I found myself thinking it would make more sense to sweat a little information out of him first. Get a detailed list of who else was involved. Rather than just eliminating him, we could wrap up his whole cell. That made sense.

Yet my boss had been adamant that the job was urgent. Maybe what I'd found out would change his mind; then again, maybe it would just convince him that I was losing my stomach for this kind of work. He clearly thought I'd hesitated on the Thurington job. The last thing I wanted was to have my boss lose confidence in me. A killer who hesitates to kill is no good as a government executioner anymore. And I damned sure didn't want to lose my government job. I had no idea what the fuck else I could do for a living.

Dan came out of the community center, part of a small group following the Verdoyer woman, getting a few final pointers or just hanging on her every word as long as possible. Maybe environmentalists have groupies, I don't know. She looked like she was trying to make a clean escape, nodding agreement to something one of Dan's associates said, looking at her watch, obviously trying to be polite but really wanting to be somewhere else. I suspect she just found the whole thing as pathetic as I did, less than a dozen people at a community center in the middle of nowhere acting as if they could have some kind of impact on the bureaucratic glacier of the EPA and USG. They might as well have been standing on a railroad track waving for a freight train to pull over.

Of course, in this case, I was driving the locomotive.

She finally managed to get away, got in her vehicle and drove off. I'd been betting she was driving the little Toyota Prius hybrid sitting in the parking lot, but she surprised me, climbing instead into a big black Chevy Suburban. I guess there's no reason why tree huggers shouldn't be hypocrites like everyone else.

Dan and the others hung out in front of the community center for about 15 minutes, talking, laughing, acting like people who'd just come out of a cinema or ballgame. Nothing they did looked threatening, just a bunch of do-gooders feeling good about spending a rainy Saturday trying to make the planet a better place. I've seen pictures of Mohammed Atta. He didn't look like such a bad guy, either.

Following Dan after that was an anti-climax. He drove straight home, carrying the package in with him and staying for about an hour. When he left, the package remained inside. I didn't need to tail him anymore. He was headed to the bar to work the extra-busy Saturday night shift with his weekend helper. No need to confirm that. Anyway, I was now more interested in the package. Finding out what was in that would answer a lot of questions.

Breaking into Dan's house in daylight a few minutes after he left was too risky, though. I had all evening for that. Besides, I was hungry. Following Dan all day hadn't given me any opportunity to eat, and my stomach was growling. I decided I needed a generous helping of meat. Fortunately, there's a Red Hot & Blue in Fairfax, a local barbecue chain founded in the eighties by some Reagan Republicans who claimed they couldn't find decent barbecue in Washington. That's bullshit, of course. You can get a great side of barbecued ribs in D.C., but you have to be willing to go to neighborhoods where Reagan Republicans don't feel comfortable. So they'd opened Red Hot & Blue's franchises in pricey areas where people didn't mind shelling out thirty bucks for a plate of charred meats and beans. The places made damned good ribs, though. I picked up an order to go. There was still some beer at my apartment. I figured a good southern meal of ribs and beer was just the ticket before heading back to Dan's for a little breaking and entering.

Back at my apartment, I needed to take my mind off the job for awhile. Best would be to head back to Dan's late, maybe 11:00 or so. He'd be at the bar until after 2:00 the next morning, so I had plenty of time. But sitting thinking about what I'd seen that day was just confusing. I turned on my cheap TV hooked up to its stolen cable. I don't watch it often, but it's just the kind of escape that's perfect when waiting to do a job.

The History Channel was running a documentary about the failed efforts of Germany's generals to assassinate Adolf Hitler. That looked good, combining two of my interests; bumping people off and officers being idiots. I settled onto my beat-up sofa with the ribs and beer. The show was rich in detail, exploring biographical facts about some of the key plotters, explaining the flaw that kept the first bomb from blowing Hitler's plane out of the sky and the bad luck of Stauffenberg's bomb not having been properly placed. Apparently several other attempts to kill the bastard with grenades and land mines failed when he didn't coordinate his schedule properly with his would-be executioners. The narrator—the voice was some

Hollywood actor I'd heard a million times but couldn't put a name to—emphasized repeatedly that Hitler survived all this purely through dumb luck. I was unconvinced. The simpler explanation is that all the key conspirators were officers. They fucked it up. Big surprise.

After *Keystone Kops Fail to Kill Hitler* came an even more interesting historical item on the assassination of the Archduke Ferdinand that led to the First World War. This one had a different narrator who failed to get the point, too. The voice kept droning on about how Ferdinand was a liberal who would have reformed the empire if he'd lived long enough to take over for his asshole father. Since there has never been a single liberal who ever succeeded in doing anything but making things worse when they got a shot at running the show someplace, I have my doubts that fat Ferdinand would have somehow made everyone in the Balkans kiss and hold hands.

But the real story was the assassination itself. Three Bosnian nationalists got advanced copies of Ferdinand's route through Sarajevo and set up an ambush to throw bombs at his car. But Ferdie's people changed the route, negating their efforts. So they called it off and headed their separate ways. Then, lo and behold, one of the plotters, Gavril Prinzip, was walking along minding his own business when there, right in front of him, was Ferdie's limo with the fat Prince and his wife sitting in the back, soft top of the car down, exposed to the whole world. If Gavril had been a German officer, I'll bet he'd have saluted and spent the rest of his life talking about the day he "almost" killed Ferdinand. But he was just a poor dumb kid from the country who'd never attended a fancy military academy and been told that someone else is supposed to shine your shoes and wipe your ass. He pulled out his handgun and blazed away. The rest is history.

I tossed the remnants of my rib dinner into the garbage, washed the barbecue sauce off my hands, and headed back to my car, grabbing a dark rain jacket and stuffing a mini mag light I always carry for night jobs and a pocket leatherman I'd picked up at REI a couple years back into the jacket's pockets. I also grabbed a taser I keep taped behind the garbage disposal under the sink. It never hurts to be prepared. I wasn't packing my brand new Bersa Thunder, by the way. Prinzip's assassination of Ferdinand was his last operational act. He was arrested and died four years later in prison of tuberculosis. Leaving Dan's bullet-ridden body for the police would just mean an investigation and, who knows, some cop might get lucky and find a clue leading back to me. I'd find a subtler way.

Breaking in was as easy as before. I left the lights off—no reason to get a nosy neighbor wondering why Dan was strangely home on Saturday night—switching on the mini mag light, making sure all the blinds and drapes were closed. Fairly confident I could now ransack the house without being noticed by neighbors or passersby, I nevertheless switched off my mag light and sat on the living room sofa in the dark for half an hour. In the unlikely event someone noticed me breaking in and called the police, they'd simply find the place locked and dark without a peep coming from inside. Then they'd politely tell the neighbor to stop imagining things and leave.

No cops arrived. I relaxed, switched the mag light back on, and ran through logical hiding places from my memory of having broken in before. I played the light over the shelves with the stereo, past the records, looking for any sign of a false wall. Nothing. I pivoted slowly in the center of the living room, casting the mag beam up and down the walls. The beam shot through the door to the kitchen, illuminating the counter where I'd found the stack of mail before.

The shopping bag was sitting right on the counter. I went into the kitchen. The black-wrapped parcel was inside the shopping bag. Instinctively, I stepped back. It was all too easy. Was this some elaborate trap? Was Dan working with Sharon's people, setting me up in a complicated sting? I half-expected the lights to come on suddenly with people springing from behind the furniture yelling "Surprise!"

No lights came on. I played the beam around the kitchen, looking for something, anything. No tripwires, no booby traps, no signs of a surveillance camera—although they can make those things almost invisible these days. The inescapable conclusion was that Dan had just set the bag on the counter and gone about his business as if nothing out of the ordinary was going on.

I removed the package gently from the bag and set it on the counter, inspecting it closely under the mag light beam. It was just black garbage-bag plastic sealed with black plastic tape. Whoever had wrapped it had done a good job, sealing it so it didn't get wet in the rain under that foot bridge. I ran my hand along the taped seals. No wires, nothing to suggest it would blow up if I opened it. I picked it up, flexed it gently. It bent like a thick sheaf of paper. That ruled out narcotics or explosives. Cash?

I stuck the mag light in my mouth and pulled out the

pocket leatherman, opening the knife blade and slitting the taped end of the package carefully. It was thick gauge plastic, making it a delicate operation to cut through it without damaging the contents. I made an incision at the base and then all the way up one side. I was sweating as I folded back the plastic and finally got a look at Dan's secret treasure.

It wasn't cash. Inside were about three inches of documents. Government documents. The top one was stamped "SECRET/EYES ONLY."

Dan was a fucking spy.

I'm ashamed to say my pulse was racing. Not a very professional response, I'll admit. But wild thoughts raced through my head; Dan stealing secret plans for the H-Bomb and passing them to al Qa'ida, getting hold of the army's deployment plans and sending them to Iraqi insurgents, handing our country's vital economic and technological secrets to the French. Sweat stung my eyes; I wiped them to clear my vision, to read what national secrets Dan had gotten his hands on.

The top document had nothing to do with America's nuclear arsenal. Nor did it outline war plans or sensitive laser technology or anything like that. It was a policy document from the Office of the Director of the Environmental Protection Agency.

"What the fuck?" I talk to myself when I'm confused.

I leafed quickly through the stack of papers. They were all EPA policy memos, all marked "SECRET/EYES ONLY." I flipped back to the first document and read it more closely. I was sweating profusely, panicked slightly that Dan had found a source willing to expose the EPA's most secret activities—namely, the work done by people like me.

The first memo was addressed to the Director for Inspections, Toxic Chemicals Division. The subject line, "Improving Inspection Efficiencies," was misleading. The memo instructed that particular inspections department to implement cost saving measures consisting of canceling all site inspection activity by EPA staff. Future inspections of chemical industry compliance with toxic waste disposal would be outsourced to the private sector. As I waded through what I now recognized as government legalese and bullshit, it became clear that "private sector" meant the very chemical industry that was being inspected.

Memo two was addressed to the Water Quality Enforcement Division. My joke about being sent to inspect Death Valley because it had no water turned out to be not far from the truth. Because of the "controversies over definitions of water purity" in current EPA guidelines, Water Quality Division efforts were to be indefinitely refocused on "baseline studies" to establish new guidelines. Step one was to identify "pristine areas in the continental United States as yet untouched by industrial, agricultural, or residential development activity." You didn't have to be an environmental scientist to know that finding areas like that would be virtually impossible, especially since "national parks, national forests, and sensitive areas set aside for natural preservation" were excluded "due to political sensitivities."

Memo after memo directed the various elements of the vast EPA bureaucracy to stand down on meaningful environmental protection. It was documentary proof of exactly what tree huggers had been complaining about for years. Not that any of it surprised me. EPA do-gooders had been making nuisances of themselves with productive American industry for decades. I had always assumed they were simply tolerated to provide cover for the real work of the EPA, my work—and what I assumed had to be the work of other compartmented EPA programs—protecting Americans from the real environmental threats; terrorists, spies, and traitors. Somebody high up in the government had finally had enough, I figured, and was reigning the phony EPA in and restoring them to their meaningless front job activity. It's a fact of government life that for every civil servant doing a critically important job, there are ten bureaucrats trying to shove idiotic regulations down people's throats to keep them from accomplishing anything. My experience in the army had taught me that. It also explained the Internal Revenue Service. The only way any of it made sense was if incompetent government was just cover so people like me could operate in the shadows.

Dan Stigler and company wanted to blow the lid on all that, demand accountability from the EPA. And once they forced the Agency into the business of playing pollutant policeman, they'd no doubt start digging into the EPA's real mission. I damned sure couldn't allow that. There were still too many assignments out there, too many enemies biding their time for the opportunity to bring the country to its knees.

Plus, if people like Dan Stigler reined in the EPA, where the hell would I find a job?

I checked my watch. It was almost 12:30. Dan wouldn't be home for a couple hours at the earliest. I checked his refrigerator; fortunately there was a six-pack of Budweiser. I grabbed a beer and the sheaf of papers, went back to the living room and sat on the sofa. Popping the top on the Bud and switching off the mag light, I sat back in the dark and relaxed. It would be a long wait.

The rain was finally letting up outside. Sitting in the dark, I hefted the taser. It's not the same as holding a .9mm Browning, but it has a reassuring feel. The taser's a remarkable weapon, capable of bringing down a lumberjack without leaving a mark. Just having it in my hand brought a renewed sense of focus. I'd have no trouble handling Dan when he arrived. But this was no longer a simple killing. Dan had a source, a traitor inside the EPA passing him classified information. Before I got down to business, Dan and I were going to have a talk.

I dozed off and on, sitting there in the dark. It didn't concern me that I might fall asleep, have Dan surprise me when he showed up. I've never been a sound sleeper. The slightest change in my environment and I'm fully alert. Some people might consider that a problem, maybe an inability to relax completely. I figure it's a sixth sense for danger. Whatever, I was wide-eyed and alert at 2:47 a.m. once I heard Dan's Subaru pull into his driveway.

He was whistling as he put the key in the lock and opened the door. Probably some tune that had been playing on the juke box at the bar. It sounded country and western, maybe a Garth Brooks number. He came in and closed the door before switching on the light. I was just sitting on the sofa, waiting. He saw me and froze.

"Hello, Dan."

He didn't say anything, just stared like a deer caught in headlights. There was a chance, of course, that he'd open the front door again and bolt. I'm betting that's what most normal people would do if they happened upon someone sitting uninvited in their living room at three in the morning. Dan was no normal person. He stood still, eyes concerned, obviously going over reasons why I was there, no doubt looking for a harmless explanation. But I was sure he knew.

"Good night at the bar?"

"Paladin." His voice was flat, the kind of flat that says fear. "What the hell are you doing in my house?"

"What, after all these months, we're not good enough friends that I can drop by for a visit?"

"You broke in?" Then he saw the stack of papers beside me on the couch. His shoulders slumped.

"Yeah. Wanted to talk to you about these." I picked up the top memo, held it up for him. "Pretty interesting reading."

"You read 'em?"

"Yes, I did." He was still standing, confused. Probably coming up with some line of bullshit to try to explain the documents. Maybe he was just wondering what I had to do with any of this. "Why don't you sit down? You're making me nervous, standing there like that."

"I don't want to sit down. I want to know why you broke into my house and what the hell you're doing here." He was getting over the shock. Acting indignant was a nice move, though predictable. Any good fighter knows that just getting your balance back after taking a good punch isn't enough; you've got to sting the other guy right away before he starts using you as a punching bag.

But I'm a good fighter, too. I stood up, slowly, took a couple of steps toward him. He drew back. I didn't give him a chance to run. Quick as a cat I grabbed him by the front of his shirt, pulled him across the room and shoved him into a padded armchair next to the sofa.

"I said sit down." I stood over him for a minute, letting him know I'd frown upon it if he tried to get up. Dan's a wiry guy, tough enough in his own way. But he was no match for me, and he knew it.

"So I was thinking maybe you could explain to me why you have a stack of classified documents here in your house." I sat down on the sofa again, easing back the confrontation level. Lots of people who watch too many bad cop shows on TV think the best way to make someone talk is to start beating the crap out of them. I know better. Establishing a level of fear is good—I'd accomplished that already—but a real interrogation is just a conversation. You want to get the guy talking, not bleeding.

"I don't have to explain anything to you. You fucking broke into my home."

"Right. So you said. Maybe you should call the cops."

"Maybe I should." He was breathing heavy, eyes darting wildly.

"Before you do, you might want to consider the fact that espionage is a crime."

"Espionage? Aw, give me a break."

"Lots more serious than breaking and entering."

"What are you talking about?"

"Punishable by death in wartime."

"That's ridiculous. I'm not a spy."

I held up one of the documents, pointed to the classification. "What's that say?"

"Look, I can explain." He wasn't talking about calling the cops anymore.

"Okay." I sat back on the sofa. "I'm listening."

"A customer left those in the bar a couple of nights ago." His eyes were still working overtime, a sure sign of someone making up a story. "I brought the stuff home to see if there was an address or phone number."

"You didn't think it was odd, them being all taped up in plastic?"

"It was just a shopping bag with a package inside. I didn't even know they were documents until you told me. You're the one who opened them up and read them." It was a nice try. He was still trying to regain the initiative, put me on the defensive.

"Funny thing, though. Looks exactly like the package you picked up in McLean this morning." I looked at my watch. "Sorry, yesterday morning."

"How'd you know about . . . " His face went white. But I hadn't knocked all the fight out of him yet. He took one more shot. "What's all this to you, Paladin? You're not a cop."

"I'm not? Tell me, Dan, what am I exactly?"

"Aw, come on. You work at the EPA. You do water quality inspections or some such crap. I don't have to talk to you. Get the fuck out of my house."

He started to stand up. I was on him in a heartbeat, pinning him back in the chair, forearm shoved into his Adam's apple. I help him there until his face started turning purple.

"You're right, Dan. I'm not a cop. I work for the EPA. But I don't do water quality inspections or any other crap like that . . . "

His eyes were beginning to bug out.

"What I do for the EPA is highly classified, just like those EPA documents I found in your kitchen . . ."

He was making a gurgling sound.

"In fact, I'm doing my EPA job right now . . . "

I could tell he was about to pass out. I stopped choking him, stood up, towered over him for a minute, and sat back down on the sofa.

"So I think you should talk to me about this . . . "

He was sucking in air, limbs limp in the chair but eyes wide with fear.

" . . . because we're friends, Dan. And I don't want to hurt you."

"I think you broke my windpipe," he rasped, rubbing his throat. He was getting his breath back, though. "I'm not saying anything. I want a lawyer."

I laughed. It wasn't an act. That was really funny.

"I told you, Dan. I'm not a cop. I'm not gonna read you your rights or any of that crap. And I'm not gonna arrest you."

"You're not?"

"You don't get off that easy."

"What are you gonna do?" He'd stopped rubbing his throat.

"That depends on you. Cooperate and maybe I won't do anything at all."

"And if I don't? I've got rights. You can't just break into my house, push me around, threaten me."

"Really? Seems to me that's exactly what I'm doing."

"I mean, you've got no right to treat me like this. There are laws."

"Not for spies."

He hesitated, stammered; "That's n-not right. Even if I were a spy, you'd have to let me call a lawyer, charge me, all that crap."

I leaned forward, looking into his scared-shitless eyes. He was right on the edge, almost ready to crack. He just needed a little nudge. I grinned at him, a big, evil grin. "Not any more, Dan. Spies, traitors, enemy combatants, these days we just wrap 'em up in orange velcro and ship 'em someplace where they never bother anybody again."

"You can't do that to me. I'm an American citizen." It wasn't much of a protest. He was whispering.

"If you're lucky, you'll still be breathing when we ship you out."

I could tell he was going to try to bolt one more time. His eyes telegraphed it, darting for a quick look at the door, a dead-giveaway that he was calculating whether he could make it. I knew he'd try to chance it. Desperation makes people stupid. He almost made it to his feet before I reacted. This time I tasered him. He slumped back in the chair like a corpse.

Tasering always gives you a couple of minutes while the victim's muscles recover. I strolled casually into the kitchen, grabbed another beer, popped the top and returned to the sofa. I took a few swigs while I waited, watching him come out of it. I doubted he'd try to run again.

"What the hell was that?" Muscle coordination had returned to his vocal chords.

"This little thing?" I held up the taser for him to see. "Just something they issue people like me to deal with people like you."

"You coulda killed me." He sounded sincerely afraid. "I got a bad heart."

"Then you should be more careful, Dan. Avoid exertion. Take deep breaths. Relax. And whatever you do, don't piss me off again."

"I need some water."

"First things first. Who's giving you these?" I pointed the taser at the documents.

"I don't know."

I tasered him again, then drank some more beer. It was another couple of minutes before his eyes refocused on me and I knew he could hear me.

"Now that was a wrong answer, Dan. See, we're gonna play a little game. I ask you questions and you give me the right answers. If you give me enough right answers, I'll get you a glass of water. Every time you give me a wrong answer, well . . . " I held up the taser.

"Iiiarcherea . . . " He was trying to talk, but his muscles were still zapped.

"Take your time, Dan. I didn't quite catch that."

"I . . . I s-said . . . I really . . . don't know who'sh . . . giving me the stuff." I reached forward with the taser. He tried to draw away, but he still hadn't fully recovered from the previous jolt. "No, stop. I'll tell you."

I pulled back. "I'm all ears."

"Look, there's this reporter. She knows the guy. He leaves the stuff for me, I give it to her. She figured it wasn't safe for him to meet her, hand her documents. Figured he'd get in trouble. So she asked me to collect the stuff."

"Now that sounds like a load of crap." I hefted the taser, like I was considering it.

"I'm not lying, Paladin. Honest to God."

"How'd she meet you? She do a feature story on redneck bars?"

"She's an environmental reporter, writes for some Internet magazine or something. She came and talked to a group I belong to."

"Keep Fairfax Green?" His eyes gaped. "There's no point lying to me, Dan. I already know more than you think."

"Yeah, well, sure . . . she came and talked to the Keep Fairfax Green committee. She's writing a book about the EPA being in collusion with corporate polluters."

"And then after the meeting she just waltzed up to you and asked you to start picking up classified documents from a dead drop. Sure, Dan."

"No, I approached her." His eyes were pleading now. "I'm chairman of the committee. We're pretty well known in environmental activist circles."

"Well known for what?"

"We've organized the largest letter-writing campaign in the country. That's what the committee was formed to do. We get lists from other environmental groups, national groups, e-mail addresses. There's about thirty committee members who send out e-mails."

"E-mails."

"We send letters for people to print off, sign, mail to Congress."

"Don't tell me, a national campaign to save Fairfax from all the hot air spewed by Senators and Representatives? Asking them to give shorter speeches?"

"We're serious, Paladin. It's a national campaign to persuade as many people in Congress as possible to pressure the administration into signing the Kyoto Protocol."

I didn't say anything. It was like I'd been sucker-punched. Everywhere I turned, I kept running into the fucking Kyoto Protocol. I wondered if I had wandered into some bizarre parallel universe where my cover story was suddenly reality. Maybe I was supposed to stop interrogating Dan now and run through the EPA's anti-Kyoto talking points with him. Then I could include that as a highlight in next quarter's KPPRI report. I downed the rest of my beer. Drinking was the only thing that made sense.

"I can show you the letter we send out." Dan had obviously interpreted my stunned silence to mean I still didn't believe him. I let him talk. "Thousands of the letters have been sent to Congress. I'm betting it's a real headache for someone in the administration."

I had a pretty good idea who that someone was. "You still haven't explained to me what the fuck any of this has to do with picking up bundles of secrets from under footbridges in McLean."

"Look, this reporter, she comes and talks about how basically this isn't about the government not understanding about greenhouse gasses and global warming. She says she's gathering evidence that fat cats in the administration know damned well their policies are ruining the environment. Instead of trying to fix it, they're colluding with big corporations, lining their pockets at the expense of the environment. At the expense of the world."

"Christ, Dan, you really believe this crap. I'd have thought you had more sense than to buy into all this tree-hugger bullshit."

"You read those documents. I haven't seen the ones you've got there, but I've read some of the stuff I've picked up before. It's fucking unbelievable. Cover-ups of toxic chemicals dumped in playgrounds. Inspection reports buried about cyanide in public reservoirs, the inspectors reassigned to administrative work."

"I still don't follow how she got you involved in stealing government secrets."

"That's what I'm telling you. After her talk, I went up to her, asked her what I could do to help. It was pretty clear that all the letters in the world weren't going to change anything. I wanted to do something, make a difference. Then she tells me she's got a friend at the EPA who wants to help, blow the lid on what's going on there. But he's afraid, says whistle-blowers get hung out to dry. He's gotten too afraid even to meet her."

"So she comes up with this spy vs. spy crap and dupes you into playing along."

"That was my idea." The poor sap's chest actually puffed out a bit. "I'd seen this TV movie about some spy who left documents for the Russians in a public park. I told her to contact her friend, tell her he could leave stuff for her somewhere, I could pick it up and send it to her."

"They caught that spy, Dan. Didn't that occur to you?"

"Yeah, but he was some national security type. Of course they watch people like that. But who's gonna watch me . . . " His voice trailed off.

"Exactly."

"Anyway, she thought it sounded like a good idea. So'd the EPA guy, apparently."

"How long have you been playing delivery boy, then?"

"About three months. He makes a drop every couple of weeks."

"So tell me who he is."

"I can't. She wouldn't tell me. Said it was better if I couldn't identify him."

"Makes sense." He looked relieved. Nobody likes to rat people out. He thought he was off the hook. "So who's the reporter?"

"I can't tell you that."

"Dan, you have to tell me that." I didn't even bother

to threaten him with the taser. I just gave him a hard stare that told him it was either her or him. His call. "Give me her name and I'll leave you in peace."

He thought about it for a long two minutes. I kept quiet. Betrayal is something people have to wrap their minds around, come to terms with. I figure there are some people who won't do it. Graham Fielding would never give me up, for example, just like I'd protect his back-room business with my last breath. But Dan was different. He'd already betrayed his government. I doubted he'd have any qualms about betraying a journalist.

"Rebecca Goldstein. She writes for the *Online Environmental Watchdog*."

He could have been lying, of course. I'd have made up a name. But the Keep Fairfax Green committee meetings weren't secret, and I was pretty confident I could confirm just what environmental reporter had spoken to them three or four months back. There was really nothing else for Dan to tell me.

I reached across and tasered him again. I needed time to think.

It was about four in the morning. If I was going to kill Dan, I needed to do it quick and get out of his house while it was still dark. I'd make it look like suicide, of course. Rig a noose from a bed sheet and hang him, lay him in the bathtub and slit his wrists. Either job would be easy. I'd just taser him into submission first. I'd even brought the letter from Fairfax informing him of the impending rezoning that was going to put him out of business. Leaving that on the counter would provide ample evidence that he had good reason to kill himself.

One thing kept bothering me, though. It was pretty

clear Dan wasn't a terrorist. Hell, he wasn't even much of a spy. Passing stolen EPA documents to an Internet journalist doesn't really compare with giving the H-bomb to al Qa'ida. Dan wasn't much more than a harmless crackpot, really. He'd just had the bad sense to make problems for my boss. How was he to know that the guy in charge of dealing with the public about the Kyoto Protocol just happened to be the same guy running the EPA's Murder Incorporated? I didn't see how any of that justified killing him.

I sat staring at him slumped back in the chair while I thought through everything. He looked really peaceful.

"It's a tough decision I got this time, buddy." I don't know what made me want to talk it over with him. Maybe I wanted him to appreciate the big favor I'd be doing if I let him live. He didn't respond. His eyes didn't even move.

"Dan? You hear me, Dan?"

It'd been more than five minutes. He should have been showing some signs of recovery by now. I reached across and picked up his hand, then let it drop. He was totally limp. I felt for a pulse. Nothing. I put my ear to his chest, listening for a heartbeat. Not a sound.

He was dead. Stone cold dead.

"Son of a bitch, Dan. You weren't lying. You did have a bum ticker."

There was nothing else to do. I finished my beer, collected both empty cans and the documents and shoved them all in the shopping bag still sitting on the dinette table. Before I left, I placed the rezoning letter on the kitchen counter. No reason to keep it any more. Then I picked up the shopping bag and walked out the front door without looking back. The neighborhood was pitch black. I strolled casually back to my car, walking as quietly as possible to avoid waking the neighbors. I didn't need to hurry. It'd be hours before anyone came looking for Dan when he didn't show up to open the bar.

The mind's a funny thing. Letting Dan live had seemed like a real option to me for awhile, but it wouldn't have been tenable. He'd learned too much about me, for one thing. And if I'd walked out with him still breathing, he'd have been on the phone in an instant warning the journalist, the committee members, everyone he could think of. With him out of the picture, things would be a lot simpler. Sure, I'd kidded myself, almost convinced myself that I couldn't do it. Deep down I knew I'd tasered him that third time hoping I'd get lucky. Like I always say, I'm a lucky guy.

Chapter XI
The Truth about Lies

I GRABBED A FEW HOURS SLEEP when I got back to my apartment, but I was up and out the door by ten in the morning. I hate sleeping away a whole day, even when I've been up all night. Sleep when you're dead, I say. Like Dan.

I'd finished the assignment, but it didn't feel like I'd wrapped anything up. Too many loose ends. A mole in the EPA was not a positive development, and I was curious to learn more about Rebecca Goldstein, if that was really her name. But I wasn't going to go off half-cocked on a private investigation. First, I needed to talk to my boss, run these developments by him and see just how much he really knew about Dan Stigler's little spy ring. He might tell me to stand down, hand the matter over to some other department. I'm not exactly an investigator, after all.

It also seemed like a good idea to warn Riffelbach about Sharon and company nosing around his affairs. Whatever they were up to, it made the office even more off limits for us to talk. If I wanted to have a private conversation with him, first I'd have to write up the Stigler assignment and leave word that it was time for another lunch meeting at the Wafle Shop.

I headed to the office, hoping Sharon wasn't there with another telephone repair team. She'd said she'd be in New York. By now I knew she was an accomplished liar.

But the office was dark and empty. I powered up

my little machine and began dashing off the usual euphemisms. Except it all had an eerie tinge of reality this time. Here I was typing standard bullshit about Kyoto Protocol discussions I'd had with "subject of File 38^/55-45-65@4B239," unable to put out of my mind the nagging thought that I really had discussed Kyoto with Dan.

I'd been right to complain that assignments should always be strangers. Nothing would have suckered me into talking to Mohammed Mohammed, for Christ's sake. To remain effective at my job, I realized, I was going to have to be a lot more disciplined, a lot more detached.

I saved my accounting and write-up to the disk and locked it back in the safe. There was nothing new there, no assignment disk, no alias envelopes. Unusual, really. I couldn't remember many times in the last year when there hadn't been at least one job pending. Sometimes I'd actually found two or three assignments in the safe. Riffelbach had been occupied recently, though, in and out of the office a lot more than usual, according to Sharon. Not that I minded having a break. A couple of quiet days would do me good. Of course, he'd probably have something for me the next time I checked. And I'd see him tomorrow at the Wafle Shop. I left the normal yellow post-it on his computer screen on the way out.

His desk was even cleaner than ordinary. He's a neat freak, sure; never a stray memo or file left lying out in the open. I figure that's a habit people in compartmented work develop, making sure everything is secured before they leave. I certainly don't have any loose paper or computer disks lying around on my desk. But even his trash can had been spotless. And the office felt, well, vacant. It bothered me. I decided I was being paranoid. The cleaning crew had probably been in Friday evening.

My stomach was growling, a combination of not having had enough to eat during the previous 36 hours and some residual complaining from the ribs I'd scarfed down the night before. What I needed was a decent lunch. Spur of the moment, I hiked over to Chester's.

Ordinarily, I'm not someone who seeks out popular places. I'm a loner. But sitting in a restaurant surrounded by people talking and eating suddenly had an appeal. I was experiencing the oddest sensation; maybe it was loneliness, like I'd lost a good friend or something. Or maybe I was just hoping Chester's would rekindle memories of that evening with Sharon. Anyway, a good steak wouldn't do me any harm.

The place was pretty full; any steak joint within a mile of Capitol Hill is always jumping. Washington's elite love their red meat—especially if some corrupt lobbyist is picking up the tab. The twenty-something hostess with too much make-up and way too much exposed cleavage told me they could probably find a table for me if I was willing to wait an hour. I noticed an empty seat at the bar.

"Can I get food service in there?"

"Certainly, sir." She said "sir" like it was a synonym for "old dude." Hell, after less than four hours sleep and everything else I'd been through the last two days, I probably looked none too good.

"Thanks. I'll just get some lunch at the bar."

Instead of the waitress who'd been tending bar a week ago, I found myself sitting across from a weathered looking bartender in his fifties wearing the Chester's uniform black pants, black vest, white shirt and black bow tie. He had all the appearance of an upscale Dan Stigler. I didn't know if that was a good or bad sign.

"What might I get for you?"

"Menu and a beer."

"We have quite a few on draft and more in the bottle. Want me to run through the list?" He had a thick accent, maybe English or Irish. I can never tell the difference.

"Not really. You got anything that's not brewed by Harvard MBAs?"

He laughed. He actually laughed.

"You're in luck. Management just started importing a decent Scottish ale. *McKenna's*. Guess they think it sounds sophisticated. Joke is it's a cheap workingman's pub brew back in Scotland. 'Course they charge 9 dollars for a glass here."

"It any good?"

"I like it. But I'm just a working stiff."

"Okay. I'll try it."

He drew me a generous pint and placed it next to a menu in front of me. The beer was good, bitter and strong.

"Not bad. Thanks."

"Thought you'd like it. Let me know when you're ready to order." He didn't bother to run through any specials. I appreciated him for that.

"Ah, I'll just have a rib-eye, pink in the middle but not bloody."

"Chips with that?"

"Huh? Potato chips?"

"Oh, bloody hell. Sorry, still forget sometimes you don't say chips over here. Fries or baked potato?"

"Fries."

He disappeared with my order into the kitchen. I sipped my beer slowly, realizing that I'd have to find a new place to drink. Dan's bar had become a fixture in my life. Chester's didn't feel like an adequate replacement. The beer was good, and this bartender didn't seem so bad, but looking around I could tell it wasn't really my kind of place. Two red-cheeked, puffy-faced men sitting at a table close to the bar were pretty typical of the clientele. They were both dressed in expensive, black wool suits, but no ties and their collars open on their white, silk shirts. They probably thought that made them look casual, but it just highlighted their over-sized Adam's apples, pasty skin and bodies bloated from too much scotch and red meat and not enough exercise. I caught snippets of their conversation.

"He needs to play ball with us on this one."

"It's a lot of money. There's an election coming up."

"Aw, hell, it's just 20 million. That's chicken feed. Besides, we just need him to make sure it doesn't get tied up in committee. We've got the votes on the floor."

"Yeah, well, getting it out of committee's gotta be worth something."

"Don't worry. There'll be contributions. It'll be worth his while. Be something in it for you, too."

"That goes without saying. Keep in mind, he can hold the bill up in committee damn near forever."

None of their discussion shocked or surprised me. It's not exactly a secret in Washington that the legislative branch runs on kickbacks and extortion. Working for an executive branch agency like the EPA was a lot more straightforward. My steak arrived. I dug in. I was hungry.

"So which part of the government do you work

for?" It took a second for me to realize the question was directed at me. I looked up. The barman was standing in front of me, drying glasses and placing them on a rack over the bar.

"What makes you think I work for the government?" Nosy bartenders were getting to be a thing with me. Maybe I was spending too much time in bars.

"Doesn't everyone who comes in here work for the government?"

"Probably." I decided to give him the benefit of the doubt, assume he was just being friendly. "EPA."

"Don't get many of you coming in here. Lots of congressional staffers, folks in from Treasury and Energy. But you're my first EPA customer."

"Guess we're not as corrupt as the rest. We can't afford 9 dollar glasses of beer very often." Who was I kidding? Between my salary and padded expense accounts, I was rolling in dough.

"You should try being a lobbyist." He looked over at the table I'd been eavesdropping on. "They seem to be able to afford just about anything."

"What about you? You're not from these parts." I took a bite of my steak, savored it. "That's not exactly a Virginia accent."

"Scottish."

So I'd been wrong. English, Irish, Scottish; they all sound like limeys to me. "How'd you wind up tending bar in Washington, D.C.?"

"Decided it would be a better career than tending bar in Scotland."

"Why's that?"

"In case you haven't heard, Scottish folk tend to be very bad tippers." He picked up my almost empty glass, refilled it and replaced it next to my plate.

"Thought you Washingtonians might be more generous."

"Well, you're working the right bar if you want customers with too much money." I washed down another morsel of steak with a big swig of ale. "Lucky you were able to find a gig in such an upscale place."

"It's the accent. Manager hired me because he said I would bring an air of class and sophistication."

"I didn't know Scots were known for their class and sophistication." It was the kind of smart-ass comment I'd made all the time at Dan's. It didn't occur to me until after I said it that he might be offended.

He raised an eyebrow, like he was trying to decide if I was serious or just giving him a hard time. "We're not. But the manager thinks I'm bloody English."

"You didn't straighten him out on that?"

"Not likely." He leaned across the bar and lowered his voice. "Know what the bleedin' moron says to me? He says, 'You sound like that Sean Connery dude. You Brits all sound sophisticated.' Me Scottish homeland twice insulted in one interview."

I finished my steak and downed the rest of the ale. No point telling him I'd been making the same mistake.

"Get you another one of those?"

"No, thanks. Just the check. Got a few errands to run."

He went to the register to print my tab. The two fat-cats were still discussing their cut of taxpayer dollars. I needed some fresh air. When I got the check, I noticed the Scot had only charged me for one beer. Maybe he'd forgotten the second one, or maybe he'd believed me about not being corrupt enough to be able to afford the place. I left him a generous tip. Might as well continue to feed his illusions about

Washingtonians.

"Been nice talking to you"—I looked at the nameplate on his vest—"Gavin. My office is close by. Maybe I'll stop by for a drink again sometime."

"My pleasure. But if it's my charming personality that's bringing you back, come at lunch. Management deploys my sophisticated accent solely for the lunch crowd. Evenings, you'll find two young lasses with oversized tits."

"I'll keep that in mind."

A bellyful of steak and beer had proved restorative. I walked out of the restaurant and noticed for the first time that it was actually a nice, sunny Sunday. The rain of the last three days had finally cleared. Taking a deep breath of clean, sweet air—a rarity in Washington—I headed up the street intent on taking a long, relaxing hike . . . and ran right into the rude waiter from dinner with Sharon the week before.

He was obviously in a rush, probably late to start his shift. He hadn't seen me and I hadn't seen him. We walked directly into each other.

"Watch where you're going, asshole." He didn't look at me when he said it, just tried to get around me.

Instinctively, I caught his arm and spun him around. "Watch your mouth, punk."

"Hey, lemme go. What's your fucking problem?"

"Guess I don't like being called asshole." I had a firm grip on his upper arm. It felt soft, like a woman's. I could have snapped him in half like a twig. He finally looked up at me.

"Hey, I remember you. You were in here last week with that black chick."

Hearing him refer to Sharon as 'that black chick' pissed me off even more. I made a fist, getting ready to punch him.

"Yeah, and I remember you. And I still don't like being called asshole."

"Let go my arm, prick." He was getting mad. He grabbed my wrist with his free hand and tried to wrestle loose. I tightened my grip until it started to hurt him.

"Call me another name. Then I'll break your arm." I could tell I was smiling.

Anger turned to panic, then fear as he realized I could make good on the threat. He didn't say anything, though. Pride's funny. All he had to do was mumble "sorry" and I'd have let him go. But he just couldn't bring himself to do that. Not until I really hurt him. And I might have. I was primed to pull him around the corner out of sight and beat him within an inch of his life.

Instead, I let him go. He stood motionless for a moment. Shock, probably.

"You need help, mister." He ran into the restaurant. I wasn't really listening.

Out of the corner of my eye, I'd noticed a man on the other side of the street. He was about my height, my build, maybe a few years older, wearing jeans, black Timberland street shoes, short-sleeved brown polo shirt. Tough looking, muscular, but clean. Cop or spook clean. He'd been watching. He was smiling. Laughing, almost.

I'd seen him before. He'd been sitting in a park just outside my office earlier that morning, reading the Sunday paper. Joe Clean sitting in a park enjoying a lovely Sunday morning. I lost all sense of professionalism and stared at him in disbelief. He stared right back. Then he grinned. And waved.

I had a fucking tail.

It's unnerving, finding out you're being followed. You start wondering what you've done to call attention to yourself. It never happens when you're expecting it, either. All the jobs I'd pulled, I'd checked thoroughly to make sure I was surveillance free, never spotted anyone. I'd picked up a dumb-shit mugger when I was just out for some exercise, but that had reassured me I know what I'm doing. Then on a Sunday when I'm doing nothing more than finalizing paperwork and having a decent lunch, I find myself shadowed by a guy who obviously spends as much time in the gym as me.

He was good, too. I took off up the street away from him, walking at a brisk pace, made a quick right up a side street and stopped, waiting to confront him when he rounded the same corner. He never came around that corner. I waited five minutes. Nothing. I turned around and continued up the street, figuring he'd dropped me since he'd seen that I spotted him. But suddenly there he was again, waiting for me at the next intersection on the other side of the street, casually leaning against a lamp post. I glared at him. He shrugged his shoulders and gave me a sad-sack look that said "Don't get pissed buddy I'm just doing my job."

I was feeling mean. I took him into one of Washington's crime-ridden southeast neighborhoods. For an hour I cut through side streets where punks waiting to make their next crack cocaine sale glared at us, probably figuring us for cops. I glared back at them, looking threatening. They left me alone. They left him alone, too. He probably looked meaner than me.

Nearing the old Navy Yard, one of Washington's worst districts, I jaywalked across a street and reversed direction to get another look at him. I spotted him about fifty yards behind me. He rolled his eyes as I walked past, letting me know he was aware I was playing games.

We were close to the Green Line Navy Yard Station. I decided to play subway with him, headed down to the platform to wait for a train. He followed close now, not even trying to be subtle. A train pulled up. I stood there, waiting to let him sweat whether I was boarding or not. He didn't sweat. He got on the train and stood directly in one of the doorways so it wouldn't close. It's a nice trick. If I boarded the train, he was already on. If I decided to let it go, all the doors would close except his, the automatic announcement would warn people to stand clear of the doors, and he'd jump off. He'd obviously played this game before. I got on the train and took a seat. He grinned again. I guess he was enjoying himself.

Then he surprised me. He walked toward me and took the seat right behind me. There were a couple of civilians in the car, so I didn't figure him to try anything. Even so, I braced myself. If he wanted a fight, I'd give him one.

"This has been a lot of fun, buddy." He sounded sincere.

"Glad I could provide some entertainment." I didn't turn around. "I hope you haven't been following me all this way to ask me out. I'm straight."

"Really? Straight? Oh, you mean you're not gay. Me neither." He was leaning forward in his seat, talking low so only I could hear. I could have popped him in the mouth with my elbow, maybe broken his jaw. I decided against it. It wasn't an easy decision. "Still, nice of you to lead me on a sightseeing tour of some of Washington's historic areas. Very educational."

"So where'd you learn how to tail someone? FBI school of obvious surveillance? Christ, I'm just a mid-level civil servant and I picked you up right away."

"Mid-level civil servant, huh? Boy, we do have a lot in common." He chuckled. "Hey, I did you a favor, buddy. I let you spot me. I decided I better distract you before you killed that kid outside the restaurant. You having a bad day or something?"

"I just don't like smart-ass kids. Don't like being followed, either."

"Noted. Don't get me wrong. You want to beat up somebody who's rude, I don't care. It just seemed like overkill. I mean, he's really no match for you and your mid-level-civil-servant judo skills." He made a whistling sound, like he was impressed. "I guess you bureaucrats have to stay in fighting shape for all those interagency coordination battles, huh?"

"You got a point you're trying to make?"

"Nope, not me." The train was pulling into L'Enfant Plaza. "Hey, isn't this your stop? You can catch the Orange Line here. Head out to Fairfax."

"I'm waiting to see where you get off. Figured I'd follow you for awhile."

"Oh, you'd get bored. I'm riding up to Gallery Place. Gonna catch the Red Line and head home. Told the wife I'd be back early afternoon and we'd go get ice cream or something."

"How sweet. Give her a big kiss for me." I got up and headed for the door.

"Be seein' ya, Paladin."

I stood on the platform and watched the train pull away with him still sitting inside. He waved goodbye.

So I really would have a lot to talk over with my boss the next day. Assuming I wasn't being followed and could make the meeting. Of course, if I was followed, there are plenty of ways to shake surveillance. I know a few tricks.

I went home and spent the afternoon cleaning and checking the action on the Bersa Thunder. Yeah, there's more than one way to lose a tail.

Monday morning I left my apartment before nine and went hunting; hunting for surveillance. The little .22 caliber Bersa was tucked reassuringly into the waistband of my trousers, magazine full and a round in the chamber. I knew guys in the army who always carried their sidearm with the chamber empty, they were so afraid of shooting off their own foot or their dick. If you're that afraid of a gun, you shouldn't carry one. Especially with an automatic, because when the time comes you need to use it, the last thing you want is to lose precious seconds chambering a round. There's a safety to keep you from blowing your balls off.

I had on a jacket and tie. The jacket covered the Bersa's handle protruding over my belt. The tie made me look like a respectable businessman. Civilians don't feel threatened by a guy with a tie, so it reduces the likelihood some convenience store clerk would watch me suspiciously and catch a glimpse of my piece.

My plan was simple. I'd spend three hours on foot headed to the Wafle Shop. That would give me plenty of time to spot somebody following me. I didn't intend to be subtle, either. Brisk walks through malls, in and out of subway stations, hop a bus and get off at the next stop, reverse direction unexpectedly. I'd use every trick I knew. And if I spotted someone—Joe Clean, another mugger, anybody—well, that's where the Bersa came in. Maybe I'd just lead the guy into an alley somewhere and kneecap him. I wasn't necessarily feeling lethal. But I was going to be surveillance-free before I made my lunch meeting. My boss and I had a lot to discuss: a mole in the EPA; spooks crawling all over the phone lines in the office; Sharon turning out to be a plant; Joe Clean tailing me on a Sunday. We'd need a little privacy.

Those three hours were maybe the most frustrating of my life. I was meticulous. I started the moment I left my apartment, walking two blocks, hitting myself on the forehead like I'd forgotten something and turning around to find an absolutely empty street behind me. Still, I went back to my apartment like I was getting whatever it was I'd forgotten and set off again a few minutes later. The area around my apartment was so empty I got paranoid the cops had cleared the neighborhood in anticipation of shooting it out with me. But I didn't see any cops, either.

I hiked through Fairfax, picked up a cup of coffee at a Starbucks, kept walking east toward Merrifield. I stopped in a Men's store to browse ties, looking through the front window for anyone waiting for me to come out. The street was empty. A few blocks later I went into a Home Depot, checked out a few power tools, then cut over to the garden section and left via the separate exit. Once outside, I ducked behind a concrete column in the garage and waited. Ten minutes and no one came out behind me. I continued walking through some quiet neighborhoods to Dunn Loring Metro Station. From there I took the Orange Line, then the Blue Line to Pentagon City. Once in the mall, I hopped on the escalator to the second level and at the top immediately reversed direction on the adjacent down escalator, checking out everyone who was coming up behind me. Everyone turned out to be two girls in their early teens, obviously skipping school. There was no one following me.

Not being tailed when you're expecting it is worse than spotting surveillance. You start wondering whether you've lost your professional edge, start questioning your own powers of observation. I actually found myself trying to recall if I'd seen the two teenaged girls anywhere else, wondering if terrorists or spies were recruiting middle-school kids to do their dirty work. But they didn't follow me out of the mall, either. Finally, I decided I really was clean. I couldn't figure it. Why follow me one day but not the next? It made no sense.

I decided not to question luck or fate or whatever was watching out for me, headed back to the Metro and rode to King Street Station in Alexandria. From there I walked to the Wafle Shop. I arrived right on time and took my usual table. I'd worked up quite an appetite, could almost taste the pancakes, bacon and eggs I always order.

Exactly five minutes later, Joe Clean walked in carrying a newspaper and sat at a table on the other side of the patio. He didn't look at me, just ordered coffee and started reading. My hand went instinctively to the butt of the Bersa. Before I reached it, a voice stopped me.

"Richard Paladin, glad you could make it." A man took the seat usually reserved for my boss. I looked across at him. It was the man who'd met Sharon at the coffee house Saturday before last. The man who'd returned to pick up his wife and kids from the library. Now I knew why I hadn't been followed. They'd known where I was going all along.

"I'm afraid you've mistaken me for someone else. Sorry." It was worth a try. He'd never met me before. Maybe he'd be confused long enough for me to get away. I started to stand up.

"Dick, you know my friend over there isn't going to let you leave." I looked over. Joe Clean was watching me now. The Bersa was almost willing itself into my hand. A thought flashed through my head that I should pump three rounds into Joe Clean first, then take care of the control officer across from me. I sat back down instead.

"Well, might as well have lunch. You're buying, right?" There'd be plenty of opportunity for the Bersa later, I figured. Maybe I could learn something first.

"Naturally." He smiled, sat back, relaxed, noticed me scanning the street in front of the restaurant. "Your boss won't be joining us today, I'm afraid. He's been unavoidably detained."

"Too bad." It was no surprise. The only way these guys could know about the Wafle Shop meetings was if my boss had told them. I wondered if they'd sweated him, how much else he'd given up. Time to play dumb. "We were planning to go over the next phase of KPPRI. That's the Kyoto . . . "

"Yes, yes." He cut me off. "The Kyoto PR initiative. I'm quite familiar with it."

"We just submitted the last progress report. Wanted to get a jump start on next steps, maintain the momentum."

"Ri-ight." He was scanning the menu. "Tell me, Dick . . . by the way, do you prefer Dick or Richard?"

"Richard'll do."

"Okay, then. Richard." He smiled, like he approved. "So what's good here?"

"Don't know. First time I've eaten here."

"You don't say."

"I hear the spinach salad is good, though."

"Spinach salad. That sounds healthy."

He signaled the waitress over and ordered a bacon cheeseburger with fries.

"Something to drink?"

"What's your draft beer?"

"All we got is bottles."

"Heineken?"

"Sure." She looked at me. I ordered my usual.

"So this is really your first time here?" He was watching the waitress head toward the kitchen. She wasn't all that attractive. I figured he was just letting her get out of earshot.

"That's what I said."

"Funny. You ordered without even looking at the menu."

"It's a waffle joint. I'm sure they've got pancakes, eggs, and coffee."

"Good point." He stopped talking while the waitress brought his beer and my coffee. She poured his beer in a glass and left. "It's just your boss told me he's been meeting you here regularly for over a year."

"No shit. What else he tell you?"

"Not a lot, really. Filled me in on how you've been helping him with the Kyoto program and all that. I take it you are really the point man for the program."

"So they tell me."

"Changing the demographics of Americans' views on the Kyoto Protocol."

"That's what KPPRI is all about."

"So tell me, Richard." He took a sip of his beer. "How familiar are you with the thirty-eight fifty-five program?"

"I have no idea what you're talking about." I didn't.

"File three eight carat stroke five five dash four five dash six five. Ring a bell?"

I waited a second, tried to look like I was searching my memory. It rang a bell, of course. More like tolled a bell for my clients. "Oh, sure, that file. It's people who might potentially be helpful influencing public opinion on Kyoto."

"Close. Very close, in fact."

"Guess you know more about it than me. I've seen a couple of entries from the file. That's about it."

"Thirty-eight fifty-five is a data file containing the names and relevant identifying details of anyone who has ever come to the attention of the U.S. government by expressing disapproval of the administration's refusal to sign the Kyoto Protocol."

"Sounds like what I just said."

"Your boss was assigned the program to develop an initiative to turn public opinion around on this issue. Some senior policy type came up with the notion that analyzing the kinds of people who favored Kyoto could be instructive for designing a PR campaign to change their minds."

"You're just describing KPPRI. I'm familiar with it, remember. I'm the program manager." It sounded like he'd bought the cover story. Maybe he didn't know as much as I'd feared.

He sat back in his chair and sighed, stared off into space like he was searching for the right words.

"Look, Paladin, I'll be blunt. The thirty-eight fifty-fives are Kyoto Protocol sympathizers. They're not terrorists, spies, or enemy combatants. They oppose U.S. policy. On Kyoto. That's it."

"Again, you're not telling me anything new." Actually, I was sweating.

"KPPRI is not a cover for something else."

I just sat there silent. I think I'd already known where this was going.

"For the last year you have been, er, reaching out to people who believe the U.S. should sign Kyoto and start reducing greenhouse gas emissions."

I stared at him. I really didn't know what to say.

The waitress arrived with our food.

"Hey, this looks pretty good." He picked up the burger and took a big bite, chewing with a grin on his face like he hadn't had a decent meal in weeks. While he chewed, he poured ketchup over his fries, picked one up and shoved it in his already full mouth. Obviously he lacked Riffelbach's dainty table manners.

I poured maple syrup over my pancakes and dug in. Hell, I was still hungry. Might as well eat and let him do the talking.

"Man, they make a good burger here." He swigged some more beer. "Pancakes look good, too. Maybe I'll bring my wife here. She likes a good breakfast."

I knew what he was doing. He'd dropped his bombshell. Now he was making small talk, waiting for me to get impatient, start asking questions, make denials, slip up and say something stupid. I kept eating.

"You know, Paladin, this is the point where you're supposed to tell me you're just a mid-level civil servant doing your job and you have no idea what I'm driving at." He'd stopped calling me 'Richard.' He was still smiling, though. Clearly, he enjoyed his work.

"Sounds to me like you've got both sides of the conversation covered pretty good." I slopped a bite of pancake in the runny part of my eggs and shoved it in my mouth.

"Ah, there's no point playing games with you. You're no fun at all." He'd eaten about half his burger and seemed to be losing interest in it.

"I've been told that before." I stayed focused on my food. "I do have one question, though."

"Now we're getting somewhere. Shoot." He leaned back and took a swig of his Heineken.

"You got a name, or should I just keep thinking of you as 'asshole'?"

He stared for a minute, giving no real reaction. "How about you call me Frank?"

"Okay. Frank. The asshole."

"Whatever you prefer, Paladin. Funny name, 'Paladin.' Means 'knight,' if I remember correctly. French, isn't it?"

"My momma always told me we're Americans."

"Right. Born in the USA. You and Springsteen." He set his bottle of Heineken back on the table and leaned forward. "So how about I tell you a story?"

"Whatever makes you happy. You're the one paying for lunch."

"Well, once upon a time, there was this odd little man who worked for a big U.S. government agency. Let's call it the EPA."

"Okay."

"He'd been working his way up the bureaucracy for years, always the good little soldier doing what he was told, getting rewarded by moving up the government service ladder, taking that first management position, eventually getting his own little office to run. Quite the success story. Along the way, he gets a wife, family, bigger and bigger mortgage. All the stuff that comes with success."

"Is this autobiography?"

"Oh, no. Let me continue. One day, he gets called to a meeting of real government big shots, suits who can give him that last big promotion, move him into the senior executive service, give him that free ride on the government gravy train that all good civil servants dream about."

"Lucky him."

"Except they don't have his train ticket for him just yet. First, they've got a job for him. A very thankless job. An impossible job, in fact."

"Don't tell me. They want him to convince people taxes are good."

"Oh, worse than that." He was really enjoying himself. Some people are natural storytellers. "They want him to make a problem disappear. They want him to turn polling numbers that say a lot of people overwhelmingly hate something their government is doing into numbers that indicate everyone loves their government's misguided policies."

"This isn't much of a story. That's the kind of crap that goes on every day in government. Tell me something new."

"How's this, then. Our hero is already close to the edge. Seems he'd been counting on the big promotion for a few years already. The last big mortgage was a little too big. And he's been loading up his credit cards, figuring he'll pay 'em off when the big promotion comes. But now he's mired in this program that's got real high-level attention, and he's not gonna get that promotion if he doesn't show some results."

"Is this where I'm supposed to start crying?"

"Well, you might be interested in this. As the bills stack up and the pressure mounts at work, he goes a little crazy. He's got access to lots of records, databases with names, social security numbers, that sort of stuff. Information like that just piles up in government offices, as you know. He's kind of a computer guy anyway. So he starts a little side business, phonying up credit cards and such. They call it 'identity theft' these days. He just wants to take some of the financial pressure off."

I didn't like the sound of that.

"And then one day he has this epiphany."

"Huh?"

"Sort of a revelation. Maybe he can't change peoples' minds about their government. But there are other ways to change the demographics. He gets to thinking that he doesn't have to make people switch from the 'anti' to the 'pro' column, he just needs to get them out of the 'anti' column. Reduce the numbers on one side of the equation."

"So how does he do that?"

"Dead people don't get to be in a column."

He stopped talking and stared at me. I guess he was waiting for a reaction.

"Wow. Crazed EPA administrator becomes serial killer. You're wasting this story on me. You should pitch it to the *National Enquirer*."

"Nah. They only print fantasy. This story's all fact."

"One thing I'm not clear about." I stopped eating, too, looked him in the eye. "What's your interest in this? Who exactly are you, anyway?"

"Sorry. I'm the one who gets to ask questions today. Not you."

"Well, if you want this conversation to continue, you'll show me a badge or something. For all I know, you could be some kind of foreign agent trying to subvert the workings of a U.S. federal agency."

"What, you think I'm a Russian spy?"

"Maybe Canadian."

"Canadian. That's a good one." He chuckled. "Actually, I work for the EPA. Just like you."

"Sure you do." I glanced over at Joe Clean. "Just which EPA section do you work in that you rate your own personal goon?"

"Can't tell you." He grinned again. "It's a secret, compartmented program. You don't have a need to know."

"The EPA doesn't have secret, compartmented programs. It's an environmental agency, not the secret police."

He leaned forward and lowered his voice. "You of all people know just how wrong that statement is."

"Okay, let's assume I believe you. Let's assume I buy your story about the EPA bureaucrat turned mad killer. That would make you some kind of EPA internal watchdog, spying on your colleagues."

"Those would be good assumptions."

"Sounds to me like you're no more competent than any of the other yokels I work with at the office."

"I'm hurt. Whatever would lead you to insult me in such a way?" He looked more curious than offended.

"Well, the way I figure it, a decent internal affairs shop wouldn't need six months of spying on someone who's forging credit cards and murdering people before they decide to take action."

"Six months? How do you figure six months?"

"You planted Sharon in the office six months ago."

That surprised him. He had a good poker face, but his eyes gave him away. He looked down at his plate, fingered one of his fries.

"What makes you think she has anything to do with this?"

"She likes to meet a friend for coffee at a little cafe near the Arlington Central Library."

"Fuck." He was annoyed. At least I'd accomplished that. "Guess somebody's going to get a refresher class in spotting surveillance."

"Nobody's perfect."

"You seem to be pretty good at it. You scared the crap out of Jimmy."

"Jimmy." Sometimes I'm slow. I didn't follow. "Who the hell's Jimmy. That your goon over there? I didn't know I spooked him the other day."

"No, Jimmy's the kid whose arm you almost broke in Clarendon."

Now I was surprised. The petty thief hadn't been a petty thief after all. Stupid of me to fall for it. "Actually, he was pretty convincing as a mugger, cheap switch-blade and all."

"That's because he is a mugger. He just does favors for me every once in awhile. And we keep him out of jail as long as he doesn't kill anyone. Except now he doesn't want to play anymore. No great loss."

"Sorry. Next time I'll try to be nicer."

"There won't be a next time. We're shutting KPPRI down."

We were getting to it now. It was pretty obvious I'd been working for a rogue operation, and its cover was blown. From what I'd heard so far, it was clear my boss had told them everything. That explained Joe Clean tailing me the day before. He'd probably been waiting at my office for days to see when I'd turn up, file my paperwork, signal a meeting at the Wafle Shop.

It wasn't the proudest moment in my life either, I'll

admit. Finding out I'd been killing people whose offense was signing petitions to stop global warming was, well, embarrassing. I didn't have any illusions what that meant for me. I inched my hand slowly toward the little .22 automatic. At least I could make a run for it.

"I'll stop playing games with you, Paladin. Yes, your boss has been under investigation for six months. But not by me. Sharon was assigned by another office—and don't ask me about that one, either. They were looking into some financial irregularities. Your boss's spending habits attracted attention, not to mention his constantly accessing IRS and social security files he had no business accessing. They thought it was just a simple case of fraud and graft. Then they stumbled on the KPPRI program. Couldn't make sense of most of the paperwork—your reports and accounting are masterful bullshit, I must say."

"I'll take that as a compliment."

"I meant it as one. Anyway, they decided to interview some of the people you'd met with for Kyoto discussions."

"Oh." I could imagine how those interviews had turned out. Or hadn't.

"Yeah. Seems that people you meet have a pretty high mortality rate. One-hundred percent, to be exact."

"Guess I'm a jinx or something."

"Or something. They handed the whole mess over to my department."

I wrapped my fingers around the butt of the Bersa. "And you've arrested Riffelbach and are now here to take me in."

He looked surprised. "Whoa, there. Let's not get ahead of ourselves. Who said anything about arresting anybody?"

"You're holding my boss somewhere, interrogating him."

"I prefer to say we're 'debriefing' him."

"Cute. Guess you figure on taking me somewhere for 'debriefing,' too."

"Not much point in that. We already know what's been going on."

"So you're not planning on questioning me?"

"I'm here to tell you to stop. Stand down."

"That's it?"

"Not entirely. We'll be sending your boss away for awhile. We've got a nice sanatorium for government executives who've been under excessive strain."

"You expect me to buy that? He organized all this on his own, total rogue operation, and you're just going to send him somewhere to have a few therapy sessions?"

"What, you think we should arrest him, have a big public trial and announce to the world that the EPA's been assassinating people who disagree with U.S. policy?" He glanced around, concerned to make sure no one had overheard him slip up and use the 'a' word. "Let's just say that a lot of very senior people in the government prefer that we handle this quietly."

"So they don't care that innocent people may have been killed?"

"Innocent people?" He made a face as if I'd offended him. "Don't make me laugh. They were in the thirty-eight fifty-five file in the first place because of their opposition to official government policy. Nobody's crying over a few malcontents getting ki . . . meeting with unfortunate accidents."

"Yeah. I guess not." I took my hand off my gun. I had to admit, it was silly for me to suddenly defend the very people I'd killed. "Still, I don't like having been played for a sap. I signed on to fight our enemies, not get rid of a few pathetic tree huggers."

"Don't beat yourself up. It's a mistake any of us could have made." He shrugged his shoulders. "There's always collateral damage in a war."

"So what happens to me?"

"Well, that's the question, isn't it? We've been debating that back in my office. Some people see you as a problem we should just make go away."

"If that means what I think, I'll warn you, I'll put up a fight." I looked back at Joe Clean. "You better have more than that guy around if you're gonna try shoving me in the trunk of a car."

"Now, there you go again. I never said anything about that sort of thing. We're not gangsters, you know."

"Yeah, right."

"The discussion is about giving you sort of an early retirement package. Pay you off to disappear."

"So you're here to give me a bundle of cash and a goodbye kiss? That's nice."

"I'm not one of the ones advocating that approach."

"Look, you want me to disappear into the setting sun, I can do that. You want to pay me off, too, I won't object. But I can take care of myself."

"I'm sure you can. By the way, stop using those credit cards your old boss gave you. Unless you want to get arrested by some Podunk police department for identity theft. Riffelbach was a gifted amateur at credit card theft, but an amateur all the same. Those things are ticking time bombs."

There went my plan of hitting ATMs on my way out of town. I had to say, though, I had found his forgeries damned convincing. Anyway, I still had a decent amount of cash in the freezer.

"As for you riding off into the sunset, I'd advise you to hold off. Personally, I think that'd be a waste of talent." He paused a moment, thinking. "You asked if I'm with some kind of EPA internal watch-dog. I'm not, really. My department was called in on this because we do work that's, well, somewhat similar to what your boss had you doing. Frankly, you've got surprising skills. We might be able to put some of those skills to use."

"What, you want me to start bumping off journalists who don't like the Patriot Act?"

"It's a thought." I stared at him, trying to decide if he was serious. He was deadpan for a good minute. Then he laughed. Sort of. "I'm joking, of course. Look, you're quick on your feet, good at spotting a tail, obviously capable of following orders even when they don't make a lot of sense. I think we can find something for you to do."

"For the EPA."

"It's a big agency. We protect the environment in many ways. Listen, why don't you lay low for a couple of days . . . hell, take the rest of the week off. Give us a chance to sort a few things out."

"What, I just hang out and you'll be in touch? How do I know you're not just waiting for me to drop my guard, have Joe Clean over there snap my neck, then say I fell off the Key Bridge?"

"Do you ever drop your guard, Paladin?"

"Good point. I try not to."

"So shut up and pay attention. This is what I want you to do. Take the week off, but stay in town. Some of my colleagues would get nervous if you decided to take a trip somewhere. I'm telling them you're working with us to clean this mess up. If you take off, well, there goes my credibility."

"That'd be too bad."

"Sure would. Somebody might panic and put you in a few police databases as a pedophile or something."

"Nice."

"Anyway, just go to your office next Monday. We'll have had a chance to straighten everything up there by then. Maybe even get a new supervisor assigned, get the staff adjusted to their boss's stress-related breakdown."

"They won't wonder what happened to me?"

"Why would they? You're out of the office more than in. They'll just figure you're off on another of your mystery trips. Or they'll assume you heard about your boss's misfortunes and are taking the opportunity to skip work even more than usual."

"What about Sharon?"

"What about her? She's already been reassigned."

"Oh." That was to be expected, of course. She'd only been there as part of the investigation. Still, I must have looked disappointed.

"Oh, my God, you falling for her?" He rolled his eyes. "For Christ's sake, Paladin. You want a girlfriend, go cruising the bars for some bimbo."

"Right. Not a problem. I'd have just liked to say goodbye."

"That's not going to happen. Don't try to look her up, either. She's not briefed in on any of this. As far as she knows, her department wrapped up a petty corruption investigation. They've already got her working another assignment."

"Sure thing. I'll be a good boy." Why was I relieved

Sharon hadn't learned about my real work? Maybe I had fallen for her. "Okay, I'll show up for work Monday next week. I guess I touch base with the new supervisor to see what it is you have in mind for me?"

"Absolutely not. Don't talk to anyone there. Just go to your office. We'll leave you instructions."

"What, you'll just stick a post-it on my computer screen telling me I'm now a bag man or secret errand boy?"

"You'll figure it out." He signaled the waitress to bring the check. Neither of us said anything while she added it up and handed it to him.

"How was everything?" She didn't really seem that interested.

"Burger was quite good. One of the best I've had." He smiled at her, looked across at me. "How were those pancakes, Richard?" I was 'Richard' again.

"Not bad. I've had better."

He handed her a wad of tens and waved off the change. I guess the taxpayer was picking up the tab.

"Don't get up." He got out of his chair. "And by that I mean, of course, wait here five minutes before you leave."

"Don't worry. I wasn't going to follow you."

He walked out. Joe Clean threw a twenty on the table and followed him.

I sat there wondering if I'd made a mistake, not shooting them both.

Chapter XII
EPA Killer

KILLING TIME is not something I'm good at. I'd gotten accustomed to always having an assignment. Working out at the gym, taking those five mile runs, doing research at the library, it's always been with a sense of purpose and accomplishment driving me. Now I was just waiting to see what my new EPA masters had in store. Of course, the fact that I didn't trust them kept me sharp. But watching your back twenty-four hours a day is not a mission. It's just survival instinct kicking in.

I'm not good at doing what I'm told, either, despite what Frank the asshole had said. Sure, I'd been doing my job pretty much by the book the last couple of years, faithfully executing assignments and steadily filing my paperwork. The only time in my life I'd been a good soldier and followed orders. And what had that got me except the big mess I was now in? Graham had been right, of course. Officers just get grunts killed, then they get promoted, even at the EPA. My boss landed me in hot water, and his fellow bureaucrats rushed in to protect him. I was betting he'd spend a couple of years in that sanatorium and then be right back running another EPA outpost. Meanwhile I'd be doing scut work for some EPA goon squad. If I was lucky I'd be doing scut work. I figured there was still a pretty good chance I had an appointment with a bullet or was destined for a dark cell in some secret prison. But that's just the way the world works. I'd done my share of latrine duty in the army.

I wasn't going to run, not just yet. I decided to stick around and see what this mystery EPA spook section was playing at. Besides, I still had those loose ends nagging at me. Joe Clean's boss had told me to lie low, but he hadn't said anything about staying away from the library. No reason I couldn't do a little digging into Rebecca Goldstein.

He had told me directly to stay away from Sharon. I drove to her apartment building in the District that evening, not even bothering to check for surveillance. If Joe Clean was following me, all the better. Let him report back to his leash-holders.

The building had one of those security doors so someone inside has to buzz you in if you don't have a key. I looked through the name plates by the buttons but none listed "Denovo." Number 6 was blank; that had to be Sharon's. I rang it. No answer. I rang the other five. Two people activated the intercom and asked what I wanted. I ignored them. Someone else just buzzed me through. Why do people bother with locks?

I bounded up the stairs. A guy on the second floor stuck his head out his door.

"Cable company," I yelled as I rushed past him. "Just checking a loose connection on the roof." He went back inside his apartment, closing the door behind him.

I knocked on what I figured was Sharon's door. Still no answer. I picked the lock and let myself in.

The place was empty, stripped bare. It was a nice one-bedroom apartment, hardwood floors, decent little kitchen. It was clean, too. If someone had just moved out, they'd left the place pretty spotless. It was possible, of course, that I had the wrong apartment. But I knew this was Sharon's building. I'd watched her leave it that morning just over a week ago, after walking her to it the night before.

On a hunch, I went into the kitchen and opened the refrigerator. It was full. Fresh produce, a bottle of white wine, open carton of milk. I smelled the milk, drank some. It was still good. Sharon had probably bought it a few days before. She'd cleared out fast. I wondered if I'd ever see her again.

I left the apartment without bothering to lock it, went downstairs and knocked on the door of the nosy neighbor on the second floor. He opened the door cautiously, peered out at me.

"Say, do you know if the lady upstairs is at home? She called in a problem with the cable. I can't find anything loose on the roof and wanted to check her connection inside, but she's not answering."

"She moved out Saturday."

"Huh? No way. She called in a problem this morning."

"Don't know what to tell you. Moving company took out all her stuff Saturday."

"Crap. I must have the wrong building. Sorry to bother you."

Back at my apartment I spent most of the evening thinking about Sharon. She'd been lying to me all along, right up to the last time I saw her when she lied about spending the weekend in New York, obviously just keeping me away from her and her apartment while her spy buddies whisked her away. Maybe I should have been mad. She'd been ready to sleep with me but not be honest with me. That probably would piss most guys off. Not me. I've lied to women my whole life. Being bamboozled right back by one for a change was quite a turn-on.

Still, the smart move would have been to put Sharon behind me, collect up my cash, and leave Richard Paladin and the EPA twisting in the Washington wind. I could probably have talked Graham into putting me up for a couple of weeks, settled in Kannapolis for awhile, maybe pick up some money teaching backwoods survival skills to the survivalist wannabes who bought assault rifles from him. It wasn't a bad idea, really; but all I could think was that it just took me further away from Sharon. The only chance I had of ever finding her was to work with people who knew who she really was and where she'd gone. That meant playing along with Joe Clean's boss.

So I was stuck waiting for next Monday, finding ways to kill time. Like I said, it's the one thing I'm not good at killing.

Tuesday morning with nothing better to do, I decided to buy a book. Even a guy in great physical condition like me can only run and lift weights so many hours a day. Sure, I could have vegged in front of the cable for hours at a time in my apartment. I'm no egghead, but even I know that's the quickest way to fry your brain. On the rare days I spent in my office, I'd occasionally overhear some of the EPA yoyos assigned there talking among themselves about some sitcom or cop show they'd watched the night before. Or they'd repeat what some FOX News or CNN pundit had said about same-sex marriage or Brittney Spears. Looking at people around me over the years had pretty-well convinced me that watching too much television makes you stupid.

There's a Barnes and Noble about a mile from my apartment, of course. I'd walked past it numerous times before, always wondering how those places stay in business. Most people I've known over the years never read anything they couldn't buy off a 7-11 magazine rack. Graham had been the exception, but every book I'd ever seen him read was old and beat-up, like he'd inherited it from his grandfather or found it in a garage sale. Somebody must buy books in those places, though; they keep building more of them.

I hiked over, still watching for any sign of Joe Clean or some other goon. Actually, I realized it would be fitting if Frank chose this moment to have me bumped off or spirited away to that dark cell, nipping in the bud my newfound desire to improve my mind. But I made it to the store without incident. This was actually the first time I'd been in a book store for something other than checking to see if anyone followed me in or hovered outside waiting for me. I went up to the front desk, hoping it worked like a library.

"Excuse me. Where can I find a book called *Decline of the West*? It's by some guy named Oswald something-or-other."

"Huh?" The guy behind the counter looked like I'd awakened him from a deep sleep. "What are you looking for?"

"*Decline of the West*. It's a book."

"Westerns are in the fiction section, rear of the store to the left."

"Thanks."

I browsed the Westerns with no luck. The only authors I recognized were Zane Grey and Elmore Leonard. In the army, some pinhead would occasionally be reading a paperback by one of those guys. The titles seemed pretty stupid. I picked up one called *Dry Gulch Creek* and flipped through it. The plot seemed to be about a cowboy whose best buddy steals his girl so he shoots him. Then he has to lam out of town pursued by a posse. I flipped to the back to see how it turned out. The girl tells him she loves him just before they take him out and hang him. That wasn't exactly the kind of story I needed to read.

Another kid was stocking books in the next aisle. I tried my luck with him.

"I'm looking for a book by some guy named Oswald something. *Decline of the West*. Kid at the counter said it would be with the Westerns, but it doesn't seem to be there."

"*Decline of the West?* Oh, yeah. Came out a couple of years ago. Current events section is up by the front desk. There're a lot of commentaries on post 9/11, all that sort of stuff."

That didn't sound right either, but I looked anyway. I didn't find anything called *Decline of the West*, but the kid had been spot on about 9/11 commentaries. Every fucking pundit and academic lame-brain in America seemed to have published an analysis of what 9/11 really meant. I didn't need a book to tell me that. I already knew. It's a fucking dangerous world and you'd better kill the bastards who hate you before they kill you.

I wandered through the store hoping to get lucky. I still couldn't figure out what B&Ns sold that kept them out of bankruptcy. There were hundreds of books on gardening, cooking, woodworking. Lots of people do these things, sure, but do they really buy books so they can read about them, too? I stumbled across a book by

Rush Limbaugh. At least I'd heard of him. His picture was on the front. I'd never realized he was such a fat, dumpy-looking jerk.

Eventually I ran into an older woman who looked like a manager. By older, I mean she wasn't a teenager.

"Excuse me. I'm trying to find a book called *Decline of the West*."

"By Oswald Spengler?"

I almost gasped. "Yeah, that's it."

"I don't think we have it. Let me check." She strolled over to a computer station off in a nook, typed in the title and clicked search. It popped up several entries, obviously different editions. I'd followed and was reading over her shoulder. Each entry said "Out of Stock."

"Sorry. You could try one of the university book stores. They might carry something like that for a western civilization or philosophy class. Or I could order it for you."

"How long would that take?"

She consulted the screen, typed in a few more instructions, got an answer. "Probably get it for you in three weeks."

"Three weeks? No thanks. I was planning to read it this week."

"Sorry. You could try Amazon."

"Amazon. Sure." I'd heard of it, too. Yet another reason to wonder how B&N stays in business. Of course, it's possible B&N is just a front. Hell, maybe they're really in the same business I'm in. Was in.

"I haven't had anyone come in looking for Spengler before. You studying history or philosophy?" She looked skeptical. I suspect I don't look like a philosophy student.

"Nah. Just interested in getting a different perspective on how messed up everything is." I started to leave. She'd be no help.

"Have you read Huntington?"

"Huh?"

"Samuel Huntington's *The Clash of Civilizations and the Remaking of the World Order*. If you're interested in Spengler, I'm betting you'd find it interesting, too."

"You got a copy of it?"

"Oh, I'm sure we do." She entered more instructions, looked at the results on the screen. "It should be right over here. Let me get it for you."

I followed her to an obscure section of the store. She scanned a few shelves, reached up and pulled down an impressively thick paperback.

"Here it is. Give it a try. I really enjoyed it myself." No shit, she batted her eyelids. At first I'd thought she just really wanted to make a sale, maybe was short on this week's quota. I was wrong. Frank the asshole had been full of shit, recommending I cruise bars to pick up a bimbo. The only half-way intelligent employee I'd found at B&N was signaling me that she wouldn't mind at all getting nailed by a guy with some impressive muscles who came in looking for a philosophy book. I filed that away.

"Thanks. I will." I took the book up to the counter and bought it. She was only the second person in my life who'd ever recommended a book to me. Taking her word for it sure beat trying to find one on my own.

Attached to the B&N was a Starbucks. From my observations around the country, there's a Starbucks attached to every B&N. After buying the book, I stopped in, bought one of the larger thermos containers they sell and paid to have the kid working the coffee bar clean it and fill it with the bitter swill Starbucks passes off as regular coffee. I planned to spend the day sitting in a nice park reading and drinking coffee. The coffee and the book were important. People see a guy sitting in a park, they think 'pervert.' If he's got a book and a thermos of coffee, they figure he's some kind of tree-hugging intellectual. I preferred being mistaken for the latter.

I hiked over to 123 and caught the bus to McLean. Once there I found a nice bench in McLean Central Park and settled in. I had a good view of the parking lot.

It had been two days since Dan had passed away. I was playing a hunch. Rebecca Goldstein might have heard the news by now. Maybe she didn't know Dan had picked up the documents from the park before he died. She might just come looking for them. With nothing better to do, I figured to pass the time staking out the place, see if I got lucky.

I quickly discovered that Sam Huntington wrote some pretty dry, academic prose. The first few pages were a real struggle for me. Hell, on page one I came across the word *Weltanschauung*, which sure as shit is no word in any dictionary I've ever consulted. Not that I've consulted many over the years. But he was writing about characters I recognized; Russians, illegal immigrants from Mexico, Muslims. I forced myself to keep reading, one eye always glancing at the parking lot in case someone pulled in.

As I read, some of what was there struck a chord. He specifically talked about the decline of the West. I'd been observing that my whole life. And I couldn't help but nod agreement to this observation: *The survival of the West depends on Americans reaffirming their Western identity and Westerners accepting their civilization as unique not universal and uniting to renew and preserve it against challenges from non-Western societies.* Of course, he lost me on the very next sentence. *Avoidance of a global war of civilizations depends on world leaders accepting and cooperating to maintain the multicivilizational character of global politics.*

"What crap." I felt like I was speaking directly to him. "Avoid a global war my ass. We're in a fucking global war, you moron."

I kept reading, fascinated someone so smart could understand so clearly that hate, envy, and mistrust dominate not just the lives of people but of civilizations as well, and yet avoid the obvious conclusion that survival demands getting rid of those people who hate, envy, and mistrust you. Academics really do live in ivory towers. If this Huntington guy had spent just a few days in my world, he'd have come to more sensible conclusions.

By sunset, I'd struggled through about a third of the book. That and finding a secluded bush where I could piss after drinking a whole thermos of coffee was all I accomplished. The only other park visitors that day were women with baby strollers. I watched them all anyway. Maybe Rebecca Goldstein was smart enough to pass herself off as a mom walking her kid. But none of them headed down the path toward the footbridge. Finally I caught the bus back to my apartment, fixed myself a sandwich and drank a beer before hitting the rack.

The next day, Wednesday, I filled my new thermos with coffee I brewed myself, stuffed the thermos and book in my rucksack and returned to the park. Maybe the green-loving journalist would never show, but I was improving my mind at any rate. Again, all I accomplished was plowing through another third of the book. That and learning that McLean Central Park is one of the most underutilized green spaces in northern Virginia were my major accomplishments. It explained why Stigler had selected it as a drop site, though.

Thursday looked to be the same. I'd been reading for more than an hour and was considering giving up. All I was getting out of Huntington was a headache. He spent page after page amassing evidence to convince me that the people of the world generally hate each other. Christ, watch Fox News some evening and you'll figure that one out.

A car pulled into the parking lot. I kept my nose stuck in the book but watched closely out of the corner of one eye. It looked like another disappointment. Instead of a woman, a middle-aged guy sporting big black-framed glasses and wearing a rumpled dark suit got out. Definitely not Rebecca Goldstein. Still, I kept an eye on him, wondering what business a guy in a suit had in a park. He glanced around, then stood for almost a minute staring at me. I flipped a page and tried to look like I was totally focused on the book. It worked. He lost interest in me and headed up the path into the woods.

I'd already scoped out a short-cut through the wooded area to the bridge. As soon as he was out of sight, I put the book down on the bench and hurried as quietly as possible to a bushy area I'd identified as a nice concealed look-out. I made it there just ahead of him.

He stopped at the footbridge, just like Dan had five days before, doing a slow 360 to make sure no one was in the area. I remained perfectly still behind my concealment. He laid down on the bridge, again just like Dan, and stuck his arm underneath, feeling around.

When he didn't find anything, he panicked, jumped off the bridge and crawled underneath, rummaging around the mud and moldy leaves for a good fifteen minutes. He didn't find what he was looking for, of course. The documents he'd left there were now sitting in my apartment. Finally, he gave up, brushed off some of the mud and leaves, and headed back to his car. His rumpled suit was now a mess; maybe he'd finally take the time to get it cleaned and pressed.

Once he'd gotten out of sight, I retraced my steps quickly back to the bench, opened the book and pretended to be reading. He walked straight back to his car and drove away, but not before I'd gotten a good enough look at him to remember him if I saw him again. I even got his license plate number.

I couldn't believe my luck. I'd gone looking for a third-rate environmental reporter and bagged what surely was the EPA mole instead. It was his lucky day, too. A week ago, I'd have turned him in. Today, with the EPA in the process of closing down my program and debating just what to do with me, I planned on keeping what I knew about this little espionage ring all to myself for awhile. Knowledge is power, after all.

Friday I set out to tie up one last loose end. After spending the morning doing some serious weightlifting at Pris's—no point letting myself go—I headed back to the Arlington Library to do some Internet research. The place was quiet; I had my pick of terminals. I Googled *Online Environmental Watchdog*. It wasn't first on the results list that popped up: that was something called the Environmental Working Group. I had to scan down a couple of pages to find it.

I found a website called www.oew.org, but that

proved to be the page of the *Organisation für Eine solidarische Welt*, some German do-gooder group. Since my German is non-existent, and since I didn't figure Rebecca Goldstein was writing for a German web site, I went back to the search results page.

Eventually there it was, www.oewdog.org. I loaded the page.

Oewdog.org was pretty vanilla as web sites go, no music or flashing advertisements. Pretty disappointing, really. I'd kinda hoped it would turn out to be a fancy E-mag funded by rich Hollywood tree huggers or something. Somewhere in the back of my head I'd been rolling around the notion that it might be worth something to Rebecca Goldstein to keep me from blowing the lid on her espionage connection, sort of a fallback if things went badly at the EPA come Monday. One look at oewdog.org told me I wasn't going to get rich bleeding someone who wrote for an organization that devoted most of its home page to desperate pleas for donations. And there weren't even any links to feature articles on the main page.

I clicked a small "Newsletter" icon in the bottom left corner of the screen. This took me to a page of announcements; a book signing tonight by some writer I'd never heard of in Eau Claire, rally against global warming scheduled for a week from Saturday in Oshkosh, week-long seminar about acid rain next month in Madison. It was obviously a Wisconsin-based group. I was beginning to think Dan had misled me, given me the name of some harmless organization that had nothing to do with his journalist crony. Then I spotted another link down the page. *Smoke and Mirrors at the EPA* by Rebecca Goldstein.

It wasn't a bad piece of investigative reporting. She

detailed numerous examples of coal-burning power plants across the United States that had received clean bills of health from the EPA despite overwhelming proof collected by Agency inspectors that the plants were taking no steps whatsoever to remove pollutants from the emissions they were spewing into the atmosphere. She quoted from numerous inspection reports, noting that all seemed to be marked SECRET/EYES ONLY, asking rhetorically why EPA inspection reports were classified at all. And, of course, she'd obtained a juicy memo from an EPA Deputy Secretary instructing a department head to "rein in your department's out-of-control inspection teams." It was pretty damning stuff, at least in the eyes of people who actually believe the EPA exists to police polluters. Sad that she was relegated to writing for an organization so obscure that it doesn't even make the first page of a Google search for it by its exact name.

Her byline included a brief bio. *Rebecca Goldstein has been writing about environmental issues for more than a decade. She has a Bachelor of Arts degree in environmental journalism from the University of Southeastern Wyoming State.* I almost laughed out loud. Hers had to be the lamest resumé I'd ever read. But she sure had a dynamite inside source. That made me wonder who Rebecca Goldstein really worked for. Her bio was about as credible as, well, Richard Paladin's. I made myself a promise to look her up some day.

She was lucky, of course, that she'd never made my assignment list. If KPPRI hadn't been shut down and my crazy boss spirited away to a sanatorium, I'm sure it would have just been a matter of time.

That weekend, I fought going stir crazy. Having nothing to do makes me antsy. It didn't help that I spent both Saturday and Sunday morning out on long, serpentine hikes looking for Mr. Clean or someone else behind me but spotted absolutely no one. Whatever EPA division was now in charge of me was either extremely cocky, convinced I had no option but to play along, or damned good at surveying me without being spotted. Neither possibility was reassuring. Back at my apartment, I passed the time cleaning and checking the action on the Bersa. That didn't help much, either. I felt like a third-rate prize-fighter, eager to get in the ring and punch somebody but worried I was maybe overmatched.

By Sunday afternoon, I could tell I was getting jumpy. I'd been walking for almost three hours with no indication of any surveillance at all. I found myself staring intently at everyone else on the street, looking desperately for some sign of suspicious behavior. Some old lady out for a stroll happened to look up at me staring at her. She gasped and scurried away in the opposite direction. I quickened my gait to get out of the area before she had a chance to call a cop. Just at that moment, a skinny, pimple-faced kid standing next to a dumpster stepped out in front of me.

"Hey, mister . . . "

I grabbed him by the arm, spun him around and shoved him up against the dumpster.

"You want something, punk?"

"Ow! Lemme go. You're gonna break my arm!"

"You'll be lucky if that's all I do."

"Jesus, mister. I was just gonna ask if you'd buy me a six pack. I got the money, but they won't sell it to me."

The dumpster was sitting in the parking lot of a convenience store. I looked at the kid more closely. He was maybe fifteen. His eyes were big saucers of abject terror.

"Aw, fuck, kid. I'm sorry. Thought you were someone else. Wait here and I'll get you some beer. My treat."

He stood frozen while I went into the store. I bought three six packs of Miller Genuine Draft in cans and a frozen pizza. While the clerk bagged everything up, I noticed a local newspaper, the *Fairfax Times*, stacked on the counter.

"One of these, too." I picked up a copy of the paper.

"They're free."

"Great. Thanks." I stuffed the paper in the bag and headed back out to the parking lot. The kid was still there. I couldn't tell if he was really waiting for the beer or just frozen stiff with fear. I pulled out one of the six packs and handed it to him.

"Gee, thanks mister." He grabbed it and scurried away like I was carrying bubonic plague.

"Don't mention it." I needed to get off the street before I snapped some civilian's neck. The best thing, I figured, was to head home, eat some pizza and drink one shit-load of beer. That way I might be able to wind down enough to get some sleep.

Back at my hovel, pizza in the oven and a fresh can of beer in hand, I flipped through the paper I'd picked up. I wasn't too sure what I was looking for. Local rags don't usually interest me. I could care less who gets the Fairfax lawn of the month award. But I'd picked up this paper by sheer instinct, and my instincts don't lie. Sure enough, there on page three was a little column that seemed written just for me.

Local Bar Owner Dead at 57.

Dan Stigler, owner and operator of Dan's Bar in Fairfax, was found dead of an apparent heart attack in his home last Saturday. Police discovered the longtime Fairfax resident in his home after an employee of the bar notified them that Mr. Stigler had failed to arrive to open his bar and was not answering his telephone. Mr. Stigler was divorced and had no children. Police are attempting to locate the former wife or another relative.

It was the shot of self-confidence I'd needed. *Apparent heart attack.* Whatever else, I could still pull a job and walk away clean.

"See you in Hell, Dan." I raised my can of beer in his honor and drank it in one long swig. I couldn't think of a more fitting send-off.

Monday morning I woke up with one thought, that I should throw my cash and possessions in my car and get as far away from Washington as possible. I was kidding myself, of course, to think there was really a job waiting for me at my EPA office. Maybe they were rehabilitating my boss, but he was part of the EPA officer corps. I was a grunt. Grunts don't get forgiven. Frank's outfit hadn't tried to take me in at the Wafle Shop or anywhere else during the last week because they were avoiding a public scene and possible publicity. Once I showed up at my office, they could make me disappear with no one the wiser.

I'm not someone to run from a fight. You can't hide from the government forever, not even in North Carolina. Eric Rudolph can vouch for that. I took a long shower and dressed for the office, gray slacks, white shirt, tie, blue blazer. Today I'd look the part of a typical EPA wonk. On my way out the door I shoved the Bersa into my trousers and dropped a handful of extra .22 hollow-points in my blazer pocket. I wasn't going make it easy for them.

I took my time walking to the Metro, stopping along the way for a cup of coffee. There's at least one Starbucks per square kilometer throughout the Washington area, I figure. Got myself a blueberry muffin, too, and sat enjoying it with the bitter Starbucks brew. Subways are packed before about 10:00 a.m. in Washington. It's not a good idea to ride a subway car crammed to overflowing with Washington's unique mix of civil servants and Midwestern tourists when you've got a pistol bulging out of your pants.

Eventually I made my way to the Metro station, again checking to see if I was followed. I wasn't. Maybe Joe Clean's master had called off the dogs in hopes I'd make a run for it. He was certainly tempting me. I stood for a long time on the platform, watching trains go by, wondering why I was being so stupid. For some reason I found myself humming the theme from an old western, *High Noon*. "Do not forsake me oh my darling." As a kid I'd loved watching that film on our beat-up old black and white TV. Maybe I identified with the marshal because he was as alone as I've always felt. More likely I just admired someone who made a living killing people.

I boarded an Orange Line train toward the city. I didn't switch to the Red Line for Union Station, though, riding all the way to Capitol South instead. I'd make the longer walk to the office from a direction they wouldn't be expecting. At least, I hoped they wouldn't expect it. All the odds were against me; having the element of surprise might improve them a bit.

Rather than walk right past the Capitol

building—the place is always teeming with cops—I skirted a few blocks east before heading north. It's more residential, so there wasn't the bustle of people running from one office to another. More opportunity to spot a tail. I was kidding myself again. No one would follow me at this point. They knew where I was going. I stopped at a street corner for a minute to think, lay out a plan of attack. Walking into an ambush is never smart, but if you're prepared, sometimes you can turn the tables. I touched the handle of the Bersa for luck.

Then I noticed where I was. Somehow I'd walked directly to Sharon's old building. Staring at the door leading to her apartment, the door where I'd kissed her that night, the door she'd walked out of on her way to her secret meeting the next morning, a wave of regret washed over me. My life the last couple of years seemed to have an air of inevitability; taking the EPA job, Sharon meeting me at Chester's, Gladys Thurington pulling in front of that fire truck. But I couldn't help thinking that things could have been different. If only my boss had been more careful. If only I'd gone upstairs with Sharon that night. It's not fate or God or luck; it's the choices we make that put us in miserable mud-filled foxholes in the middle of hurricanes. And once we're there, we still get to chose whether to take the consequences like a man or slink away like a coward.

I walked briskly to my office.

Of course, my internal pep talk wasn't going to make me act like a complete fool, either. A block away I went on full alert, checking my surroundings for anything out of the ordinary. I looked closely at every car, dumpster, alleyway, recessed door for anyone out of place. I did a full, slow circuit of the building. If there was a SWAT team or some elite assassination squad laying in wait for me, I couldn't spot them. That didn't reassure me much. A small team waiting for me inside could easily call in backup positioned blocks away. But the odds would be less against me during any initial confrontation. I pulled out the Bersa, flipped off the safety and ducked into the foyer of my building. Still no one. I moved away from the door, out of sight from the street, waited ten minutes. No one followed me in.

I slid my hand with the Bersa into my jacket pocket to hide it, safety still off. It was unearthly quiet in the building. Somebody was up there in the office, though. All the doors were unlocked. I walked through the foyer to a hallway leading to the back stair, climbed them to the door opening to the corridor with my old boss's office. I slipped in and walked as quietly as possible, looking into my old boss's digs—it still looked pristine, unoccupied. Likely they hadn't assigned anyone yet, keeping the place clear until they'd taken care of me. I eased forward to Sharon's desk, now empty and bare. I noticed that the stupid stuffed frog I'd given her was gone. Had she taken it with her? I found myself hoping she had, but knowing some of Joe Clean's fellow spooks had probably spirited everything away like they'd removed every personal item from Riffelbach's old space. For the first time, I knew she was really gone.

The sound of a door opening behind me snapped me out of my reverie. I spun around, finger on the Bersa's trigger.

"Paladin. Didn't know you were coming in today." It was Millpond, the runner, coming out of the bathroom. He was wearing running shorts, running shoes, a t-shirt with *Capitol 10-K* blazoned on it. I loosened my grip on the .22, thumbed the safety on, grateful I'd caught myself before blowing his guts out. "You've been out for awhile. Guess you haven't heard."

"Heard what?" I glanced around again. We seemed to be the only two people in the office.

"Lots of changes. New supervisor starting next week."

"What happened to Riffelbach?" I was curious what they'd told him.

"Off to some year-long senior executive preparatory seminar, I heard. Go figure."

"Yeah, go figure."

"Sharon's gone, too. No telling when they'll find a replacement for her. Too bad, really. I'd been thinking of asking her out."

"Thought you were married."

"I only said I'd been thinking of it." He looked embarrassed.

"Where'd she go?" I had a crazy notion he might know. I was wrong.

"Big mystery. She just never showed up last week. We all got an e-mail Friday saying she'd been reassigned to a field office."

"Which one?"

"That's the mystery. It just said field office. Didn't say which one."

"Strange." I looked around. The place really was empty. "Where's everybody else?"

"Foster called in sick. Reed's in training all week. I'm the only one here today. Except for you, now."

"Should be a quiet day, then."

"Actually, I'm glad you came in. I was going for a run and was afraid I'd have to lock up. With you here, I can leave my keys. I don't like running with keys in my pocket."

"Glad I can help. Go enjoy your run. I'll be here when you get back." I doubted that, actually. Millpond's presence was probably the reason I hadn't been waylaid on arrival. Once he left, I'd be all alone. "Well, guess I better check my inbox, see what's piled up."

"Right." He gave me an odd look. I realized that in more than a year, I'd never had anything in the inbox on my desk. Except for that KPPRI report Sharon left for me. I was beginning to see that as the beginning of the end. "Well, I'll be back in an hour or so. Training for the MCM, you know."

"MCM?" Did everyone in the government speak only alphabet soup?

"Marine Corps Marathon. You should do it some year. Everyone says it's quite an experience."

"I'll bet." Hell, maybe I would, if I lived that long. He headed out the door. It was just me now. I went into my little office and sat down in front of my ancient computer. If they were going to come crashing in for me now, it was as good a place as any. I took the Bersa out of my jacket pocket and held it in my lap, waiting.

I sat there for half an hour, staring through the door of my office into the open space where Sharon used to sit typing or filing memos. I was barely breathing, listening for any sound, ready to go down in a blaze of glory, hollow-points flying. Getting antsy, I got up and found an office with a window, looked out on the park across the street. It was empty. I went back to my office, placed the Bersa on the desk in front of me, and sat down. It was beginning to look like I wasn't going to be waylaid after all. I couldn't decide if I was relieved or disappointed.

Was it possible Frank had been straight with me? This was going to be the first day of my new career as secret EPA errand boy? If so, there'd be instructions somewhere. I looked around for a note or letter, checked the drawers of my desk. Nothing. I looked at the two-drawer safe next to my desk. It was locked, of course. But Riffelbach had probably given them the combination. Hell, he'd obviously spilled everything else.

I spun the dial and opened the bottom drawer. Inside was a legal-size manila envelope with 'Paladin' scrawled in thick black marker on the outside. That hadn't been there before. I picked it up carefully, examined it, ran my hands along the seams for a wire or anything else out of the ordinary. Not finding anything wasn't all that reassuring. Professionals like Frank's people can make a letter-bomb that looks and feels perfectly innocuous. I dug through my desk and found a pair of scissors, carefully cutting an opening on the end opposite the flap. It didn't explode. I resumed breathing and looked inside. It wasn't a bomb.

I dumped the contents on the desk. Two smaller envelopes fell out. I picked up the one with 'Open Me First' typed neatly on the front and hefted it. It didn't feel like a letter bomb, either. Of course, maybe Frank had a real sense of humor, knowing I'd be real careful with the big envelope and then drop my guard with the second. I took a chance and opened it.

Inside were several credit cards, a couple of driver's licenses, and a note.

These may prove useful. No worries. They're professionally backstopped. Not like the crap your old boss was supplying you.

Confused, I opened the second envelope. It contained a floppy disk. This had to be my instructions. I booted up my computer, inserted the disk, double-clicked the document file that was all the disk contained.

My hard drive whirred, loading the word processing package, accessing the file. A document popped up on my screen.

It was a photo, name, biographical details, work and home addresses. I stared at the photo of a middle-aged man who lived in Scranton, Pennsylvania.

I'd been given a new assignment. I wasn't going to be an errand boy after all. I don't know why I was surprised, why I hadn't expected it. How had Frank put it? "Surprising skills." I've got exactly one skill that's hard to come by. Bag men and errand boys are a dime a dozen. Riffelbach's rogue operation had brought me to the attention of an authorized lethal EPA program. Yeah, they could put my skill to use. Governments always need killers.

I smiled. Sometimes I forget; I'm a lucky guy.